Slay Four
RISING

Laurelin Paige

Hot Alphas. Smart Women. Sexy Stories.

Editing: Erica Russikoff at Erica Edits

Proofing: Michele Ficht

Cover: Laurelin Paige, Melissa Gaston, and Tom Barnes

Formatting: Alyssa Garcia at Uplifting Author Services

Beta Readers: Candi Kane, Melissa Gaston, Amy "Vox" Libris, Roxie Madar, and Liz Berry

SLAY FOUR
RISING

ALSO BY LAURELIN PAIGE

Visit www.laurelinpaige.com for a more detailed reading order.

Man in Charge Duet
Man in Charge - October 2020
Man in Love - November 2020

The Dirty Universe

Dirty Filthy Rich Boys - READ FREE
Dirty Duet: Dirty Filthy Rich Men | Dirty Filthy Rich Love
Dirty Sexy Bastard - READ FREE
Dirty Games Duet: Dirty Sexy Player | Dirty Sexy Games
Dirty Sweet Duet: Sweet Liar | Sweet Fate
Dirty Filthy Fix
Dirty Wild Trilogy: Wild Rebel, Coming 2021

The Fixed Universe

Fixed Series: Fixed on You | Found in You | Forever with You
Hudson | Fixed Forever
Found Duet: Free Me | Find Me
Chandler
Falling Under You
Dirty Filthy Fix
Slay Saga Slay One: Rivalry | Slay Two: Ruin
Slay Three: Revenge | Slay Four: Rising
The Open Door

First and Last Duet: First Touch | Last Kiss

Hollywood Standalones
One More Time
Close
Sex Symbol
Star Struck

Written with Sierra Simone

Porn Star | Hot Cop

Written with Kayti McGee under the name Laurelin McGee

Miss Match | Love Struck | MisTaken | Holiday for Hire

For Amy "Vox" Libris,
for always telling me my words are a blessing,
especially when I fear they're a burden.

PROLOGUE

Five months before the end of Revenge, Book Three

CELIA

E dward wrapped his arms around me from behind, complicating my attempt to tie the belt of my robe.

"For someone who's spent the better part of a week on a pleasure island, you're awfully handsy." I tilted my neck, encouraging him to nuzzle in.

He nibbled along the skin I'd exposed. "A week with sex happening all around me while I slept alone in my cabin. You better believe I came home greedy."

"Hurry up with your shower then so you can have your way with me."

"You sure you won't join me?" He was already undressed except for his boxer briefs, and the heat of his skin at my back as well as the hardness of his body made my belly curl low with desire.

But there was a buzz in my head, and I needed a few minutes to sort my thoughts before abandoning them entirely to wanton ways. "If I join you, you'll never get clean," I said, nudging him to the task with the promise of what would come after.

"That's very likely true, bird." He turned me into him and kissed me deeply, making his own promises before pulling away abruptly. "I'll hurry."

"I'll be here."

I wandered over to the sink to begin my nighttime routine of makeup removal and moisturizing, eyeing my husband in the mirror as he stripped from his underwear and stepped into the glass walk-in shower. He was magnificent to look at, and I admired the view with full attention until the whir of my thoughts grew too distracting, and I gave myself into them instead.

Edward had said he'd come home greedy. Considering how highly he prized honesty, it was almost strange to hear the lie cased in the statement. Not that it was a bold-faced falsehood, and not that I didn't understand his reasons. It was for me. He was romanticizing the trip on my account. He didn't want me to have to think too hard about why he'd really been there, about the perversions he'd had to interact with. Didn't want me to think about my uncle Ron and the sick things men like him were into.

Grateful as I was for Edward's desire to protect me, the shield only worked on the surface. It allowed me not to have to talk about it. I could avoid the questions that pressed like a heated iron at the edges of my mind, wanting to straighten the wrinkles of my imagination that were surely as terrible as the truth.

But not talking about it meant the acrid thoughts remained inside me, seeds of poison ivy that would grow if given the right soil.

Old habits dying hard, my instinct was to make that ground infertile, to close off. To become numb. I'd been working through the things my uncle had done to me, but as much as I trimmed and hacked at the memories, I could never cut them away completely. The pips remained inside me, sprouting unexpectedly in the sun, and the urge to withdraw would shiver through me.

It was a funny thing, the fight or flight response. Most people who knew me would probably say hands down that I was a fighter in every instance. I would have said the same before Edward. It was ironic that he showed me the error in that presumption considering how often he drew me to fight with him. I certainly did deal with many threats with a bulled head and sharp tongue.

The truth, though, was that when the threat was severe, when it brought on intense levels of emotional pain, I didn't fight at all. I fle . Like the bird that he'd always seen me to be, I abandoned feeling and took flight to a sky of gray and numb. It had been a practiced skill, one I hadn't been very good at on my own. I could still clearly remember the day I'd begged my friend to be my mentor, when the baby boy inside me had decided to make a much too early appearance to the world. I'd been nearly twenty weeks along, one day later and his death would have been called a stillbirth instead of a miscarriage. Whatever the appropriate term, the result had been the same—my womb had once been full of life and with that life gone, it was full of pain.

"Teach me, Hudson," I'd said when I'd woken from sorrowful dreaming to find him at my hospital bedside. Even the burn of the IV at the back of my hand was intolerable, and his games—experiments, as he called them—

beckoned to me like the whispered praise of a magic healing elixir. *"Experiment with me."*

"What? Why would you want me to...? I'm not experimenting on people I know anymore."

"Not on me," I'd corrected. *"With me. I want to learn how you do it. Teach me."*

"No. That's absurd."

"Please." It wasn't just in the wording that I begged. My entire body leaned forward in supplication, as though he were my messiah. The only one who could release me from my heartache.

"No." But his features had furrowed as if he was thinking about it. *"Why?"*

"Because I want to be like that."

"Like what?"

"Like someone who doesn't feel."

He'd had mercy on me then, and he'd taught me. He'd taught me so well that not feeling had become second nature. And even after Edward had tethered me with an invisible collar, forcing me to stay grounded when the pain grew too great, the impulse still niggled inside me, and I had to take deep breaths and center myself so that I wouldn't thrash against my leash, longing for the gray, numb sky.

Tonight, the urge was especially strong, a driving beat pulsing in my blood, increasing in volume as if to drown out the myriad of memories accompanied with Ron's grooming. The swing, the baths, the first orgasms. The attention from strangers, their eyes, their hands, their mouths. The look of disgust and disbelief when I tried to tell my father. My wings fluttered. The wind called.

Deep breath in.

Deep breath out.

Feel the feeling, find the anchor, stay on the ground.

I dropped the dirty wet wipe and my hands went instinctively to my belly, ensuring my breaths were full and from my diaphragm. The pain washed in like the tide overtaking a dry stretch of land, but then it slowly began to pull out again, and a newly familiar desire was left on the shore. The desire to replace emotion with emotion. To relieve the fullness of anguish with the fullness of joy.

I wanted a baby.

And Edward would allow it, but only on his terms, terms that I was unable to concede to. He believed too deeply that unburdening my sorrow required balancing karma. I supposed I did too, in a way, we just had different ideas of how to go about that balancing. He wanted to make the people who'd hurt me in the past suffer for their sins. I wanted to look forward and replace the pains of the past with happiness in the future.

We'd fight about it again, he'd promised me that. After Ron was taken care of, which would happen soon if all went right. But Edward fought dirty. He fought dirty, and he always won, so this time I promised myself to fight just as dirty in return. I thought of it as an act of love, really. He needed the challenge from me, and I wanted to be able to deliver.

So when he got out of the shower and wrapped a towel around himself, I set the trap. "You have the nurse practitioner on the schedule to come by Tuesday for my birth control, but I have a meeting with a vendor at the same time that can't be changed."

Edward had been arranging my shots for me since I'd been living on Amelie, when I'd been his prisoner. He took care of me in many ways now as he did then, because he liked it and because I liked it, so I didn't automatically believe that he continued this particular arrangement because he didn't trust me.

I was about to find out for sure

"No problem. I'll have Charlotte get it rescheduled."

"Thank you." I waited a beat then turned toward him. "On second thought, could Charlotte make me an appointment for a full gynecological exam in the office instead? I'm due for a pap smear and all of that. The doctor can renew my birth control at the same time."

He raised an eyebrow, and for half a second I thought he suspected. "I didn't realize the time had flown so quickly. Of course you're due for your yearly. I'll get that scheduled immediately. Sorry I hadn't thought of it myself."

I turned back to the mirror and smiled at his reflection behind me. "You would have," I assured him. "Don't beat yourself up. Let me have the rare victory of thinking of it before you."

Again he wrapped himself around me, the scent of his body wash making me weak in the knees. "Yes. Have your victory. I do know how you need those wins."

I appreciated that he could laugh at himself, and I chuckled with him, but the humor I felt was for an entirely different win. Because, while I had every intention of going to that doctor's visit, I knew that changing the scope of the visit would make it much easier to hide the fact that I had no intention of getting that shot.

I'd have my baby just as Edward had had his revenge. It would be on my terms. No obstacle too great to overcome, even if the obstacle was my husband. I knew that once I was pregnant, he'd come around. The same way he'd ruined me, I'd ruin him and we'd both be better for it.

This time when I met his eyes in the mirror, the urge to fly felt different, as though my wings were unfurling and readying to fly *toward* something, not away. The sky above me wasn't gray or numb—it was sunlit and cloud free. I was no longer Edward's little bird. I was a phoenix, and I was rising.

ONE

EDWARD

A suit-clad arm shot out to hold the lift doors open as I approached.

"Thank you," I said in earnest as I slid inside the crowded car, the words out of my mouth before I had time to assess who the saintly gentleman had been. "Ah, Pierce. Edward Fasbender. It's a pleasure to finally have a real meeting."

I held out my hand to Hudson Pierce, the CEO of Pierce Industries. We'd seen each other in passing before, maybe even shaken hands once or twice, but we'd never really spoken. We had plenty to speak about, though, which was why I'd made the four o'clock appointment with him.

Subtly, I glanced at my wristwatch. Was I running early?

Three forty-seven. Perhaps he was just returning from

lunch.

Hudson smiled as he took my hand, an expression that didn't reach his eyes. Not because he was cold, necessarily, but because he was guarded. The way men in his position had to be in order to survive the dog-eat-dog environment they existed in. I imagined my own expression was as severe as his.

"Yes, I'm glad for this opportunity as well," he said. "I must admit, though, if I'd known it were you I was holding the elevator for, I might have let the doors close. By the time you arrived upstairs I would have been safely in my office, and you would have had no idea how late I was running this afternoon."

Stoic but had the ability to laugh at himself. I appreciated that in a rival, if that's what he was to be. Hopefully, I'd know by the time I left his office later this afternoon

"I'll make a stop at the little boy's room, if you'd like. Pretend I never saw you."

"Ah, but that would never do. You and I would both know the truth. I have to accept that my first impression has already been made. Excuse me for a moment." He pulled out his mobile and hit a contact that must be called frequently since it was at the top of the list. "Patricia, it's me. I'm headed up now. Edward Fasbender is with me. Would you make sure the coffee is fresh and…" He looked to me, an eyebrow lifted in question. "That there's water for tea?"

I shook my head. "Coffee's fine.

"Nevermind the tea. See you shortly."

The doors opened and half the people in the car emptied out before they shut again.

"It hasn't been a bad impression," I said when Hudson had pocketed his mobile again, moving to occupy the space that had opened up. "You did hold the door to the lift for a stranger."

"I'm surprised I had enough sense about me for even that." Hudson's features relaxed, and now I glimpsed the man underneath the mask. There were shadows under his eyes, his lids appeared heavy. "Twins," he said in explanation. "I went home for lunch, hoping to sneak in a nap. They're only a month old, and I haven't timed it for sure, but I don't think a full hour passes that they both stay asleep. It's why I sent my brother in my place to your gala on Friday. I would have been a zombie if I'd gone myself."

Being a parent with a newborn brought an exhaustion like no other. I'd been spared much with Hagan and Genevieve. Because I'd been the type of asshole father who left the upbringing to my wife and the children's nurse. Marion's insistence on separate rooms only helped feed into my detached style of parenting—I didn't have to be disturbed by the sound of a baby's cries over a monitor.

Still, I hadn't been immune to the fatigue. It had spread through the household like a contagion. I remembered it vividly, lethargy setting into my body at the thought like muscle memory.

"You didn't miss anything at the gala." The charity auction had been merely a diversion for Celia, something to keep her mind off the press about her uncle's arrest as well as something that would show her name in a good light. "I did see Chandler at a distance. I didn't get a chance to speak with him directly, but my daughter connected with him. I suspect it was more of a social conversation than anything pertinent."

"Knowing my brother, I'd suspect that as well."

I wasn't sure how I felt about Genevieve hitting it off

with a Pierce, but at least it was something to keep her preoccupied. Hagan had pressured me to bring her to the States as we aggressively pursued Werner, and though I'd conceded, it had been reluctantly. Perhaps she'd be focused on this boy now instead of trying to involve herself in what would likely eventually become cutthroat business.

"As for the lack of sleep, I can only imagine what that must be like," I offered in sincere sympathy. "Congratulations and consolation. My wife is pregnant, and I've been dreading the coming exhaustion since she told me of her condition. I'm much relieved at the moment that we only have a single baby on the way. I don't think I have the stamina for more."

"You find it when you need it. Even if it has you running late to the office on a Wednesday." His back straightened and the weariness disappeared from his features, tucked behind his mask of professionalism once again. "Please accept my congratulations to you as well. I'd only just heard that Celia was expecting."

I surmised what that news must have meant to Hudson. He'd claimed to be the father the first time she'd conceived, hiding that it had actually been *his* father who'd knocked up my wife. He'd likely been relieved when she'd lost the baby since it had alleviated him of his duty, but if he was a decent man—as I supposed he was—he'd probably felt guilty for feeling that way when the loss had hurt Celia so terribly.

The news that she was now pregnant must have lessened that guilt if not eliminated it all together.

It would have been better for negotiation if he still carried that shame, but there was nothing I could do about that. "Yes, she's four months along now."

"She must be thrilled."

"We both are," I lied. Because that's what people were supposed to say in these situations. It was uncouth to grumble about the coming of a baby. And it showed weakness to allow anyone to believe I wasn't on board with it. Men with power such as I had didn't have unwanted children. They got rid of them, or they got rid of the women who conceived them.

Truthfully, I didn't want to get rid of either.

Celia was mine for all of eternity, despite the contention that wound around us concerning her pregnancy.

And it wasn't her baby that was unwanted, really. It was all the rest of it. The trickery. The deceit. The secrets she refused to share. The clipped conversations between us. The sliver of cold space that separated our bodies every night in our bed at the Park Hyatt.

The discord in my marriage leaked into every aspect of my being. I'd become meaner over the weeks. Brutal. Defiant. She argued to go home to London as soon as the charity was over. I insisted we stay in the States. She refused to give me what I needed to continue seeking vengeance for the past. I refused to drop the pursuit. She wanted to let control of her father's company go to whomever Hudson Pierce chose to lead it. I wanted to be the one he chose.

She'd got to have her baby. I should get to have what I desired as well. I was determined that I would.

Another stop of the lift and when the doors shut this time, it was only me and Hudson in the car. Fueled by thoughts of Celia, by the dissension coursing through my veins, I turned to my would-be nemesis. "I'm not going to waste either of our time here, Hudson. You know from my emails what I'm after. It should be an obvious choice to put the company in my hands."

He opened his mouth and then closed it, and I could practically see the gears spinning in his head, trying to decide what excuse to give me, perhaps. Trying to guess what I knew about his possession of the majority stocks.

He was aware that I knew he owned them and that Warren Werner was in the dark. I'd made that clear in my correspondence so far. I hadn't yet admitted that I knew *why* he owned them. I was curious whether or not he'd bring it up himself. Throwing accusations at a man's wife took guts, but it was also a dirty move. If he chose to expose my wife's manipulative past, I might be impressed. I'd be equally impressed if he continued to step around it. Whichever choice he made would tell me a lot about the man. Would tell me what I was up against. Would help me prepare my own weapons.

"I have great respect for Warren and the company he ran," Hudson said finall , all traces of informality gone from his tone. He was pure businessman now. Focused and sharp. "It would be quite desirable to see Werner Media continue in that direction, and I understand the attraction of keeping it in the hands of family. I am not, however, yet convinced that your motives are as noble."

Impressive. Without mentioning Celia at all, he'd managed to hint at her possible intentions while throwing the accusations at me instead. He was smooth, that was certain.

"Then I need to do a better job of persuading you of my business plan." The business plan wasn't the problem. In our previous communications, I'd given him a five-year and ten-year prospective. He'd returned with a number of aims he wanted to see added. Some of them had been ridiculous asks, but I'd implemented them all. It was a solid plan.

What Hudson needed would have to be given off-page. Behind closed doors. Just between the two of us.

The lift opened, and I followed him across the hallway to a waiting area with frosted glass walls. He paused to greet the woman behind the desk.

"Coffee's still brewing," she said. "I'll bring it in shortly."

"Thank you, Patricia." He turned back to me, gesturing for me to follow as he opened the solid wood doors revealing a luxurious office space behind. "It's not what you intend to do with Werner Media that I'm concerned with," he said over his shoulder. "It's how that will affect Pierce Industries."

Rather than lead me to the comfy seating area, he sat in the oversized chair behind a magnificent wooden desk, staking a clear position as king. He held all the power here, and he wanted to be certain I knew it.

It made my insides seethe with envy. I rarely encountered a situation where I wasn't the one sitting on the throne. Even if he gave me the reins to Werner, we still wouldn't be on equal footing. He'd still have the majority shares.

But I'd get those too. One day. Somehow. I had patience.

For now, I'd have to accept the inferior role. I sat in the chair facing him. "I can assure you, Accelecom has no interest in taking any predatory action against your company. I've conceded to every one of your conditions, Hudson. Our position should be quite obvious."

He eyed a messy pile of papers on his desk and his brow creased, as if he were annoyed that any of his belongings would fall out of complete order. He straightened them, his gaze quickly scanning the room lingering on a spot behind me.

I followed his line of vision to land on an ordinary coat cupboard. When I turned back to him, his attention was focused on me, whatever had distracted him apparently gone from his mind.

I took that as a cue to press on. "What more can we do to prove good faith?"

He steepled his hands together, leaning back in his chair and considered.

My jaw twitched, and I realized it was time to make a choice. I could sit here and listen to a list of unfounded demands, or I could cut to the chase.

"Let me be candid," I said, leaning forward. "I'm well aware of how the Werner shares ended up in your hands. Celia told me."

His eyes widened ever so slightly. "She told you everything?"

"She did." On the subject of Hudson Pierce, at least, she'd been forthright.

But there was someone else from her past that she'd kept secret, a mysterious man she'd referred to as A in her diaries. A man who had used her to play devious games on the innocent simply for entertainment. A man who had taught her to be manipulative and cold and unfeeling.

He wasn't convinced. "I'm curious what exactly she said."

He was being cautious, but I could understand if there was a bit of curiosity as well. I also was curious about his relationship with my wife. I would love to hear his version of events. Whether or not he'd justify the way he'd led her on before sleeping with her friend. If he'd take full blame for her running to his father's bed or if he'd pass that blame to her. I especially wondered how he'd discovered about the games she played, and wondered what specific reasons he had for thinking he needed insurance to keep her from coming after him and his family.

Honestly, I wouldn't have been surprised to find that his side of the story painted Celia in a much harsher light. I knew what kind of woman she'd been. I knew what kind of woman she still could be if not nurtured and cared for.

Guilt stabbed between my ribs. I hadn't done a good job of caring for her lately. There had been too much hostility between us, and the will to nurture her had been eaten in the flames of that fir

I'd shirked some of my duties, it was true. But I was here because of her. *For* her. I focused on that, stepping carefully as I spoke of her past misdeeds. "She's told me about the ways she's preyed on innocent people around her. It's clear that she attempted to play you as well, and that you required leverage to protect yourself. It might not mean anything coming from me, but I can assure you that she isn't the same person she was when you had to make that move, and I'm certainly not a man who would allow his wife to behave like that in the future."

He scrutinized me with narrow eyes, his expression calculating the risk of trusting me. "You're sure that she isn't currently playing you?"

She had played me in the end, hadn't she? Though forcing a baby on me should hardly count. It was par for the way we negotiated with each other. The games between us would likely be deemed as sick to anyone on the outside.

None of that was relevant to the conversation. "I'm certain that any way she *is* playing me has been welcomed and deserved. Point being, she has no interest in playing *you*."

"But you see how I can't take that on blind faith. You could be in on the game along with her. Or you could be a man blinded by a pretty woman. The Celia I knew would never stand for a man 'allowing' her to do anything. It's suspicious that you believe you have such complete control of a woman I've always thought of as a dragon."

"Dragon?" I let out a gruff laugh. She'd tried to convince me of the same and failed. "Hardly. She's a little bird. Menacing only if you're an unearthed worm."

I sobered. "However, I do understand your plight. Which, I believe, gives you even more reason to want me in the lead position at Werner. You lose your power over her as soon as Warren steps down. If I were to replace him, your thumb would be on her once again."

He nodded an acknowledgment. "Or the two of you have figured out a way to ruin me from the inside out. I have a lot of money wrapped up in Werner. It behooves me to see it do well."

"Please. Even if I ran Werner into the ground, it wouldn't ruin you. Pierce Industries is as solid as they come."

"Unless you discover a way to bring both companies down."

It wasn't on my agenda, but if it were necessary, I would do just that. It was possible he might see that in my eyes, which I wasn't sure was a bad thing. If he thought I was against him, he had even more reason to keep me in his sights. *Keep your enemies closer* and all that.

I let silence be my response, allowing it to fully settle before I spoke again. "There's no way anything I can say will persuade you one way or another. All I can do is offer you a solid business plan and give you my assurance that I want to see Werner succeed, and that I am fully convinced that with the power of Accelecom behind it, I can take Werner to levels you've never even imagined."

It took a beat, but eventually he smiled. "I do like that sort of certainty in my CEOs," he admitted. "But I'm going to need more time to make a decision. You're not the only candidate I'm looking at."

I refused to let any disappointment show on my face. It was standard phrasing. It didn't mean that I hadn't gained any ground. It didn't mean I didn't have him exactly where I wanted him.

He confirmed my confidence a second later. "You do currently have a nice lead, however. So let's discuss next level. The prospects you've shown me are ambitious compared to the ones I've had drawn up myself. I'd like to look closer at the discrepancies."

"You can only reach as high as you dream," I said smugly. "I'd be happy to justify the differences. It would please me to show you where your team has been small-minded."

"I would find that quite interesting. Do you mind?" He stood, signaling me to stand as well. "My chief financial advisor can show you the projections she's put together. Her office is just down the hall. Let me walk you ove ."

I followed behind him like the moon in the shadow of the sun. On the surface, he may have appeared to have the superior position. But the sun only ruled the day. Everyone knew when the night dawned, the throne belonged to the moon.

Two

Celia

I stepped out of the sunk-in tub and grabbed a towel from the oversized bathroom counter. While I greatly missed the house in London, the Presidential Suite at the Park Hyatt was nothing to frown at. We'd been here for more than two months, and I was already addicted to the luxury amenities and sleek modern design.

I'd give it all up, though, in a heartbeat, to have things go back to the way they'd been in England.

No, that wasn't true. I wouldn't give it *all* up.

I put my hand over the bump that had just begun to protrude noticeably from my abdomen. I couldn't feel my baby move yet, but I was always aware of her presence. She'd changed my body completely, high-jacked it like she was an alien invader. Besides the constant exhaustion and the intermittent nausea, nothing about who I was felt the same. Food tasted different. The taste *in my mouth* was different. The temperature of my body was different. My head spun differently. My muscles and joints ached differently.

I hated it, and I loved it. I'd already decided one would be enough because of how miserable the ordeal of pregnancy was. I also already knew without any doubt that she would be worth it.

"Totally worth it," I told my belly. I imagined she found the sound of my voice comforting, so I spoke to her often like this. Or maybe I spoke to her because I knew she couldn't respond, unlike my husband who had taken to spending long stretches of our time together in silence. There was a sexiness about the way he brooded, as there was about almost everything he did, but knowing I was to blame for his taciturnity put a damper on the visual benefits

Would he be like this forever? Distant and withdrawn. He didn't pick out my clothes anymore, didn't dictate my days. Didn't command me or boss me around.

And I resented him for it, which was ridiculous since almost everything I did was meant to push him away. If he tried to care for me like he once had, I'd most likely argue or ignore him outright, and since he surely knew that—because didn't he always know everything?—why would he make an effort to connect?

I didn't even know why I pushed him away anymore. At first, I'd been angry. He demanded to know the identity of the man who'd taught me The Game, and if it were simply because he wanted me to share everything with him, I would have told him long ago. But it was because of his stupid quest for vengeance. A quest that had come to mean so much to him that he'd lost sight of the person he claimed to be looking after. Me.

And that felt worse than the anger. That hurt.

Add to that his secrets—what he'd done to Camilla's husband, the lengths he'd gone to for other acts of justice. I was scared on top of hurt. Not for what he'd do to me, but what he could do—what he *would* do—to Hudson. To my father. To himself.

But then I found out I was pregnant, and my anger and hurt and fear became centered around something else. Some*one* else. Around her, the child living inside me that I was certain was a girl despite not having confirmatio yet. She was everything, and I'd hoped beyond hope that she would be everything to Edward too.

And for a moment, when he'd walked into my parents' apartment and declared his love to me in such beautiful words, I really believed it was possible everything would work out. *"I'm better at your side,"* he'd said, *"and I believe you're better at mine."*

But then I told him I was pregnant.

His response to that announcement stung so sharply it erased anything he'd said before that.

"How is that possible?" he'd asked.

"No birth control is infallible."

"You didn't get your shot."

I hadn't expected him to put the pieces together, but when he did, I couldn't lie. So I'd said nothing.

And he'd walked out of the room.

We hadn't recovered from that. Nine weeks later and we lived in a shell of the marriage we'd once occupied. I didn't know how to go back to what we were, and maybe he didn't either. Point was, neither of us made much effort to try. We'd fallen into a wretched cycle—he wouldn't reach out so I'd do something to make sure he didn't reach out the next time and sure enough he wouldn't and then I'd do something else to make sure he wouldn't again.

We'd been good lovers. I truly believed that. But we'd been even better rivals, and we fell easily into that well-worn groove.

"He'll come around," I said, as much for my sake as my baby's. "He loves us too much to stay away forever."

Please, oh, please let that be true.

With a sigh, I toweled off, staring at the pile of panties and tank I'd brought into the bathroom with me. It had become a standard bedtime outfit for me—not purposefully provocative, yet still revealing in a way that caught Edward's eye. He tried not to notice, I could visibly see him trying, but he always did. His eyes would skate over the bare skin of my legs, lingering at the V of white cotton at the top of my thighs.

It was a passive-aggressive move on my part, wearing what I knew would grab his attention when we were barely on speaking terms. It hadn't yet worked in my favor though. No matter that he couldn't resist looking, he somehow was still able to resist the need to touch.

He was fantastically good at self-denial. I'd learned that from the first time we were enemies. It put me at a disadvantage because I did not have that skill. And I was desperate for him. Desperate for his words and his care and his regard and his love, and definitely desperate for his touch.

But there was no way I'd beg for it.

Which meant my passive-aggressive behavior had to become decidedly more aggressive-aggressive.

Ignoring the clothing, I wrapped the towel around me

and opened the door, planning to walk out to the living area where Edward had been working before I'd gotten in the bath in search of a bottle of water or acetaminophen or a nighttime snack. And if I dropped the towel when I reached for whatever item I was after, and Edward had to face me completely naked, well, whoops.

Except when I stepped out of the bathroom, I discovered Edward, still dressed in the suit and tie he'd worn for whatever business he'd done today, was in the bedroom. Which was unusual since he generally waited until I was asleep before he came to this part of the suite. Even stranger, he was standing at my side of the bed.

And any thought that he might be having the same ideas as I was were seemingly confirmed by what he was holding in his hand—my newly purchased pink Lelo vibrator.

"Really, Celia? You think this little thing is going to satisfy you?"

I forgot I'd left it on the nightstand before I'd taken my bath. I'd lain there for nearly half an hour, contemplating using it before I'd abandoned it for a soak instead. In fact, I hadn't used it even once since I'd bought it two weeks earlier. It wasn't that I thought sex toys were immoral or that masturbating was a form of cheating. The prospect of using it just increased my feeling of loneliness. I wanted to play with my husband, and the inanimate object was sure to be a poor substitute.

Forgetting to put it away suddenly seemed fortuitous.

While there was absolutely no hint of seduction in his tone when he'd spoken, he'd at least engaged. It was progress I intended to use to my advantage.

I nodded at the object in his hand. "I have a better bet

at getting off from that than from a husband who refuses to touch me."

"I told you before I'd fuck you."

The offer had come in the middle of a terse conversation and had been so full of venom I'd ignored it. It pricked to hear it again, recognizing it as a weapon. A way of shifting blame. *The problems between us are you, obviously. I'm here. I offered.*

Well, fuck him and his "offer." I didn't need him cold and hard. I'd do better with the toy.

"No need to trouble yourself," I said. "I wouldn't want to put you out." I spun back to the bathroom to grab the lotion I'd left there on the counter.

When I returned, Edward was still where I'd left him, but now he had the vibrator pressed to his nose, sniffing.

I shivered, knowing what scent he was looking for. The indecency of the act caused arousal to pool between my legs.

I hated him for that. For having such an effect on me. Hated him almost as much as I loved him.

"Are you equally loathe to put this toy out? It hasn't been used." His smile was smug, and I hated him for that too.

I marched across the room and snatched the toy from his hand. "Maybe I washed it."

"Pussy scent doesn't wipe away that easily."

"I only just bought it. I had it out because I was planning to use it now." It was a challenge. An attempt to make him jealous. To make him plead, *please don't use it. Use me instead.*

What he actually said was nothing like that at all.

"Good idea. Now that you're all nice and clean you can get yourself dirty."

I spun away from him and set the lotion on the night-stand, using that as an excuse so he wouldn't see my dis-appointment knit across my features. This was how every conversation went with him these days. Barbs and jabs back and forth. Never a winner. What did I have to do to make that change? What did I have to say?

I took a deep breath and tried to listen to the conver-sation objectively. Tried to hear what his goal was in this exchange. Edward was the last person on earth I'd call pas-sive, but was that what this was? His version of walking in and dropping the towel? His way of saying he wanted me as much as I wanted him?

I turned back toward him, and with less hostility, I awkwardly held out an olive branch. "Would you rather it were you dirtying me up?"

He was three feet away, the closest he'd been for any real amount of time in weeks, and I was nearly naked, a fact I was very aware of as his eyes skimmed down my face, down my neck, to the top of my breasts. I held my breath and silently begged for him to make the next move.

He stepped a foot closer, the heat between us as thick and solid as a wall. "Would *you* rather it were me?"

My jaw tightened. Of course he would force me to be the vulnerable one. That was the true goal of these battles, wasn't it? Both of us intent on the other being the first to bend. The first to be exposed. The first to say something honest.

If there was ever going to be a chance for us, a chance to be the family I knew we could be, then one of us would eventually have to take that risk. It could be me. Maybe even it should be.

"You can," I whispered. "If you want." It wasn't the complete surrender that was needed, and I knew it. I was chickenshit, too scared to say what I really felt. *Yes, I want it to be you. Make me dirty, Edward. Love me like you used to.*

My heart pounded with anticipation as his heated gaze drifted once more over my face, lingering on my lips before dropping lower to my abdomen. I saw the change in his expression as he remembered what lay hidden behind the towel, underneath the expanding stretch of flesh. The last victory taken in our war, and it had been mine.

He stepped back, cold sweeping in between us like an arctic front. "You've already made the purchase. It would be a shame to waste the money." He glanced at the vibrator still in my hand. "No matter how disappointing the experience might be. Two of my fingers are wider than that, and you're not usually satisfied until you have at least three.

There he was, the devil I'd married. In full-blown splendor. Taunting me with what he wouldn't let me have.

It brought out the devil in me as well. "Size is less important than what's done with it. This should do just fine.

"Since you're so good at knowing what you need, yes, I'm sure it shall." The words dripped with sarcasm as he turned away from me, removing his jacket as he walked to the closet. As though he were done with me and my "needs."

"It will," I said, wanting his attention back, as cruel as it had been.

He hung up his jacket then shifted back to face me. Undoing his tie, he threw me a challenging stare. "What are you waiting for then? Go on."

"I'm waiting for you to leave."

"Leave? I'm done with my work. I thought I'd retire early tonight."

God, he was infuriating. He'd probably only come in the room to get his reading glasses, or some report that he'd left on his nightstand the evening before. The only reason he was staying was to prove I had no real intention of getting myself off.

But I'd bought the damn vibrator, so I did have the intention, even if I hadn't used it as of yet. And if he wasn't going to give, I'd take care of myself. "Stay then. You can pretend I'm not here, like you always do. Turn the light off, will you?"

I dropped the towel, and somehow managed to stay standing tall underneath his gaze.

"I'd rather keep it on," he said, his voice deeper than it had been a moment before. It was barely noticeable, the change in timbre, but it was there, and it bolstered me.

I baited him. "So you can watch?"

"So I can judge."

The upward curl of his lip got me low in my belly, a tug of desire so strong that any inhibitions about masturbating fell away. Besides, I'd done this before. On our wedding night. I'd played with myself while he watched until he couldn't stand it anymore and he'd taken over. Then he'd fucked me, and nothing between us was ever the same.

Maybe that would happen again.

"Suit yourself," I said, laying on the bed, my shoulders propped up by the headboard. I pressed the button on the toy, increasing the power until the buzz was quite loud and strong. It was a steady vibration, the default out of twenty possible settings, and while I would have experimented more with which one I liked if I were alone, I left it as is and shoved the pulsing tip between my legs.

"Oh my God." I closed my eyes, the sensation against my clit more intense than Edward's fingers. Which wasn't necessarily a good thing. It was almost too intense, and if I weren't trying to prove some point, I would have turned the damn thing down.

But I *was* trying to prove a point, and beyond that, I had grasped something that I hadn't been able to get hold of for weeks—my husband's attention. I was desperate to keep it, even if it meant enduring the brutal buzz against my sensitive nerves.

I lasted all of ten seconds before I had to lift the toy ever so slightly to give myself a break. Fortunately, my knees up like they were, I was pretty sure Edward couldn't tell. Not that I was even sure he was actually watching since I wasn't about to look at him. It was enough to imagine that he might be.

I tried the tip against me again and had to immediately jerk it away.

"Too much for you?" Edward's voice cut through the haze of sensation.

So he *was* watching.

"Fuck you, it's perfect." I tried a new tactic—pressing the head of the toy to the spot next to my clit instead of directly on it. This, I could manage. This sent enough vibration to my hotspot without being overwhelming.

And now I could concentrate on the real source of my gathering pleasure—Edward. His eyes were more effective than a vibrator ever could be. It turned me on to be watched by him. It felt sexy and naughty and almost like cheating. Combined with the steady pulsation of the toy, an orgasm was building, slowly but surely. My back arched up off the bed as I let out a sigh.

"You're faking."

"I am not." I shot him a glare, which was a mistake because then I saw how hard he was, how the crotch of his pants tented with his cock at full mast. He couldn't be wearing underwear, and hell, that was hot.

I forced myself to look away, but I kept the image in my mind. Imagined more. Imagined him taking his cock out, about fisting it with one strong hand, about him crawling over me and sinking deep, deep...

"Open your knees."

No way. "Undo your pants."

"Already undone."

At that, my head swung back toward him. Sure enough, his pants were undone and his cock was in his hand, just as I'd imagined. There was no looking away from him now. He'd caught my gaze and trapped it.

"Open your knees," he demanded again.

I wanted to hold on to his eyes too much to deny him. So I opened my knees, showing him everything between them. Which meant I had to move the vibrator to my clit again so that he wouldn't know I hadn't been able to handle it.

Of course I jerked almost instantly.

He stepped closer. Closer still, his stare boring like a hot laser onto my pussy. "Turn down the vibration," he ordered when he was at my side. I clicked it down a notch. "More." Another notch. "One more."

I clicked the button again, and it was better now, but I

handed the toy toward him anyway. "You could take over."

"I'm busy." He reached over to the lotion at my bedside and pumped a dab into his hand, then he spread it over his cock with the downward glide of his palm.

Yes, he was indeed busy.

"You could be busy with me," I purred, no longer able to restrain myself.

"I *am* busy with you." He stroked leisurely up his length. "Put it inside you."

For a fraction of a second I thought he meant his cock, and my breath hitched with anticipation. But before I could reach out and pull him to me, he nodded to the vibrator still in my hand.

"Oh." I brought it down to my entrance and worked the head inside the hole. He'd only been somewhat exaggerating when he'd made fun of the small size—it was a fairly innocuous vibrator—but it had been months since I'd had anything inside me at all, and I was tight.

I was also sensitive. The pregnancy alien that had invaded my body had done especially strange things to my lower regions, and the vibration of the toy against my inner walls made my entire pussy tighten and buzz, even with just the tip buried inside.

It was already enough for me, but it wasn't enough for Edward.

"Deeper," he ordered, and because I could rarely ignore this particular commanding tone of his voice, I pushed it in a little farther.

It still wasn't enough. "All the way," he said sharply.

I whimpered as I pressed it in as far as I could. I felt so full. So tight. So on fire

"Good," he said, and I almost came right then I was so happy I'd pleased him. "Now fuck yourself with it."

I did as he told, shoving the object in and out while his dark hooded eyes watched in earnest.

"Harder," he said, and I complied. Then, "Pretend it's me," and I increased my tempo yet again, and let out a moan at the erotic sound my juices made as the toy slid in and out. "Fuck. Yes. Just like that." His own strokes quickened, matching mine. "Touch your clit with your other hand."

My fingers nudged against the sensitive bud, and my knees involuntarily pressed together, as if to push away the intensity of the sensation.

My husband wouldn't have that. "Keep your legs open wide so I can see."

I took a breath and eased them back down. I was panting now. So close to coming. So close to falling apart and breaking down and letting him have every last piece of me, even the parts I'd managed to withhold.

"Edward…" Tears pricked at my eyes.

"Say it."

"What?"

"Say what you want to say."

He knew. He knew everything that was inside of me, and he was determined to reel it out.

But it wasn't that easy. The words were lodged so far inside that I couldn't recognize their form. "I don't know what that is."

"You do."

I shook my head, trying to shake off the overwhelming

feelings that pressed like high waters behind a dam. "I need to come," I said, focusing on the physical.

"That's not it." His voice was coarse and insistent.

"Edward..." I blinked up at him, my eyes darting from his to the brisk jerk of his hand. "I need..." you. I need you inside me. I need to feel you driving hard and deep into my cunt. I need to feel your skin on mine. To taste your lips. To feel your body go rigid when you rut against me with your release.

It was too much—the sensation, the sight, the emotions bottled up inside me, and I exploded like a firework on the Fourth of July. Color and light streaked across my field of vision as my body undulated against my hand. And any words that had been at the tip of my tongue, fell out of my mouth in a tangle of unintelligible grunts and gasps as pure bliss strangled through my limbs.

When I'd come back to myself enough to speak real words, I realized he was also at the brink. His face was as tight as his grip on his cock, his hand flying back and forth along its length.

I scooted quickly to the edge of the bed. "Put it on me," I begged. "Come on me. Please, Edward. Please!"

But even in the throes of pleasure, he had strength enough to resist. With a low groan, he stepped back just as white liquid spurted out over his hand.

I envied his hand. I wanted to be decorated in his cum. I wanted to be marked by him. To belong to him. To be so attached to him that he couldn't ever retreat.

I was still staring at the mess he'd made when he spoke. "You're starting to show."

My eyes moved to find is staring at my once-flat a - domen. Warmth spread through my chest. He never talked about the baby or the pregnancy unless I forced the sub-ject, and then his responses were always clipped and dis-missive.

I put my palm across my belly, as if I could hold his gaze there. As if I could connect it to the child within. "I barely notice the change, but I guess I am. I don't fit in my pants anymore."

He continued to stare for another few seconds. Heavy, silent seconds where I wished more than anything to know what he was thinking. To be in his head.

"Edward?" I said when the weight of the silence be-came unbearable.

He snapped out of his reverie, tucking himself into his pants as he turned away from me. "An excuse for you to go shopping. You should enjoy that."

I preferred when he shopped for me, and he knew it.

The moment was broken. We were back to opposing sidelines, back to our distance and our war.

I sat up, wanting to pull him back. "Tomorrow's the ultrasound. Are you still coming?"

"I said I would when you asked last time." He disap-peared into the bathroom.

"Just wanted to be sure you hadn't changed your mind," I called after him. The sound of the faucet running was my only response.

I sat for a second, trying to decide what I should do next, or if there was anything I *could* do. Maybe I should let the conversation lie. Let him get ready for bed then, once the lights were out, roll innocently into his space.

I stood and picked up the discarded towel from the floor and used it to wipe off the toy. When I looked up,

Edward had returned from the bathroom, still dressed.

Without a word, he crossed the room toward the living area.

"Where are you going? I thought you were going to bed," I asked, sure I already knew the answer. Away from me was where.

He glanced at me but looked away quickly, as if looking at me for too long was painful. "I changed my mind," he said, then left the room without another word.

I sank back on the bed and brushed away a tear. Pregnancy made them fall at the drop of a hat these days, and while they were often justified, this was not an occasion to cry. We might have just had sex without any touching, but it *was* sex. And he'd brought up my pregnancy. It was more than he'd allowed me in months.

I had to see it as a step forward. I refused to see it as anything else.

"We'll get there," I promised our baby. "One step at a time, I have to believe for your sake that we'll get there."

THREE

EDWARD

I rubbed my lips with my thumb, watching the technician as she stuffed the edges of a paper blanket inside the waistband of my wife's pants. How long had it been since I'd been at one of these ultrasounds? Genevieve was twenty-three now, so about twenty-four years.

Nearly a quarter of a decade ago. What was I doing here now at the age of forty-five?

Of course, I hadn't even been a quarter of a decade old when Genevieve was born. I'd only been twenty with Hagan.

I remembered that first ultrasound now, sitting at Marion's side in a small office in Bordeaux. The technician had used a wand that time, one that was inserted inside, and within seconds the black and white screen filled with a tiny sac of cells that resembled a sea creature more than a human, with big black holes for eyes and a body that curled in on itself.

I'd been too shocked to register any other emotions. Marion and I had become extremely close over the previous months, but we didn't even live in the same country. Our time together had been measured in a handful of long weekends on Exceso and several sporadic weeks where I'd flown in to be with her in France. The bulk of our relationship had been over the phone and via email. I'd spend a few minutes every morning detailing a list of things I wanted her to do over the course of the day, then that evening she'd send an email with proof that she had. It had been more work for her—besides the tasks I'd given she had to set up a digital camera, load the photos to her computer, write a detailed message about how the assignments had made her feel. Or, if it were convenient for me, she'd call to tell me about it over the phone while I stroked myself to release.

It had been a one-sided relationship in many ways, and I had been aware of that. I'd been comfortable with that.

Until I saw the quick pulse at the center of the creature on the screen.

"Heartbeat's strong," the tech had said. *"Measuring at seven weeks, two days."*

I'd clutched Marion's hand with mine, and without thinking about it, without imagining what our lives would be, I turned to her and said, *"Marry me."*

And as she responded to everything I ever asked, she said, *"Yes, sir."*

That had been a lifetime ago, and my current wife, whom I loved so intensely that the emotions I'd felt for Marion seemed as small and alien as that embryo on the screen in comparison, was not so agreeable.

I surveyed her now, her shirt pulled up to her tits, her swelling belly bared. While I'd known there was a baby growing inside her, it hadn't been real for me until last night when I'd seen the protrusion of Celia's belly up close. Her body was changing. It *had* changed. Her breasts were fuller, her nipples darker and more pronounced, and buried underneath her expanding skin, my child was growing.

I was going to be a father.

Again, and yet it felt like the first time in so many ways.

And I was terrified

Celia was too, I realized. If she was all the time, she'd done a good job of hiding it from me, but here and now, whatever masks she might have worn had been dropped, and I could see the fear etched on her features, her brows knit tightly above concerned eyes as she chewed on her bottom lip, much the way I was worrying my own with my thumb.

I dropped my hand and wondered if I could do anything to put her at ease.

But the barricade between us was thick, and gestures that had once come as naturally as breathing now took great effort. I glanced at her hand, resting on the table at her side, the rings on her wedding finger a blatant show of our commitment to each other. It should be easy to reach out and take that hand, thread my fingers through hers. I could do that. I *wanted* to do that.

Instead, my hands sat in my lap, as the technician put on latex gloves and then reached for the transducer. With her free hand, she picked up a white bottle with a top that resembled a mustard dispenser and shook it before turning it upside down above Celia's abdomen.

"This will be cold," she said, squeezing until a tiny

drop of jelly plopped out. The tech shook the bottle then squeezed again with similar results. After glancing around the room for another, she said, "I'm sorry. I have to get more gel. I'll be right back."

She hung the instrument in its place on the machine then slipped out into the hall, her footsteps on the hard floor diminishing until the only sound in the room was the gentle hum of the equipment.

Celia's eyes darted to the blank screen where her name flashed at the top. *Fasbender, C.* She let out a heavy sigh.

And I reached out and took her hand.

She turned to me immediately, her usual hostility completely absent, and in its place, apprehension.

"What if she's not okay?" she asked quietly, as if speaking the words any louder might make them come true.

"This is a routine checkup," I assured her. "There's no reason to believe that everything we see today won't be perfectly normal."

"But the last time…" She shook her head and swallowed. "If I'd set my ultrasound a week earlier, we would have seen that he was already gone."

I was a bloody idiot. The miscarriage she'd had years before had happened right around this time in her pregnancy. That was why she'd insisted on making the appointment for her anatomy screening as early as possible, right at eighteen weeks. Of course she was worried about it.

I scooted to the edge of my chair and put my other palm over the hand that held hers, squeezing gently. "This isn't last time, bird. This is this time, and you are strong and stubborn, and there is no way that our baby hasn't inherited that from you." I considered what I'd just said. "From both of us," I corrected.

"Mostly you," she said with a smile so bright it cut straight to my heart.

I held her gaze like that for several long beats, and when the door opened, and the technician drew my focus, my hands remained clutched to Celia's.

"Let's try this again," the tech said. She squirted gel in zigzag lines across Celia's skin, then spread it out with the transducer and settled it down on a spot near her navel.

I glanced at Celia's face, her expression breaking into pure joy before I followed her eyes to the profile of a white figure filling the previously dark screen. Unlike the seahorse that had appeared that first time with Marion, this figure was recognizable as a baby. I could make out so much of it—the curve of the nose, the indent of the eyes, tiny limbs flapping near the head

"I can make out the individual fingers," I said, astonished. Ultrasound had come a long way in the last twenty-four years. The pictures hadn't been nearly this clear.

"Ten total by my count." The technician clicked a few things on her keyboard, drawing lines and inputting numbers. "Length is right on track for eighteen weeks."

"She's growing like she should?" Celia asked tentatively.

"So far so good. Still a lot to see." The technician made a few more measurements, this time near the skull. "The head is the right size. Nothing concerning there." She moved the transducer to the torso then tapped a key and a whoosh, whoosh, whoosh sound came over the speakers. "That's the heartbeat. Sounds nice and strong."

"Told you." I squeezed her hand again. This time she squeezed back.

"What are we looking at now? Is that her foot?"

My throat felt tight. I'd never seen her so excited. I'd never seen her this aglow.

"Yep," the tech affirmed. "And I count ten toes."

As if on cue, one set of toes stretched wide. "It knows you're watching," I said, absolutely charmed by all of it.

"She's moving so much." Celia's voice was thick with emotion. I didn't have to look to know she was crying. "Is that what that flutter feeling is?

The technician nodded. "Possibly. First-time mothers often don't feel anything for another month or so, but it's not uncommon to feel it by now."

"And she's okay? Everything looks okay?" Even though she could see that the baby was moving around, though she'd heard the heartbeat, Celia still needed reassurance.

"She looks great." The tech met Celia's eyes this time, briefl , before going back to her keyboard. "A few more things I need to see to be absolutely certain. You already know the gender?"

"No," I said.

At the same time, Celia said sheepishly, "We think it's a girl."

I appreciated being included in that "we," even though we'd never discussed it. It felt hopeful. Like proof that we still were a "we," despite all that was going on between us.

I hadn't realized until that moment how much I'd worried that we weren't.

"Well, you're right," the tech said. She drew an arrow on the screen. "Right there. That's the labia. She's showing off for you. I don't always get such a clear shot."

I chuckled. "Definitely your daughter." The words said

out loud brought levity to the situation. *A daughter.* I was having another daughter. *We* were having a daughter. Together.

My breath got stuck somewhere in my throat, and I had to blink several times before I could see clearly.

The rest of the ultrasound went by in a haze. Every new view brought another wave of elation from Celia immediately followed by another request for reassurance about the baby's health.

I smiled and nodded and smiled and nodded, the whole time trying to ignore the screaming voice in my head that said, *This is really happening. You're a fuck for a father, and currently not any better as a husband, and this is re-ally happening.*

No matter what happened between me and Celia, we were now bonded forever. And I wanted that. I wanted her—both hers. The mother *and* the child. Why had it felt so much more like being collared than when Marion had gotten pregnant?

Because then I'd known my place. I'd known who was in charge. I'd known how to be the husband Marion had needed, and I'd been that for her. Until I couldn't anymore, and she slipped away.

This time it was Celia who wouldn't take what she needed from me, and it felt so much like being on the other side, like clinging to the side of a crumbling mountain, my hands clawing in the dirt.

I had to get a better grasp. I had to hold on to her, the only way I knew how.

I didn't come out of my trance until the technician went to print pictures for us to take home and hit another snag. "Out of photo paper. I apologize. The room was obviously not stocked after the last shift. I'll be quick."

The door shut, and I looked down to see I was still holding Celia's hand in both of mine. Then I slid my eyes up to her face. She was watching me. Studying me.

She stroked her thumb along the back of mine, and warmth flooded through my veins. "She was beautiful. Wasn't she?"

She held her breath after the question, and I could see it like I always could—what she needed from me along with what she thought she needed. They were less often the same thing than she would have liked. It would be easier between us if I could just be a man willing to provide the latter.

I'd almost tried the day before. I'd gone into the bedroom, meaning to tell her about my meeting with Hudson Pierce. I'd thought briefly that maybe that could be enough—Werner Media, under our control. We could go after it together, she and I, and that would be enough to repair the damage between us.

But then I'd seen the sex toy, and her—naked and newly clean—and something primal roared up inside me, and I remembered who I was. I wasn't *that* man, the one who could step aside or stand back. I was a man who stayed the course. I was a man who didn't back down, and I had to believe she loved me for that.

I shifted my hands, halting the gentle caress of her thumb, and looked at her sternly. "She needs a better home than the one we're giving her, bird."

Her forehead wrinkled. "What do you mean?"

"She needs a solid foundation. She needs her parents to have plowed down the obstacles that could prevent her from having the best life. A rich life. She needs that from her father."

"What are you saying, Edward?"

She understood, I knew she did. Still, she was forcing me to be clear.

"Tell me who he is." There was no need to say who he was. A, the nameless manipulator. The man who'd come between us.

She jerked her hand away from mine, and I instantly missed its warmth. "Oh my God. *This* today? Right *now*? I can't believe you. Seeing our baby didn't show you what's really important?"

Her volume rose, and her tone had grown sharp. I forced mine to remain low and calm in contrast. "It absolutely did show me what was important. Putting a clear end to the past. Tying up loose ends. Sharing the last secrets between us."

"So that you can go after someone who doesn't deserve it." She rolled her eyes and wiped a wayward tear from her cheek. "You have secrets too."

There was only one important secret that I'd withheld—the circumstances surrounding the death of my brother-in-law. I thought it hadn't mattered, and it hadn't, until she'd stumbled onto it, and now she was sorely due an explanation.

But keeping it to myself gave me an advantage at the moment, and I loved her enough to take any advantage that I could. "I'll tell you mine as soon as you tell me yours."

Her frown deepened, and she turned her head away. This was how many of our arguments ended, with one of us retreating into silence.

This time I kept pushing. "You don't want our baby

girl to come into our family with those things between us."

Her head shot back to me. "That's not fair, using her as leverage."

"It seems only fitting since you used her as leverage first.

"Not on purpose."

That got me, and my composure shattered. "Stopping your birth control wasn't on purpose?"

Of course it was that moment that the technician chose to return to the room. From the way her eyes flit from Celia to me back to Celia, it was evident that she'd heard our arguing from the hall.

Thank God, she had the decency to pretend she hadn't.

"Almost got it," she said as she loaded the paper into the printer. She tapped at the keyboard again and the printer came to life, shooting out a bunch of screenshots she'd captured during the visit.

Seconds passed as they continued to spit out, tense seconds that felt years long before she ripped the scans from the roll and handed them to Celia. "Here's a few of the best ones." She spoke directly to my wife, ignoring me completely as if I weren't there. "Just a few standard reminders—make sure you're taking your prenatal vitamins daily, getting enough water, as well as exercise and rest.

"And keep in mind that any undue stress at this time should be avoided." Her eyes whisked momentarily to me, just in case the message wasn't received from her words alone.

"Got it," I snapped. "Are we done now?"

Celia scowled, then quickly shook it off. "I'll keep that in mind. Thank you so much for all of this."

"My pleasure. You can use that paper blanket to clean up. Just dispose of it in the trash can in the corner." Leaving Celia to wipe the jelly from her skin, she handed the routing slip to me. "You can give this to the man at checkout."

She was out of the room before either of us could say another word, likely eager to get away from the oppressive tension, feeling good that she'd passively delivered a warning to a wife who might be suffering from abuse at the hands of her husband.

Good thing I wasn't a real threat. If I had been the type of man that she seemed to fear I might be, Celia could have been beaten for the stranger's poorly subtexted message. Didn't she understand how domestic violence worked?

I glowered at the door where she'd gone, simultaneously wondering if I should go after her to kindly educate her about her mistake and despising her for interfering where she had no business.

I didn't even notice when Celia came to stand beside me. "You heard the woman. Undue stress should be avoided."

And then I felt like an arse. Because obviously abuse didn't always come in the form of physical violence, and it was true that I had a tendency to bully my wife. It was one thing when she welcomed it. It was safe to say that these days she did not.

I breathed out deeply and turned to her, wrapping my arms around her, my forehead pressed to hers. "Let me take your stress from you," I said softly. "Let me carry your burdens. Let me do what should be done for you. For both of you." *Give in to me. I know what's best.*

She shook her head, extricating herself from my arms.

"You wouldn't want that from me, Edward. I'd be Marion, and you'd be unrestrained. I am who I am, and either that's good enough, or she is. Maybe neither of our ways are, but it can't be both."

She had a point, didn't she? There was no pleasing me. I wanted her to challenge me, and I wanted her to bend. I wanted her to have her own thoughts and opinions, and I wanted her to accept when I was right without question.

She couldn't be all of those things. No one could, and by that logic, that meant that the someone who had to change in our marriage was me.

Except it wasn't that simple. Our dynamic wasn't that black and white. I could let her win, it just couldn't be this.

But she was already gone. Without waiting for me to reply, she had grabbed the route slip from my hand, and I was once again staring at a closing door.

FOUR

CELIA

66 I 'm going to name Edward as CEO of Werner."

My father's words startled me more than his presence in the kitchen, which was unusual. He was a conventional type man who, though he firmly said otherwise, believed that there were duties best-suited for women, as well as the rooms associated with those jobs.

In my parents' house, the kitchen belonged to Lupita. She was the only one who spent any real amount of time in this area of the penthouse. Undocumented and paid under the table when she'd first begun to work for them nearly twenty years before, she was now, not only a citizen (with the help of my father's lawyer), but also practically "family," according to my mother anyway. I would echo her sentiments if I thought that paying someone a low-end salary to clean toilets and scrape dinner plates was how a person treated family. I supposed, in some ways, it wasn't any more humane than the way some members of my family treated blood—throw some token gestures of love and then put the rest of the person in a neglected box and you had a Werner daughter. Shower her with affection and then misuse her trust and her body and you had a Werner niece.

I often thought I might prefer the measly salary and a scrub brush.

Whatever she was to my parents, Lupita had always been one of the realest people in my life, and I frequently found myself huddled in her spaces when I visited. Even when we didn't speak, I enjoyed her mutterings, half English, half Spanish, as she dusted and straightened and brought order to the luxurious life Madge and Warren led.

I'd officially moved to the Park Hyatt when Edward came from London, and while he spent his days in the rented-out event space he used for his office, the suite would become small and unbearably quiet. Not that we spoke much when he was there with me. In some ways it was a worse form of captivity than when I'd been on his island. I had free rein here, but on Amelie I'd had care, and the only reason I didn't run back to that paradise prison now was because of the lack of prenatal care.

So instead, I found myself coming regularly to the apartment under the guise of wanting time with my mother, but more truthfully, it was for Lupita's companionship. Today, Mom had her weekly mahjong. Dad had been at work, presumably, and with no need to pretend to be there for them, I'd gathered my newly purchased stationery and set up a spot at the kitchen high top while Lupita organized the grocery delivery. My task was to write thank-you letters for the charity gala Accelecom had sponsored the week before. Hosting the event wasn't my favorite of assignments that Edward had given me, but it had done its job to distract me, as I was sure its real purpose was, and writing the obligatory notes now was strangely engaging.

Until my father's unexpected pronouncement, anyway.

I set down the Montblanc rollerball pen I'd borrowed from his desk and spun on the stool to face him. "What?"

"When I retire. I'm giving it to Edward. My position." He leaned against the side of the table, propping himself with his elbow, and waited for my response, which he obviously expected to be gratitude or praise or some combination of the two.

I glanced at Lupita, wishing for help that she couldn't possibly give me. She wasn't even looking my way. As if the mention of business was her cue—or perhaps just the presence of my father in general—Lupita shoved the last of the groceries in the pantry and disappeared from the kitchen, leaving us alone in her space.

I let out a slow breath, my heart pounding at my insides as I tried to manage my panic. There was no way I could let my father try to hand over his command to my husband. Hudson would never allow it, and the secret I'd managed to keep for years would come barreling to light—my father no longer owned the majority shares of his own company. Hudson did.

Changing my father's mind about anything, though, was something I'd never been good at.

Nevertheless, I had to try.

I attempted a smile. "That's so very thoughtful. But is that really what you want to do?"

"I know this business stuff is all over your head." He reached over to steal some fruit from the plate Lupita had put out for me earlier. "Trust me. It's a power move," he said around a mouth full of berries. "Merging the two companies. Werner will be bigger than ever. I'll go out with a bang."

My neck tightened as I swallowed back a bitter response to his patronizing tone. "I see why combining efforts with Accelecom can be attractive. And there are many ways to do that without a formal merger."

"I'm surprised at this reaction. You don't want Werner to stay with the family?"

"You still own the same stocks, whoever is at the helm, and Edward is not a Werner."

"He's your husband and the father of my grandchild. That's close enough. I don't understand why you'd be opposed to building a bigger and better Werner Media." His tone was stern now. He was losing patience with what he considered ignorant thinking on my part.

I leaned forward, trying not to lose *my* patience with *his* ignorance. "I'm being practical, Dad. Not letting my emotions get involved. For decades, Accelecom has been your enemy. This is a real turnaround from that. It's one thing to drop your rivalry but quite another to get in bed with him simply because he's married to your daughter. What if something happens to us? If we broke up or something."

"Are you saying there's trouble between you?" The way he looked at me I understood clearly that it wasn't going to be my side he took if there was. Ironic considering he'd been opposed to our marriage in the first place.

"I didn't say that."

Before I could expand, he jumped in with a lecture. "You have a baby on the way, Ceeley. This isn't the time to get wishy-washy about your vows. Be the daughter I raised and act responsibly. Hold on to your man no matter what the cost."

I was so infuriated I almost told him right then and there the real reason he couldn't give the company to Edward.

But then the slightest flutter happened in my belly, a feeling similar to what I'd felt when we'd seen our daughter moving on the ultrasound a week before, and I paused to let the joy of the moment sink in.

In that pause, I remembered that it wasn't just my father's ego that would be harmed from knowing the truth. It could be the first tile knocked down in a line of dominos, exposing Hudson and forcing him to take more of a leadership role. There could be good at the end of that road, but it was too much of an unknown to want to risk finding out.

"I'm not having trouble with Edward," I lied. Divorce wasn't on my radar. I didn't want to get rid of my husband, I wanted to win him back. "I am very much in love with him, but that doesn't mean things don't happen. He's been divorced before. What if he loses interest in me?"

I shook my head, not wanting to hear whatever chauvinistic response my father had to that. "My point is that marriages are not always permanent, and with the previous bad blood you've had with Accelecom, I doubt you'll get support from your board for deciding to go all in with them now."

"I hold the majority. It doesn't matter if—"

I cut him off. "Edward and I hold the majority. Don't forget they're in my name now. And it's only forty percent. If the other stockholders got together to go against you—"

It was his turn to interrupt. "Glamplay holds thirty percent, and they're legally bound to vote with me. Er, you."

They weren't bound anymore. That agreement became

null and void when Hudson purchased them.

Since I couldn't tell him that had already happened, I decided to hint that it might. "Those kinds of deals aren't permanent. Something could happen to Glamplay in the future, a competitor could buy them out or something, and you'd lose that guarantee."

My father astonished me by smiling. "You must be learning from your husband. That's indeed true, and he's right to worry about those risks. But he and I have already discussed that possibility, and we've found a way to get around it."

"You and who? You and *Edward*? You and Edward have found a way around it?" I didn't know why it was a surprise that my father had spoken about all of this with my husband before telling me. Of course he had. In fact, it probably had been Edward who had brought it up. What did I think he was working on every day in his temporary office space? Sure he could connect with London and still effectively run Accelecom from the States, but I knew he wanted Werner. Why would I think for even a second that he wasn't pursuing it just because he hadn't said anything to me?

"Yes, me and Edward. I'll admit, he's the one who brought up this particular scenario. I was quite impressed at his foresight. He's quite an intelligent man. The right man to run Werner."

Foresight, *right*. I had to agree with my father, though, about Edward's intelligence. It had been a brilliant idea to get my father involved like this. Without exposing the truth, he'd gained an ally in his quest to get the CEO spot.

I almost didn't want to ask, but I had to know. "How are you getting around it?"

"Glamplay's thirty percent only becomes an issue if it's combined with other stockholders, as you said. So we need to be sure that we have another stockholder on our side from the beginning. Then, even if the others gang up, we'll still have a majority. Edward's already reached out and met with the guy whose partnership would give us the most power."

My stomach sank. There was only one other stockholder who had enough shares to mean anything, even before he'd acquired Glamplay's thirty percent.

"What did Hudson say when Edward met with him?" What I really wanted to know was what Edward had said to Hudson, but there was no way my husband would have told my father the truth about that.

"Oh, good. You know it's Hudson. I didn't want to say his name in case that brought up any hard feelings from the past. I have to say, Ceeley, it might have been a big disappointment when you lost him to that Alayna woman, but you snagged a more savvy man with Edward. Hudson doesn't have the vision your husband does. He can't see the potential with a merger quite yet, but we're working on him."

I almost laughed. Hudson's vision was beyond what my father could even fathom. Edward was sharp too. Maybe even sharp enough to go head-to-head with my old friend, but Edward was used to having the upper hand in these kinds of dealings, and he did not have it this time.

I'd been stupid, ignoring my father's looming retirement and my husband's pattern of going behind my back to get what he wanted. I'd been too focused on my pregnancy and Edward's anger and protecting Hudson's identity, I'd forgotten to be mindful that Edward desired more than just the name of the man who'd taught me The Game.

Well, I wasn't going to sit back and let him outwit me now. Admittedly, there wasn't much I could do to interfere, but there was one move I could make.

I glanced at my watch. I couldn't make it downtown before five, especially not if I changed, and since I was wearing baggy shorts and a tank, I'd definitely have to change.

Tomorrow. First thing so I'd beat the summer heat that turned people into melting wax by the end of the day. I could go to Bergdorf Goodman now and find something that fit and was flattering, which was important. I might not have the influence I needed for the task, but I intended to use whatever tools I had. And that meant, when I walked into Hudson's office tomorrow, I needed to look good.

I turned to face my reflection in the steel wall at the back of the elevator. My hair was perfect, my eye makeup subtle, a severe shade of red on my lips. I looked exactly like the woman I once was, the dragon that used to frequently make this trip to Hudson's office

Well, except for the change at my midriff. Seemingly overnight, my belly had popped, displaying to the world the baby growing inside me. Thank goodness I'd bought a sundress. My pre-pregnancy clothes officially did not fit

I put a hand on the bump and felt immediately both centered and chaotic. This wasn't who I was anymore. The countenance I'd adorned for this occasion was a mask that no longer sat well on my face. It made me itch and fidget. My shoulders had to fight to stay lifted, and focusing my scattered thoughts was a chore.

But my baby was gravity. She rooted me to my purpose. What happened to me mattered in a way that hadn't before. What happened to her father, an equal concern. If it weren't for her, I could maybe let this whole Edward/Hudson thing play out on its own, even if it meant I had to face the consequences of what I'd done in the past. I'd done it before, and I could do it now if it were only my skin in the game.

So, for her, I would play this part. I would be the woman I needed to be.

When the elevator dinged at a floor near the top, it was a composed version of myself that stepped into the familiar waiting area and greeted Hudson's secretary.

"It's been a while, Trish," I said cooly, practicing the tone and the confidence required for the man beyond the double doors behind her. "Could you buzz me in? I need to see him."

"Uh…" I'd made her flustered, which I took as a good sign. "Did you have an appointment?"

"It's twenty past nine. If he keeps a schedule anything like he used to, he should be free right now." I meant it as a reminder that I had once been very familiar with her boss and his routines. Hudson being the methodical kind of man he was, I doubted they'd changed much. Early meetings then a break at nine for coffee and conferring with his secretary before more meetings tied up the rest of the day.

Of course, he had children now. Word on the street was that they changed everything.

Trish frowned, her expression hardening, the kind of look that preceded a dismissal.

I cut in before she tried. "Just ring him. Tell him it's me. Tell him I need to see him now. Tell him I insist." I stared at her then her phone, willing her to pick it up.

She hesitated for only a beat before she did. "Mr. Pierce, I'm sorry to interrupt, but you have a visitor that insists on seeing you right away."

I strained to hear his response but the receiver was too tight against her ear and I heard nothing.

"It's not a him," Trish said, eyeing me up and down. "It's Celia Werner-Fasbender."

The next few seconds passed like they'd been dipped in molasses. I held my breath. I tried not to move. If he turned me away, there was a very good chance I could cry, my hormones being what they were these days. In fact, if he made me wait a second longer—

"Yes, sir." She hung up the phone and pasted on her too-friendly smile, the one that said there was a whole lot going on behind it that no one in the world was privy to. "He's with someone. It will be just a moment, if you'd like to take a seat."

Every cell in my body seemed to sigh in relief as I let out the air I'd been holding. I gave her a matching fake smile, raising her a sugary tone. "I'd rather stand, thank you."

"Suit yourself."

A handful of seconds later, I wondered if that had been the right choice. Sitting was never a powerful position, and I wanted to present as strong. But if he made me wait, like he very well might, I wasn't sure my swollen feet could handle it. My fault for wearing a pointed-toe stiletto instead of choosing a more sensible pump.

But only a couple of minutes passed before the doors opened, and instead of being faced with whomever Hudson had been with, it was the man himself stepping into the lobby, as handsome and as formidable as he'd ever been with his imperious expression and his bespoke suit that brought out the gray of his eyes.

"Celia Werner. I didn't expect I'd ever see you step foot in my offices again." He didn't offer his hand, and the chilly timbre of his tone was more threatening than welcome.

What had I expected? A smile and a warm embrace? I'd been tormenting his future wife the last time we'd spoken.

I channeled the woman I'd been then and sneered. "Don't get your panties all twisted. This visit is harmless. And it's Werner-Fasbender now, which I'm sure you already know."

"Yes, I'd heard."

I felt a twinge of guilt at adding the hyphen in my name. I hadn't been using it, not just because it was Edward's preference, but because it felt right. I was more his than I'd ever been my father's.

Right now, though, as irritating and archaic as the surname construct was, it seemed useful to claim both, a subtle reminder that I had come from two powerful men, a suggestion that I had them both behind me, nevermind that it wasn't true.

He assessed me with calculating eyes, and I let him, taking a moment to study him in return. I was wrong, I realized now. He wasn't as formidable as he used to be, and while I could credit my newly found self-worth as the reason, it seemed there was something else as well. Something gentler in his gaze. Something gentler in his jaw. And the new lines at his mouth added a dose of friendly to his character. They said he was a man who could laugh. A man who *did* laugh. That hadn't been the Hudson who'd taught me The Game.

It seemed I wasn't the only one of us who'd changed.

My throat felt thick as melancholy rushed through me. I forced it down with a hard swallow before it took hold. "Are you going to keep me in your lobby all morning, or are you going to invite me in? I'll say what I have to say wherever. I just think you might prefer the privacy."

His eye twitched, a hint that my presence unnerved him more than he let on. "Very well. Come on in." He turned and I followed after him, halting when he did a few steps inside his office. He nodded to a young man I'd only just noticed. "Celia, I'm sure you remember my brother, Chandler."

"Of course I remember Chandler. My—" I blinked as I looked him over "—you sure grew up." He was a dozen years younger than me and Hudson. I'd always known him only as an irresponsible kid, but now he was a full-fledged adult, looking professional and serious in his designer suit.

He'd been graduating from high school the last time I'd seen him. Had that much time really gone by?

"It's good to see you again. It's been a while." His icy tone made it evident that he didn't remember me warmly, and I wondered if he'd learned about my part in his father's infidelity or if he was just following Hudson s lead.

It didn't really matter, I supposed. I hadn't expected this to be a friendly visit, though I'd thought I might have gotten a little credit for having stayed away as long as I had.

"Yes," I said, answering Chandler, my eyes pinned on his brother. "I've kept my distance. Haven't I, Hudson?" In case he needed a reminder.

That earned me a tight smile.

He glanced over at Chandler, and I assumed he was about to dismiss him, but when he spoke again, he said, "Whatever you have to say, Celia, I hope you're comfortable stating it in front of Chandler because I'd like him to stay."

Chandler gave a smug grin. "You won't even know I'm around."

"Afraid to be alone with me, Huds? I suppose that's fair." I smirked. He wouldn't be cruel with his brother in the room. So, really, the situation was a win for me.

Apparently, Hudson didn't appreciate my gloating. "Why are you here, Celia?"

"So we're jumping right in then. I suppose it was too much to expect we'd catch up first." It had been just something to say, but as I scanned the room, I wished for a moment we could be something else. Not friends, maybe, but something less guarded than whatever this was. We'd been close once. I'd designed his office. He'd been my first official client. We'd celebrated with champagne on the roof.

"You've changed the décor," I said, hoping I'd hid any trace of sadness from my tone. "Not what I would have done, but I like it. It suits you."

"Why are you here?" This time the question was emphatic, a warning that his patience was wearing thin.

I sighed. "Can we at least sit?"

He rubbed a hand over his chin. "Fine. Sit." He gestured toward the sofa, waiting until I sat before taking the armchair. Chandler perched on the arm of the loveseat, a silent bodyguard who, despite having grown, came across more poodle than rottweiler.

It was almost adorable how he wanted to protect his older brother. How he thought I had any power to hurt him. I had to bite back a laugh.

Then there was Hudson, keeping me to task. "Out with it, Celia. We don't have all day."

Well, here goes nothing.

I straightened my back and rested my hands on my belly like it was a talisman. "I have a favor to ask."

Hudson laughed. "That's ballsy of you."

"Perhaps. Or perhaps I just know what to say to get your attention."

"You have my attention. But it's waning quickly."

I nodded, acknowledging that he was already giving me a favor by letting me in the room with him at all, then got to the point. "I know you aren't going to go through with the Accelecom merger."

"Did your stepdaughter tell you that?"

My mask broke, and I could feel my brows rise in surprise. "Genevieve?" What the hell did she have to do with anything?

Chandler pounced. "You aren't the reason she's gotten close to me, then? That wasn't your idea?"

Hudson frowned, his gaze demanding I answer.

I was baffled. Though her room was next to ours, I'd barely seen Edward's daughter since she'd come to the States. "I didn't even realize you knew each other. Genevieve and I aren't particularly close. We definitely don't talk business. If you've already told her the merger was a no-go, she didn't pass it on to me or Edward."

That might have been a lie. It was very possible that

she'd spoken to Edward, that he had her on some mission that I was unaware of, but if so, I didn't know about it. And considering how adamant he had been not to involve Genevieve in revenge-related activity, I was pretty confi-dent what I'd said had been true.

Unless I didn't really know Edward anymore either.

I didn't want to think about that possibility.

Thankfully, Hudson distracted me from those thoughts. "If Genevieve didn't tell you, then how did you know?"

"I know there's no way you'd hand over the company to my husband." I flicked my eyes toward Chandler, wondering how much he knew, then deciding I didn't care. "It would contradict the reasons that you bought it in the first place."

"Let me guess—you're going to try to convince me to give him the job anyway."

His sardonic expression ruffled my feathers. "You really do have a bad taste in your mouth where I'm concerned, don't you? I hope you understand when I tell you I feel the same."

He took a beat, growing somber. "That's fair."

It felt like he'd given me some ground, and I did my best to stand on it, delivering the speech I'd prepared. "In answer to your question, no. I'm not here to convince you to give him the job. Frankly, I'm happy with our lives the way they are. I'm not interested in moving back to the States, and I'm especially not interested in that kind of move with a baby on the way." Nevermind that we were here indefinitely at the moment

"Then the favor you want is for me *not* to give the job to Edward?"

Guilt wrenched my intestines. "I didn't say that."

I considered backpedaling, considered trying to fight the other side, considered begging on my knees. But as much as I was doing this for our baby, I was also doing this *for* Edward, even if he didn't see it that way.

I pushed on. "Let's be clear—I'd love for Werner Media to be back in the hands of my family. I simply know that isn't an option on the table."

"Then what is it that you're asking?"

I thought about what I really wanted, for Edward to come away from this unscathed. I wanted him to let this go on his own. I wanted him to walk away and focus his energy elsewhere. On Accelecom. On me. On his baby.

Hudson couldn't grant that, no matter how much power he had.

But there was one person I could try to protect, whether or not he deserved it. "My father," I said. "This company is his pride and joy. His legacy. He wants Edward to take his place because he thinks it will make me happy, yes, but mostly because he thinks it will be good for Werner Media. He hasn't even considered giving the job to anyone else. You and I both know that you will give the job to someone else. I'm willing to help convince him that's best."

"If…what?"

"If you let him believe it's his idea."

"I'm not sure I understand."

It was satisfying to find I could throw Hudson Pierce for a loop. It gave me confidence to plunge ahead with what I knew would be a near impossible request. "I'm saying go ahead and pick who you want to pick for the job—I know you have other names in mind. I'm confident that you'll select the best person to head Werner Media in the future—you'd never let a good business fail, no matter how you feel about me. It's not in you. I just want my father to believe the decision is still up to him. Let him leave his company in a dignified fashion. Let him think it's his creative vision he's implementing, not just yours."

"What a noble endeavor," he said, and he almost didn't sound like he was mocking me. "Unfortunately, I don't know how I would begin to convince your father of anything."

I didn't either. If anyone could, I'd hoped it would be him, that he'd have enough dignity to try to keep the ruse up, especially when I'd kept my end of our bargain and left his family alone.

I was seconds from saying just that when Chandler shot to his feet.

"I'll do it. I can do it," he said. "Get me a meeting with him, and I got this."

"Chandler?" Hudson was as surprised by this as I was.

"The proposal I was telling you about. I'm confident Warren will be interested in it. I just need to be able to present it to him. Thirty minutes. That's all."

I didn't know anything about Chandler's professional abilities, but he was eager, and he wanted to try, and I was so grateful, I almost fell to my knees. "I can arrange that. If Hudson agrees."

Hudson studied me intently. I knew what he was looking for, and even though I understood why, it still stung that he couldn't just see me for who I was now instead of who I'd been. Hadn't he said the same to me once upon a time? Implored me to see that he had changed when he'd given up The Game? I hadn't wanted to believe him then.

Was this my karma? That he wouldn't believe me now?

See it. See me.

After what felt like a full minute, he gave up. "I can't figure out what game you're playing.

"Maybe I'm not playing any game," I said, my voice oddly raw.

"Wouldn't that be the most conniving scheme of all?"

"Wouldn't it?"

Our eyes locked, and something shifted. Not by much, but by enough that I could see glimpses of the man he must be now—a father, a husband. A person who did good in the world instead of harm.

Could he see something of the same about me?

"Random acts of compassion aren't like you. Thinking of anyone else's feelings isn't either." But he didn't seem to be accusing me, more he was puzzling. Then his eyes widened like he'd figured something out. "You fell in love."

Now Hudson had thrown me.

Because of course I had. Of course that was exactly the reason I was here. Because I'd met a man who had ruined me so completely that I would now care enough to ruin him in kind.

I'd loved Edward more for it. Could he love me more as well?

I couldn't think about it and not fall apart. "Do you want the meeting or not?" I asked stiffl .

"We'll take the meeting."

Relief blanketed me. My breath shuddered as I inhaled, my throat tight. "Thank you, Hudson."

Needing to get out of there before sentimentality took over, I stood. "I'll make arrangements with your secretary. No need for us to have any further contact, as far as I'm concerned."

"I appreciate that."

I beelined for the door and was halfway to escape when he called after me. "Celia." He waited until I turned back around, and it took a beat because I had to gather myself first. When I did, his eyes grazed my belly. "Congratulations on your pregnancy. I once thought you'd make a good mother."

Tears pricked at my eyes as the past slammed into me, bringing vivid memories to mind. We'd been friends. And he'd hurt me. So I'd hurt him. Then the pregnancy. And he'd claimed it. And I'd lost it. So I'd begged him for an escape. And he gave it while I'd given him companion-ship.

We'd been bad to the people around us. Really, really bad. Bad to each other, as well. But we'd been good to each other too. When both of us had needed it most.

No matter what else between us, we had that.

My vision blurred, I nodded toward the framed picture on his bookshelf of Hudson, his wife, a baby in each of their arms, a little girl tucked into his side. "Congratula-tions on your own little family," I said, amazed my voice didn't crack. "I once thought you'd make a good dad."

I went straight from his office to the bathroom, plan-ning to schedule the meeting with Trish on my way out, when I was composed.

Now, though, I needed a minute to myself. Locked in the privacy of a stall, I let the tears fall. Tears I couldn't quite explain. I wasn't sad. I was a bunch of other things all rolled into one, a muddy mess of too many emotions to name.

It felt good to let them out, the way it felt good to pull out a fresh clean sheet of paper. A blank slate. A place to start anew.

Edward had said I'd needed closure with the man who'd taught me how to play. It was why he was so determined to find out his identity, because he wanted to seek out that closure for me with hellfire and brimstone and revenge.

But this was what I'd needed. Just this. Just today.

My story with Hudson was over.

Now I could shut the book and move on.

FIVE

EDWARD

Hagan leaned over to whisper something to me.

Whatever he said, I couldn't hear it above the pounding in my ears. I was seething. Violent rage surged through my veins, my vision flashed with white hot anger, and there was absolutely nothing I could do about it but sit and continue to listen to the presentation being given to me in the conference room at Pierce Industries.

Pretend to listen, rather.

I'd stopped hearing much of the details after I'd got the general gist of the whole thing. In a nutshell, Pierce Industries proposed that Werner Media and Accelecom enter into a three-point alliance, and that, when Warren Werner stepped down, the CEO position should be handed to Nathan Murphy.

Nathan Fucking Murphy.

A man with credentials, yes, but not a man with *my* credentials. No matter what his experience, he was not the right man for the job. For the last twenty minutes he'd been sharing his plans for the company, and except for the idea of the alliance—which was clearly not his own— not a one was new or visionary. I'd given Pierce a missive with a dozen more innovative proposals. He knew that Murphy was the inferior choice, and still he chose to sell it to War-ren, knowing the old man would jump on a Pierce-backed proposition in a heartbeat.

Hudson hadn't even had the nerve to introduce the idea himself. He'd left it to his brother, Chandler, a kid, fresh out of college, with less experience than Hagan.

Worse? Genevieve had a hand in it as well.

Not only did she hand over Accelecom numbers and strategies, but she'd assisted in leading the hour-long presentation that was just now coming to a conclusion. I'd known she was spending time with the younger Pierce and had even suspected they were growing close, but never had I imagined she was drumming up the idea of an alliance that would effectively kill the merger that Warren and I had discussed.

Again Hagan whispered something at my side.

I blinked, clearing my vision before I leaned in to better hear him.

"...not what we were after, but it's better than nothing. At least they didn't leave Accelecom in the dark. It's a rather good compromise."

What had Celia said was the recipe for a perfect compromise? None of the parties walked away satisfied, something to that effect. Well, from the look on the faces of those around me, the only one dissatisfied in this particular arrangement was me.

This didn't feel like a compromise. This felt like a giant *fuck you*.

Except, I was having a particularly difficult time figu - ing out just who had done the fucking.

I looked at my daughter, smiling confidently as she expertly answered a question from Pierce's financial analyst. A burst of pride swelled out of the midst of the cacophony of rage and betrayal inside me. She'd had a part in this, but I couldn't blame her for selling me out. I hadn't treated her any better, holding her at arm's length, refusing to let her really sink her teeth into the job I'd given her, forcing her to try to stand out on her own. In many ways, I'd given her no choice but to go prove herself elsewhere.

And by God, had she proven herself, presenting an attractive strategy to men and women who had far more experience than her under the belt. She'd been bloody brilliant, and I couldn't take any of the credit for that.

Hagan nudged me again. "We could run this from London, even, which is a plus. Less manpower than a merger. Less risk, too. Merging with Werner while all this business is happening with Ron Werner isn't necessarily the wisest of moves."

I turned to face my son as I digested his words. There was logic in them, and from the point of view of the CEO and owner of Accelecom, a merger right now probably wasn't in the company's best interest.

It was from the point of view of Celia's husband that losing Werner mattered. That company belonged in her family. She may have done things that had forced Hudson to take control like he had, but he was well aware that he could still keep that control with me in charge. I'd made sure he understood.

"Look, Dad," Hagan said, his tone more direct. "Pierce could have shut us out all together. We could be going home empty-handed. We should look at this as a win."

I studied him, blinking again as I began to come to my senses. There was no betrayal. This was business. This strategy was sound. Had I been in Pierce's position, this was a move I likely would have made myself.

Honestly, I may not have even been this generous.

"I wonder if it was Genevieve who had a hand in looking out for us." I turned my attention back to her as I rubbed my thumb along my bottom lip. I'd failed her, hadn't I? She was smart and savvy and stunning, and even when I'd failed to lift her up, she'd made sure I was taken care of.

I didn't deserve her for a daughter.

And Christ. I had another one on the way. How long before I failed that one too?

My thoughts were interrupted by the shuffle of chairs as those around me stood. The meeting was officially over. For a brief second, I imagined ducking out without hav-ing to speak to anyone, but before I could really begin to entertain the idea, Warren, still seated, nudged me with his elbow.

"Edward, this is a pretty appealing scenario."

I had to make a choice—show my true feelings about this bloody plan and risk losing the opportunity of the alli-ance altogether or play nice.

Being a smart man, I made the smart decision. "It is," I said. "One I'm happy to support if you're on board."

Warren grinned and turned his attention to the other proposed entity in our alliance. "Hudson, I've got to say,

Pierce Industries as media players—quite a bold move. I like it."

"We try to be innovative whenever we can," Hudson said.

Right. Innovative. More like *safe*. His motivation had been protecting his personal best interests. Real innovation was about taking risks.

Fortunately for Hudson, Warren was easily impressed. "I'd like to study these numbers more closely, boys," he said, standing. "But if everything checks out, I think we have ourselves a solid strategy."

It was too much business for him for one day. He was obviously itching to get out of the building, probably headed for the golf course in the afternoon. Warren hadn't officially retired yet, but he'd been acting like he'd checked out for the last few years.

Sure enough, it was less than three minutes later when he'd gathered his team and was walking out the door.

"I'll walk you to the lift," I said, heading out with him.

"That went well," he said when we were in the hall and the conference room door had shut behind us. "Not at all what I was expecting. Love the idea of putting down our own digital cable. That will be very valuable to us. Nathan Murphy—have any qualms about him?"

I reminded myself I was playing nice before answering. "I hear good things about him. It's an interesting direction."

"It's not what we discussed, I know. You're still my first choice, but if Hudson's picked his horse to back, then we have a problem. Because of the risks involved with Glamplay, we really need to have more support across the stockholders."

I closed my fist and dug my fingernails into my palm. I'd been the one who had presented him with the risks of Glamplay, and now the man was acting as though he'd thought of it himself. It reminded me of another reason I wanted to be at the helm of Werner—because Warren was a douche and deserved to see his age-old rival sitting in his place.

"Now, here's an idea—you could go after Glamplay, buy up those stocks, and then we'd definitely have the strength we need to push a merger."

It was hard not to laugh. Yes. Great idea. Too bad Hudson had already had it six years earlier.

"They've refused to sell," I said, implying I'd already approached them. It wasn't exactly a lie. Hudson had made it clear he wasn't going to hand those stocks over anytime soon.

"Really?" Warren considered. "If they're not open to selling, then they'd have to vote however I do. Maybe we would have a shot at a merger after all."

If only it were that easy.

"I think your first notion was right. It's better to have Pierce on our side. We should stay the course." God, it hurt saying it.

"Then this alliance is a good idea. Show Hudson what you're made of, build his trust. Later on down the line, when this fuss with Ron has quieted down and Werner doesn't have so much media attention, we come back to the idea of a merger then."

I hated to admit it, but he had a point. This alliance was an opportunity to win Hudson's trust. Show him Celia was no longer a threat. In the future, maybe a merger. Or, perhaps, he would be amenable to selling his shares.

Werner could still be mine.

One way or another, it *would* be mine.

Bolstered by the knowledge that this quest wasn't over, I gave him the reassurance I knew he was seeking. "Good points, Warren. Good plan."

He nodded, as though my approval didn't matter as much as I knew it did. "Celia will like this too. Always a good idea to keep the wife happy."

I frowned. "Celia? Has she said something?"

The lift dinged then and the doors opened. "Nothing we haven't already discussed," he said, following his assistants into the lift. "Pointed out the risks. Said the timing was bad. Hey, we'll talk more. Come over for dinner, and we'll celebrate."

The doors shut, and I was left to wonder exactly what the conversation had been between my wife and her father.

I couldn't stand there for long, though. I had my own daughter to talk to.

Back in the room, I approached her, while she was busy un-hooking her laptop from the projector. "Genevieve. You had a hand in this proposal?"

Her face fell, guilt written across her expression. Stepping away from her task, she gave me her full attention. "I'm sorry, Daddy. I'm sure this feels like a betrayal. I know you wanted to run Werner Media yourself."

Playing nice worked with the men. With my daughter, I'd have to take it to a whole other level. There was no way I could live with myself if she had to carry this as a weight. I'd kept her away from my vengeful dealings so she wouldn't be poisoned by my rage. All the pushing away would have been in vain if I let her be poisoned by my feelings now.

Swallowing any traces of lingering emotion, I gave her the most laid-back, most unaffected version of her father I could muster.

In other words, I lied.

"I did want to run Werner Media. Until this morning when Celia broke into tears and told me she really wishes we could stay in London. I wasn't looking forward to telling her father that I wasn't going to take his position. This solves that dilemma." I smiled, hoping it was sincere enough to pull off the sham.

Her eyes shone bright with hope, and any doubts I had about deceiving her vanished. "Then you're not mad?"

"I'm not mad." Not at her, anyway. At myself, yes. And who else, I wasn't sure.

But there were other things I genuinely felt about her. "I'm surprised," I admitted. "I'm also quite impressed. A lot of work went into this. Lots of those ideas I recognize as yours. It's first-rate.

"You think so, even though you don't want me working in the business?" There was a catch in her voice, and for the first time I realized all the real damage I'd done in keeping her at a distance.

I moved closer, as if that one step could bridge all the steps away I'd taken over decades. "The only reason I haven't wanted you working in this business was because I truly thought you'd be happier elsewhere. You've had ambitious goals for Accelecom, and I feared you'd never be able to achieve what you wanted if you stayed with us, but it seems you've found a way to make them possible. I'm proud of you, princess."

Her eyes glistened, and I wasn't sure if it was me or her

who reached first, but the next thing I knew, I was holding her. Clinging onto her in a way I hadn't since she was little. Something tightened in my chest and stretched up to the back of my throat, making it hard to swallow, and for a moment, I wasn't sure that I could stand anymore if she weren't in my arms, holding me up.

We held each other like that for long seconds. When she pulled away, she swiped a tear from her cheek before she spoke, her eyes cast down at my shoes. "I know you're bluffing, Dad. You're disappointed. I know you don't like me to see your feelings because...well, I don't really know why you hide so much from me. Because you think I won't see you as strong maybe. Or because you don't think a man should show his emotions."

She looked up at me then, bravely. "Whatever the reason, I want you to know that you'll always loom tall in my eyes. You're my hero, and that's all there is to it. I'm super proud to be your daughter, whether you run every company in the world or none at all."

She'd got me. Right in the heart.

"Genevieve." I pulled her back into my arms. She'd left me speechless, and I needed another moment to simply hold her tight before I could respond.

"It wasn't all a bluff," I said, when I had enough voice to manage a harsh rasp, her head still pressed against my shoulder. "I really do have higher hopes for you than Accelecom. There are better places, better people to align yourself with." I was positive she'd have a job working for Pierce Industries before the day was over, and as much as it pained me to think it, I knew they'd treat her better than I had.

I drew away from her so I could look her in the eyes, needing her to hear this next part—to really hear it. "And

I am so proud of you. So very proud, which is entirely ridiculous because I can't take any credit for the woman you've become. I'm proud just to know you, I suppose. It's one of the greatest honors of my life."

With two straight fingers, she wiped at her eyes. "Daddy, stop. I'm working right now, and you're making me a blubbery mess." She swatted me playfully. "And shut up about not being able to take the credit. I'm all you, you prat. For good or bad, who I am is completely your fault."

"In that case, maybe you should be congratulating me." I cleared my throat, and eyed Hudson's younger brother, eager to move to a less sentimental subject. "This Pierce boy…"

"He's not a boy." She rolled her eyes, but it was her blush that gave her away. As I'd suspected, they'd gotten close.

Which made me really tempted to pull him away from his brother so I could break every bone in his body.

But I was a somewhat civilized man and reasonable enough to know that she was old enough to make decisions for herself—for good or bad, to use her words—and if this boy was one of the decisions she wanted to make, I had to let that be her choice.

There was one thing I needed to know, though. "He's good to you?"

"Mm." She peered over at him, her lips twisted. "He's trying to be. I think that's what counts. And I like him, a whole heap, so you can stop perusing him like he's prey."

A growl rumbled in the back of my throat. I expected better than "trying to be" good for my daughter.

"Please, Dad," she said, sounding a little more like she had when she'd been a teen than when she'd delivered her speech only thirty minutes before.

"Fine," I conceded. "But if he hurts you in any way—"

"I know, I know."

"You tell him that."

"Would you…?" She pushed at me with her shoulder, nudging me toward the door where Hagan was waiting with our things. "I'm good. Go. Meeting's over."

"I'm going," I said, chuckling. "I'm going."

The second walk down the hall was less tense. The episode with Genevieve had loosened something in me. Unwound me. My steps felt lighter. The weight of disappointment felt not so burdensome.

Hagan was business as usual, chattering at my side. "I set up a meeting for us next week with Pierce's chief finance officer and that Murphy guy, and I sent a text back to the London office. I'll brief them this afternoon, if you'd like. Or, if you'd rather. Oh, and I heard something."

"Heard what?"

"Gen mentioned that Celia was the one who arranged for Warren to be there today."

"Celia?" That didn't make sense. There were a dozen ways Pierce's office could contact Warren. Using Celia for a business arrangement was not the most effective method of communication.

Unless.

I stopped abruptly and looked back at the conference room just as Hudson walked out with his financial office . With a handful of strides, I was standing in front of him. "I've a question for you, if you don't mind."

"Certainly." His tone said he was only surprised that I

only had one.

There actually were several I would love to pose to him, if given the chance, but at the moment, there was only one that seemed important. "Would you have considered giving me the position if Celia hadn't intervened?"

It was a hunch. A gut feeling that I couldn't explain, but in my experience, my gut feelings very often paid out when I listened to them.

And sure enough, I was onto something. Hudson's usual austere expression had slipped into one of surprise, which might have indicated he had no idea what I was talking about, except for the way his eyes darted. That said he was hiding something. His surprise wasn't that I'd asked an odd question but that I'd known to ask it at all.

I held the higher card now, so I pressed on. "It's a fair question. After being denied a coveted position, a candidate has a right to know whether he even had a shot."

He took a slow breath in, his features composing as he did. "It *is* a fair question, and you deserve a truthful answer. I'm not sure whether she helped you or she hurt you. But she is the reason Warren thinks he has any say in this decision. I'd mark that as a victory, if I were you."

"Thank you. You've been very helpful." I ignored the outstretched hand he offered and turned back to Hagan, resuming my walk to the lift at a brisk pace, the earlier rage roaring over me in a gust.

I'd been right, then. I had been betrayed.

And the one who had betrayed me had been none other than my wife.

SIX

CELIA

I'd been pacing the hotel suite for two hours, checking my phone every five minutes while I waited for news from my father. Not that he'd necessarily update me right away. It would probably be my mother who would call and only if what happened at his meeting was interesting enough for him to tell her, and then interesting enough to *her* to pass on to me.

It occurred to me I might have a better chance of getting the story if I waited at my parents' house, and I'd called to say I was headed over earlier only to be told that Dad was going straight to the club when he was done, and my mother was headed to lunch with "the girls," whoever her gossip buddies were this month.

"Call me right away if you hear anything from Dad, will you?" I'd begged earlier.

"Sure," she'd said, distracted. Then, "You want me to

tell you about a business meeting of his?"

"It's regarding his replacement," I'd said impatiently, for the third time. Not wanting to explain more, I'd twisted the truth into a lie. "I want to know if he's changed his mind about working with Edward. So I can know if I need to prepare to comfort my husband or make reservations for celebrating."

"Oh, that's right," she'd said in a way that made me pretty sure she'd forget again as soon as I hung up. "I'll call if I hear anything."

Now, it was almost three hours later, and I hadn't heard a word.

Frustrated, I paused my pacing and texted her. **Any news yet?**

I hit send and then decided it was probably a good idea to clarify. **From Daddy?**

It took several minutes for her reply so I jumped when the notificati n pinged. **Only talked briefly. He says things are good. Ask Edward for more details. He was there as well.**

Considering I'd asked her to give me the update so that I could be prepared for Edward, her text was not very helpful.

Except that she'd filled me in on something I hadn't even thought to consider—Edward had been at the meeting as well.

Fuck.

Why had Edward been there? Chandler had asked me to get a meeting with my father. When had that invitation been extended to Edward? Did that mean Hudson had changed his mind? Was he giving over the top spot to Ed-

After our last encounter, it was possible, but didn't seem likely.

Then Edward had to have been there because my father had taken him along. Which meant he probably argued any alternative CEO suggested. Which meant Hudson had very definitely argued back, and though there were a dozen different ways I could imagine the scenario going from there, I was pretty sure many of them ended in the same way—with Edward in a rage.

There was a chance he wouldn't come straight home after. He spent most of his days in his temporary office, and even if he did come home, he might not give any indication that he'd had a bad day, seeing how he barely gave me any indication of his days at all as of late.

But if things had gone very, very badly for him, if he had any reason to blame me...

Going to my parents' house was once again appealing. Very appealing.

I turned my pacing into a purposeful stride, slipping on a pair of flats, searching for where I'd left my purse, finding it at the far end of the living room next to the sofa. After checking to make sure my sunglasses were inside, I turned to head out, muttering to myself how ridiculous I was being since, even if the meeting had gone as I'd suspected, there was little chance that I'd be connected to it at all, only to stop abruptly when I looked up and saw Edward at the mouth of the room.

Though his expression gave away nothing, his eyes said everything. They burned into me with vehement, laser focus, radiating hatred and fury and murder, and he didn't have to say a single word. He knew. I didn't know how it was possible, but he *knew*.

And here I was, trapped. Two glass walls at my back, a wall of books and a wall of concrete before me, Edward blocking the only way in or out.

Trapped.

"Good. You're here." Despite the indignation in his gaze, his tone was cold.

Scary cold. Cold that lashed and bit and bore down to the bone.

I always found him irresistible like that, when he was menacing and mean. It sparked something in the lizard parts of my being, turned me into a baser version of myself. Made me feral and restless and aroused.

At a more civilized level, it made me wary.

I swallowed, taking a careful step around the cocktail ottoman, calculating my options. Could I make it past him if I ran? Did I need to try to escape?

Did I *want* to?

"I was on my way out." This step was less cautious, as were the next two that followed.

But then he took a step of his own, toward me. "It can wait."

"It..." I was on the verge of making up a lie, but where would I urgently need to be? The doctor was my only obligation these days, and Edward had been with me when I'd made my next appointment for a month out.

Maybe I was making this into more than it was anyway. "Okay. What's up?" I forced a casual inflectio and urged the corners of my lips up, not quite a smile, but less not than before.

He moved again, toward me, stopping at the desk to deposit a small brown bag I only just noticed. The kind they used at the drugstore down the block. The shape the contents made wasn't quite discernible, but whatever it was, it stayed standing when he set it down.

"I had an interesting meeting this morning that I wanted to discuss with you," he said, and the bag was forgotten as I returned to panicking.

I pushed the strap of my purse up my shoulder, clutching to it with the need to clutch to something, and somehow managed to sound collected. "That's new. Since you don't usually talk to me about...well, anything."

"I probably wouldn't this time either, if you weren't so inextricably involved." He stalked toward me, circling round the ottoman like a lion on the hunt.

"Oh? What happened?" I reversed direction, which wasn't any better because now the couch was on the other side of me and the rest of the way around was narrow and more caged.

In a flash, he was right in front of me, heat emanating from his body now as well as his mood, and I dropped my purse and thought again of making a run for it, willed my legs to make the move, but something deeper willed me to stay still, not quite in surrender. More like in curiosity. In enthrallment.

"It's less of what happened that I'm apt to share at the moment," he said, backing me up toward his desk without laying a single hand on me. "And more of how it made me feel."

Shit. "Do you need to have a session?"

Not really the time to poke at the beast, but I never could help myself when it came to him.

And as often happened when I poked, I was rewarded. I fought not to purr as his hands gripped my hips, his touch sending electric pulses to my core and warmth up through my chest.

God, it had been so long. I wanted to lean in. Wanted to cling. Wanted to urge him to touch more.

Turned out no urging was needed. "I believe a session isn't necessary." He pressed his body flush against mine. "I can already succinctly articulate the emotion."

Delicious chills ran through me as he slanted his mouth toward my ear. "It feels," he said in a husky baritone, "like I've been fucked in the arse. By my wife."

My mouth fell open, my body ready to protest before my mind had strung any defense together.

He pushed tighter against me, pinning me with his hips while also showing off an impressive erection hidden inside his Brioni suit. Vaguely, I was aware of him reaching across the desk for the bag he'd set down earlier, then fully aware when he dug inside and pulled out a bottle of generic lube.

"I thought it only fair to reciprocate," he said.

Adrenaline shot through my system, my heart palpitating as I understood his intent. "Now...Edward..."

No words came after that because I wasn't all too sure what it was I wanted to convey. I needed a second to think.

But he didn't give me any time at all.

"Turn around." He was already guiding my body to do as he'd commanded.

I was halfway turning, so used to surrendering when he took charge, then came to my senses. "Wait. I'm..."

I blinked up at him, unable to finish this sentence as

well.

His eyes connected with mine, serious and seeking. "Are you telling me to stop?"

I should have.

I should have stood my ground, pushed him off of me, and said *This is not happening, no fucking way.*

But I was scared. Not because I thought he'd force himself on me, but because I was afraid that if I protested, he *would* stop, and while I was also very intimidated about what he apparently wanted to do to me, I was desperately wanting him, in any way he'd give himself.

Especially if he planned to give himself on his terms. That air of danger and dominance exuding from his every pore was not a detriment but, rather, a bonus.

Instead of responding with words, I simply finished turning around and leaned my palms down on the desk, readying myself for whatever he wanted to give, be it pain or pleasure or some cruel combination of the two.

"Good girl," he said, stroking from the collar of my dress down my spine, like he was petting a beloved animal.

I arched into it, seeking more as he continued over my ass, squeezing one cheek before gathering my skirt up at my waist. With one hand, he wriggled my panties down until they were stretched taut across my thighs then stepped back to admire the view.

He emitted a throaty, "Mm," a sound I echoed when he touched me, a single finger tracing my cunt. I was embarrassingly wet, dripping without any more stimulation than that. Eager, too, my hips pushing back, urging his finger inside me.

He granted me the smallest dip only to bring it back

out almost immediately, trailing my wetness up to the hole above it, the rim that had never been breached, not in this direction anyway.

He worked himself in with his thumb, if I had to guess from the shape and curve of the rest of his hand on the flesh nearby. The tracing of this hole elicited a different reaction from me. It wasn't exactly unpleasurable. In fact, it felt kind of nice, though, also foreign, and while my body knew what it wanted from a finger at my cunt, it didn't quite know what to do with one in my ass. Should I lean in? Should I pull away?

Currently, I was frozen in place, and that wasn't doing much for me.

But then his hand was gone from my ass, and he was slanting over my body, his mouth at my neck. "Who do you belong to?" he asked.

And even though I'd heard him and knew exactly what he wanted to hear in return, I said, "What?"

His hand came up to collar my throat, firml , but not threateningly. More possessive. "Who. Do you. Belong to?"

It was a thinly veiled request of consent, maybe because, while I hadn't told him to stop, I also hadn't told him to go on. I hadn't given him an outright "okay." It was admirable that he needed that from me, I supposed, though I didn't believe he would ever actually force himself on a woman, despite his tendency to dominate and control.

I also didn't suspect that was all this was about now.

He knew it would be easier for me to "let" it happen and maintain the right to resent him for it later. It gave me both my cake and the eating of it, and that was way too much for Edward to ever let me have.

If I wanted the cake, I had to *own* the cake.

And that meant answering his question with yielding honesty. "You."

I could feel the whoosh of hot air as he sighed into my nape. "Say it again."

"I belong to you, Edward."

I didn't have to say any more for us both to understand my meaning. I was his to do with as he pleased. Because I wanted to be his. Because I trusted what he'd give me. Because I needed it, too.

With my consent given, he went into action, moving his hand from my throat and standing straight up. I glanced over my shoulder to see what he was doing.

"Eyes forward," he ordered.

I lingered, watching as he undid his pants, pushing down his boxer briefs just far enough to bare his steel column of flesh. It was hot, as always, his cock impressive to look at as well as be fucked by, but knowing where it was going this time, it was also a bit intimidating.

Maybe that was why he'd wanted my eyes forward.

I shivered and turned back to the desk, leaning down on my forearms. I had a feeling I was going to need the support.

He reached for the lube next. I watched from the corner of my eye as he flipped open the lid with one hand and pulled it out of my view. A tickle of wet down my crack told me he'd poured some there. His thumb returned to push some liquid inside before his touch disappeared again.

Then I could hear the slick sound of moisture and skin as he applied it to himself. I remembered watching him the other day, staring at his hand gliding along his cock, and imagining it now behind me made a fresh pool between my legs.

Cold pressure against my tight rim snapped my thoughts back to the present, to the foreign sensation at my backend and the visitor who wanted in. My muscles stiffened, my breath caught in my lungs, as I waited for the part that came next. The shove forward, the pain that would undoubtedly accompany it.

But it didn't come.

His tip stayed poised at the entrance—the exit?—while, once again, his palm traced down my spine, soothing me. Settling me.

"Touch yourself," he said sharply.

"I can't."

"I'm not asking."

I shook my head and bit my lip. "I don't want it to feel good."

It wasn't as though I thought I deserved to be punished. I'd done what I'd done for good reason, and however it had turned out in the end, I had no regrets.

But I also knew that Edward wanted me punished, and I wanted to be *us* again, and if giving him this could pay for what he perceived I'd taken away, then I would give it absolutely, with complete capitulation and trust.

From the low groan he gave at my words, he not only understood but appreciated it.

"I'm not sure right now if I want it to feel good for you either, but the fact remains that I will tear you apart if you don't relax, and I certainly don't want that." This time he moved my hand down for me, using my fingers to caress the blazing bud of nerves, held them there until he felt confident about my finger stroke

Then his fingers were inside me, in my cunt, pushing in from behind. He crooked them to massage against my G-spot in exactly the right way, the way only he'd ever discovered, and within several seconds, I relaxed into him, pushing my hips back, begging for more.

He took advantage of my ease, and slipped the tip of his cock inside me, stopping when he got to the tighter rim inside.

"Keep rubbing," he commanded.

I hadn't even noticed I'd stopped. I'd been too focused on the new sensation at my ass. His cock, it turned out, felt definitely bigger than his thumb. Like I-do-not-know-how-this-will-ever-fit big, and panic tensed my shoulders. Rubbing myself didn't seem to help. I was too busy concentrating, too distracted to feel anything good.

Edward's hand disappeared from my cunt, more liquid trickled in around the head stuffed in my ass, then his hand returned to mine, shoving it out of the way so he could swirl firm circles over my sensitive bud

Yes. Just like that. Yes.

I'd forgotten how good he was at working my clit. Bodies couldn't remember sensation like that. Like pain. I could remember that I liked it, that it was really, really good, but I couldn't remember the exact feeling.

And the feeling was fucking fantastic. My back arched, and I moaned.

He leaned over me again, and sprinkled kisses at my neck while pushing his cock back and forth against the tight ring inside me. Wanting blatantly to be in.

Rather metaphorical, I thought abstractly.

"You spoke to him," he said, low and urging. This wasn't a question, but the next part was. "In person or on the phone?"

That's what this would be then? An interrogation? I was glad, at least, that he didn't say *his* name. It didn't belong in this act, though even keeping his name out of it, he was still here, between us. As he had been for so long.

I hung my head, resigning myself. "In person."

"Did you play the seductive role or the dragon?"

"They're not mutually exclusive."

"You know what I'm asking."

I did, but the question irritated me. "I didn't try to seduce him, Edward. His brother was there, and even if he hadn't been—"

My words cut off as he inched farther inside me. Not a lot, not the whole of him, but his crown had definitely breached that rim.

He stayed there, still, letting me get used to it as his fingers worked magic, going back and forth from my clit to my cunt. Discomfort morphed with pleasure, and pretty soon I couldn't tell if I loved his cock in my ass or I just tolerated it.

Just when I decided it was definitely more on the love side, he shoved in all the way, filling me completel .

Holy.

Mother.

Fuck.

I felt filled. Overwhelmed. Full of Edward in every possible way—in my ass, in my cunt, in my head. In my belly, where our baby reminded me of her presence with a gentle flutter. He was all-consuming, and I never felt closer to him or more taken over or more on the verge of...something...something unnamable, and all of it was so fantastic and thrilling and new and painful and it terrified me to tears.

"Play with your nipples. Breathe." He was insistent but reassuring, and without even thinking, I complied, brush-ing the flat of my palm across my clothing, which was enough to stimulate my breasts these days.

And I breathed. A deep in and out followed by another. And another.

Then everything knotted inside me relaxed, and he was still there—still so completely there and everywhere—but it was no longer unbearably oppressive. Now it was fasci-nating and tremendous and even a little comforting and a whole lot of wonderful.

"There you go. Like that. Just like that."

He started moving, slowly. With short, delicate thrusts that sent shivers down my spine, made me warm and flushed and disoriented. Spun me up toward orgasmic eu-phoria.

I was in this blissed-out stupor, dazed by feeling *so much* in *so many places* at once, when his interrogation resumed.

"You saw him, his brother was there." He nipped my ear before going on. "And you said, 'Please don't let my husband have your company. Give it to someone else. Anyone else just not him.'"

"No!" He shoved harder, or in my alarm, I'd pushed back on him, and now I wasn't responding just to his accu-sation but to the throbbing heat inside my rear. "Ohmygod,

ohmygod, no." Then I worried he'd think I meant no to the action, which even at its most overwhelming, I didn't want to stop. I tried again. "Oh my God that's intense, and no, I didn't say anything close to that."

"What did you say?" His voice was hypnotic as was his rhythm, steady and pulsing, somehow hitting that tender spot deep inside me from the other side. Stars spread across my vision. A sonorous hum vibrated in the back of my throat.

"I said I knew." I had to close my eyes and take a second so I wouldn't explode. Once I caught my breath, I rushed on. "I knew he wouldn't give it to you. So I asked him to help make whatever he decided look like my father's idea."

Edward slowed ever so slightly. His hand tangled in my hair, smoothly before giving a rough pull. "You weren't out just to fuck me?"

Does he really think...?

I was on the verge of coming when I got it. Got why he was giving me this aching pleasure when he was so entirely incensed with what I'd done, not just now but the whole last six months—stopping my birth control, running away, refusing to give up A's name.

He wasn't *just* angry. He was also *impressed*.

He wanted me to submit to him, and I did, but he also wanted me to challenge him, and I did. And maybe it was like how I enjoyed being scared of him as much as I enjoyed being cared for, two opposing emotions that pulled and tugged and stretched and made him crazy and confused and basically fucked. No wonder we'd been at such an impasse—his battle was with himself as much as it was with me, and what was he supposed to do with that?

There wasn't much I could do for his personal wars.

That didn't stop me from wanting to acknowledge it. "No," I said, my syllables short. "But admit it." Heaving breath. "You kind of admire that I did."

"That's enough. That's enough. That's enough." A mantra repeated over and over as he pounded in, in, in, his pelvis slapping against my thighs, his words a hoarse string of *That's enough*, no breaks in between. One more time he tried to say it, his voice threadbare as he thrust harder, harder, harder. "That's e—

If he finished the end of his sentence, I didn't hear it. Sound muffled around me, as though I'd been plunged underwater, or like the aftereffect of a very loud boom. All I could hear was my heart in my ears underscored with a whir as an electric storm flashed across my vision and my muscles went completely rigid.

I cried out and spiraled and convulsed, taken by a full-body climax that was at least a 9.0 on the orgasm Richter scale. I couldn't remember ever being so devastated from pleasure, so completely wrecked that I didn't know up from down. Couldn't tell if I was standing upright or a puddle on the floo .

Distantly, I was aware of clenching around Edward's cock, of his dedicated commitment to keep thrusting, to the stuttered final jab before he roared with his own release, a jagged sort of groan that I was sure would make me hot every time I thought about it for years to come.

I sort of blacked out then. Several seconds went missing from my awareness. One moment I was braced on my forearms with Edward coming in my ass, the next thing I knew, my panties were up, my forehead was against the desk, and my husband was zipped up and put away behind me.

With gentle urgency, he pulled me up, gathered me into his arms and kissed me. Complete and thorough and all him because, even though I was grateful for his lips, I was too boneless and dazed to really do anything but take it.

When he'd seemed to get what he needed, he broke away, pressing his forehead to mine and sighed. "What am I supposed to do with you, bird?"

"Love me."

He let out a gruff chuckle. "I love you too much, I think, sometimes." Without moving our heads apart, he ran the back of his knuckles across my jaw. "I hurt you."

He had that pitch of regret, and the way he was holding me, I was certain he was talking about what we just did.

"Yes," I conceded. "But not how you think. And I hurt you too."

His eyes closed briefly then opened again. "Knowing that doesn't erase our argument."

"I know."

He brushed his nose lightly against mine, then un-tangled himself from me in degrees—first his forehead, then his hand from my jaw. Then his body was no longer pressed against mine. Then it was the desk that held me up entirely and not him at all.

He turned away to the windows to gaze out.

I wasn't ready to lose him again, and I wasn't sure that I even was losing him, but I needed to know some things regardless, and this seemed as good a time as any to ask. "Will you tell me how it played out?"

He didn't turn around. "A three-point alliance between Werner, Accelecom, and Pierce Industries. An opportunity to bring our assets to the US and for Werner to break into the foreign market while simultaneously developing hardware that can compete with Google Fiber. Nathan Murphy from Mirage is being offered Werner CEO."

"And no merger."

"No merger."

It was ambitious, but also totally doable with the financial strength of Pierce Industries. Hudson had that kind of power—gigantic power. The kind that was both awe-inspiring and ominous. It was a top-of-the-game privilege to be able to partner with him.

My ribs ached with realization. "He tied us more securely to him, didn't he? He doesn't just own the majority shares of Werner but now he's linked Accelecom as well." I thought I should probably tell Edward I was sorry, but there wasn't an apology I could give that would be worth the one deserved.

"If it makes you feel any better, I don't believe it was all Hudson's idea." After giving me time to react with shock and curiosity, he went on. "The younger brother presented the idea. You'll never guess who was at his side."

But I could guess because of what Chandler had said the other day. "Genevieve."

"You knew?"

I wished I had, simply because it was rare that I had the opportunity of surprising my husband. Except I didn't really wish that, because I hated that I knew it now. Hated how much her part in this had to have hurt him. How much it must have felt like a betrayal.

On top of my betrayal.

Yes, he'd had a very, very bad day indeed.

"I didn't know," I answered truthfully, aching to say

something more comforting. "I'd heard a mention that they knew each other, and the pieces sort of fell into place."

"She sold the idea rather brilliantly. In other circumstances…" He turned back to look at me. "I couldn't bear to let her think she hadn't masterminded a good thing. I told her you were crying, begging to go back to London."

"You're as good at playing games as I ever was." I smiled weakly. He almost smiled back. A beat passed. "Then we're headed back to London?"

"Do you want to go?"

Our conversation was painfully stilted but vitally important, so I stuck with it in earnest. "Cornwall Terrace is my home now. I want to raise our baby there. Turn my office into a nursery. Redo the playroom." Imagining us in London made my sides ache with longing. "But I'm attached to my doctor here. And the trial is about to start there."

"We'll stay then," he said, resolutely. "I'll get us a connecting suite for when the baby comes. We'll go home when you're ready, after she's here."

After she's here. I couldn't bear to think we'd still be this awkward with each other when she arrived.

I had to keep him, had to pull him back before we lost this moment entirely, but I didn't know quite how. "Genevieve and Chandler, then," when I couldn't think of anything else.

"Genevieve and Chandler." He seemed less dismayed than I thought he would be.

"I'm sure that has Hudson mortified. Though, could you imagine? If they stayed together?" It was comical, so I laughed. Then reality sank in. "Even more tied together."

"Perhaps that will work out in our favor."

I gave him a stare that very blatantly said I just can't possibly see how.

"It's a wonder what being family can do to a business relationship. Your father would never have agreed to a joint venture let alone a merger before we married. Maybe Hudson would finally feel comfortable about selling us those shares."

"You still want Werner."

"I'll *have* Werner. Eventually."

Of course he wanted it. He always wanted, wanted, wanted. There was nothing ever enough to satisfy him. He would get it too, as he always did. I had no doubt. It was something I both admired and resented about him. His hunger and avarice made him powerful, powerful enough to succeed, and that was a major turn-on.

Just, it would be nice to believe he had all he needed in loving me.

Way to dream, Celia.

And since the dream couldn't be reality, I had to fight for what I could get, for our baby. "I'm guessing this will be a long game. May I propose a truce?"

He raised a brow, intrigued.

"You keep your secrets, I'll keep mine. Whatever you pursue in business is, no pun intended, your business." I wished he were closer, that I could reach out to him or that I had the nerve to go to him and throw myself in his arms. Since I didn't, I put my hand on my belly for reassurance instead. "Until she's born, at least."

His eyes went from mine to my hand resting over our child. A split second later, he was in front of me again, wrapping himself around me. "Yes. A truce. It would probably be best. For both your sakes."

I blinked back tears, wary of asking for too much, but wanting more all the same. "For your sake, too?" I asked, hopefully.

"Definitely for my sake, too."

I relaxed into him, feeling like we were finally on the same side, even if we weren't really. We were for now, united in our love for each other and our baby and our determination to stay together no matter what.

It would be hard, though, when the truce was over. When the secrets pushed their faces up against the windows, demanding to be let in.

He was thinking it as well, he had to be.

I knew for certain moments later, after he'd suggested a bath to clean us up and soothe my tail end and after I'd cooed about his desire to take care of me like he once had so routinely and after he'd promised he would again from now on. He cupped a dominating hand at my cheek and brushed his lips over mine, hot and possessive and open-mouthed.

"It's not just Werner I want," he said. "I'll want all of you, too. Eventually."

And like everything, he'd get all of me. Eventually.

I was a fool if I believed anything else.

SEVEN

EDWARD

Nothing could have prepared me for this moment.

Not the birth of my first two children, delivered so long ago in another country, when newborn practices varied in small but significant ways, when infants were immediately carted off to a nursery to be weighed and measured and cleansed instead of placed, all coated in white, waxy vernix, on the mother's bare torso to stretch and squint and whimper and root.

Not the childbirth class that Celia had requested I take with her, and I, in an attempt to honor the truce we'd made in good faith, had humbled myself to concede—a twelve-week course that had consisted of labor rehearsals and relaxation techniques and a thorough tour of our birthing facility and guidance on how to coach and instructions on how to give a good massage, that I, thank you very much, did not need.

Not the hours of late night talking when Celia should have been getting her rest but, instead, curled up next to me with a baby book on her e-reader as I caressed the expanding swell of flesh that housed a tiny human forming in our image.

Even through the preceding fourteen hours of labor—as my wife had, despite growing weary from contractions that squeezed and wrung her like she were a sponge, soldiered and triumphed while I'd made poor attempts to guide and support her—I hadn't quite grasped what we were headed for, what the end result would be. That I would eventually be looking through glassy eyes at the most beautiful scene witnessed in my forty-five years of life—my daughter in the arms of a tear-streaked goddess, a woman so evidently made to be a mother that I suddenly wondered what importance I could possibly be in her life.

How had I ever thought to keep this from her?

I was thoroughly convinced this child was more than just a blessing of joy. She'd been fated.

"Ten on the second apgar test." The nurse folded the blanket back over the baby then pulled the tiny hat farther down on her head. "Make sure she stays warm now. Skin-to-skin is best for that, but you'll want to keep that heat trapped around her."

Celia nuzzled our daughter closer. "She's doing okay, then?"

I didn't know if the nurse noted the hint of worry in her tone or not, but she was sufficiently reassuring all the same. "Her color's good, she's breathing well. She's perfect."

"Oh, thank God." More tears leaked from her eyes as she bent down to kiss our baby's head.

Without leaving her shoulder where I'd been firmly planted for the last ninety minutes, I peeked over at the hospital team still working down below. Knowing our daughter was in good health was a relief, to say the least, but I wouldn't be able to relax until I knew my wife was as well.

"Everything routine?" I asked, afraid I sounded far more on edge than Celia had.

"Placenta's just been delivered," the obstetrics doctor said, not the one we'd met with over the course of pregnancy, but the one that had been on call when Celia's contractions had begun in earnest the night before, sending us to the center with her packed bag. "There's been no tearing. Nothing to stitch. We should be out of here shortly."

That hadn't quite been an answer to my question, and I teetered between asking again and forcing myself to accept that all was fine.

Before I made up my mind, the baby nurse—or pediatrician or delivery assistant, I didn't know who was whom anymore, the room having got crowded—called me over. "Would you like to cut the cord?"

"Uh." I blinked, having forgotten about that tradition. I'd assumed the job had already been done. "Sure. What do I…?"

A pair of scissors were placed in my hands, and a spot on the cord between two clamps offered up for me. I brought up the instrument and made the cut and the whole thing took a matter of seconds and especially compared to everything Celia had done to deliver our baby, was nothing, yet I felt quite smug in that moment.

My wife called me. "Edward?"

Frankly, I'd thought she might have forgotten I was

here in the midst of her elation, which was more a refletion on my feeling of insignificance than of her preoccupation with her child, and I returned to her side at once. "I'm here."

"Look at her. She's beautiful. Isn't she so beautiful?"

I picked up a miniature hand as it curled reflexively in the air. "She's exquisite."

"I know this pregnancy was uneventful for the most part, but I can't stop feeling like she's a miracle."

"She is," I agreed. "And meant to be."

Celia's head spun toward me. Her surprised eyes also held a question that she didn't have to voice to be understood. I'd been so vehemently resistant to conceiving. Of course she'd be confused about how much I wanted our child now that she was here.

I didn't get a chance to respond, though, before Talyse, the nurse who had been with us for the past several hours, put a comforting hand on Celia's shoulder. "We've done the immediate clean up needed. I'll be back within the hour to give her eye drops and Vitamin K. Meanwhile, we'll give you three a little bit of time to bond."

Panic registered on my wife's face. "You're just going to leave her with us?"

Talyse managed to hold her laugh. "She's yours now. You'll be just fine. I'll be a click of a button away, if you need me. Let her try to nurse if she wants to, or if that seems to not be happening, you can just hold her close. Let her hear your voice. She already knows you, and that will make her feel right at home." She paused to make sure Celia had really heard her before going on. "Does this precious little thing have a name yet?"

"Cleo." Celia glanced at me. I'd been charged with de

ciding on a middle name, which I had, but I'd yet to share it.

"Cleo Wren," I said now.

Celia's expression lit up as she put the meaning of our daughter's full name together. "Small bird of glory."

I suddenly worried it was the wrong choice. "Is it... okay?"

She nodded. "I love it."

"It's gorgeous," Talyse said. "And it fits her, as this small thing is definitely glorious." She ran her thumb across Cleo's cheek. "Now enjoy yourselves."

The door shut quietly behind her as she left, and we were left alone, a little family in awe.

My own alarm began to rise. It had been so long since I'd been around a child so small, and even when I had been, I hadn't done a whole lot of engaging. Mostly because I'd been a fuck of a father, and here we were with this sweet child, sure I was about to fuck up again.

Before the panic took hold of me entirely, Celia set down an anchor. "Sit by me?" She wriggled to the side to make me room, which wasn't much, but turned out to be just enough.

I sank onto the bed beside her, throwing an arm around her shoulders, then peered down along with her at the wiggling bundle pressed up against her chest. "You did it, bird. You did this. You grew a person and brought her into this world. I'm so unbelievably amazed by you."

"I know I complained a lot this last month about my feet and my back and my bladder and well, everything, really, but it kind of feels like all that was nothing right now." She considered for a second. "Okay, that's not true.

The last few hours were the worst. I honestly didn't think I was going to make it."

"I knew you would."

She looked up at me earnestly. "You did?"

I tightened my hold around her. "Never a doubt in my mind."

Her complaints about pregnancy hadn't been much either, to be honest. Marion had been quieter, of course, as I suspected she found a certain joy in her suffering. Celia, on the other hand, had been downright miserable, and it showed, even without her saying a word. The way she moved like it took a lot of effort, the way she tossed and turned every night trying to find a comfortable position, the way her feet had swollen up to the size of logs—I'd been astonished she hadn't carped more.

I'd done what I could for her, taking care of her in the manner I had before we'd fought so terribly as well as in new ways, and none of it had seemed enough. Of everything I was able and willing to bear for her, this had been the one thing I simply could not, and it had infuriated me almost as much as not being allowed to seek vengeance in her honor.

It was funny how that had begun to mean both less and more to me.

I much preferred loving her to bickering. And the glow she carried throughout her pregnancy had made me truly doubt whether she needed the closure to her past that I believed she needed.

At the same time, as the weeks turned into months, as Celia carried the burden of pregnancy and our child became real and inevitable, my sense of purpose became more primal and fully rooted. Wasn't I supposed to be the caretaker? Wasn't I supposed to look out for her in everything? There existed a natural instinct for her to be a mother, a need that she had desperately required be met. Wasn't it natural that I possessed a similar instinct to protect and defend?

Her denial to let me be that for her, primitive as the notion might be, seemed as oppressive as I'd been in trying to keep her from having a child.

There.

I could admit it. I'd been wrong. It was impossible not to acknowledge it in the presence of the creature suckling at Celia's breast.

"Hi, Cleo. It's your mom. I've been waiting so long to meet you." She let out a giggle as the tiny mouth closed around her nipple. "Wow. That feels so weird."

"It can't be that odd," I teased. "I've sucked your tits on plenty of occasions."

She gave a glare that was hardly effective with the grin that accompanied it. "It's not the same. At all."

"I probably shouldn't find that so mollifying, but I do."

"You're such a man." Her smile lingered as she cooed again at Cleo. Then it disappeared entirely, her brow knitting ever so slightly. "Our truce has expired."

I winced. It shouldn't be the thing on her mind right now, and I felt entirely to blame that it was. "This isn't the time for that discussion."

"Actually, I think this is exactly the time for that discussion. Everything changes now, with her. We have to get used to a whole new rhythm of life, we have to develop new routines, and I can't do that if I don't know where you and I stand."

"We stand exactly where we've always stood, bird—I love you, you love me." I reached across her face to sweep a piece of hair behind her ear. "That should be all that matters."

My hand remained there, cupping her face, and I don't know if it was me or her that tilted her chin up, but soon her eyes were locked with mine. "If that's all that matters, then you don't ever need to know all my secrets."

The room felt suddenly colder, like the air had just kicked on, which was definitely not the case seeing as it was early in February with a snowstorm predicted in the coming days. What she'd said may have been a casual statement, one of her barbed jabs she was so fond of pointing in my direction, but it had the heaviness of an ultimatum.

I opened my mouth to respond, but nothing came out.

She shook her head against my palm. "You can't drop it, can you?"

"This does not need to be decided right now," I insisted, rubbing my thumb across her skin. "I'm certainly not going to begin efforts to find out what I want to know anytime soon."

"Then when?" Her voice was as sharp as her gaze. "Will you wait until she's a year old? Five years old? How about until she's eighteen?"

"Celia…"

"If you can't let this go permanently—"

I cut her off, dropping my hand from her face at the same time. "You better not be headed where I think you are. Not ever, but certainly not right now, of all occasions."

She swallowed, her eyes dropping back to Cleo who

had fallen asleep at her breast. When she looked up again at me, her expression was both softer and more resolved.

"Here's the thing, Edward—this isn't just about us anymore. Our battle doesn't just affect you and me. I could live with your distance and your resentment before, but not now. She doesn't deserve that. She deserves parents that are partners, not rivals. I won't be that for her."

"Then we won't be that for her. We are far from rivals. Just because we don't agree on everything doesn't mean we aren't a good pair."

Abruptly, she seemed to switch gears. "Do you love her?"

It gutted me that she had to ask. I had to take a moment before I could answer. "Of course I love her. How can you not know that?"

"You didn't want her."

"I wanted her. I just…" I sighed. I'd been scared, in truth. Also, I'd been a bully. "I shouldn't have leveraged a baby to try to get what I wanted. I know that. But you see, don't you, that you were also not fair in how you went around that?"

"I do see that. And I refuse to be like that anymore, a person who has to scheme to get what she needs. So if you can't give me what I need then—"

"Don't say it." She stopped at my command. Momentarily, anyway. Then was about to say more so I said it again. "Don't. Please. Please, don't." I couldn't bear to hear how the sentence ended because if it went where it so definitely seemed to be going, I didn't know if I could continue drawing air into my lungs. I'd been through one divorce, and it had nearly killed me. I couldn't imagine what it would do to me to lose Celia when the way I loved her was so much more than the way I'd loved Marion.

She nodded once, conceding. "I don't need to say it for you to know."

That confirmed it then. My worst fea .

My eyes fell to Cleo, the sun and all the stars combined. It was insane that we were talking about this right now when she was here, and she was glorious, and ours, and I loved her. More than I thought I would. More than I'd thought I was capable of loving anything.

"What is it you need?" I pushed the words out with quiet force, knowing the conversation wouldn't go away just because I wanted it gone.

It was an atomic bomb of a question, though. Because when she answered, as I was sure she would answer, demanding I give up the quest to avenge her wrongdoer, asking me to be a man that I was not and had never been, then everything between us would explode, impossible to ever put back together again.

But she didn't answer how I expected.

"It's not what I need, it's what she needs. And it's non-negotiable." She bent to nuzzle her nose against Cleo's head, then, with her eyes still centered on her, she said, "You will be everything for our daughter. Everything. You will be present. You will be engaged. You will put her before any other pursuit—before your business, before your obsessions. You will care and provide for her. You will keep her safe. You will protect her from predators. You will believe her when she comes to you in a crisis. And when the world lets her down, and she needs to crawl into your lap and fall apart, you will listen to her and console her and build her up again, but you will not destroy her monsters for her, not even if she asks you to, unless we both agree it's the right thing to be done, and—" she lifted her eyes promptly to mine "—I'm telling you right now, Edward, it will very rarely, if ever, be the right thing to be done."

It was like slamming into a wall of bricks the way her words hit me, their impact was so forceful. I was supposed to take care of her, to see what was best for her. I knew the horrors of her past and her father's role in her pain. How had I not understood that what she'd need most for me to be was a father for her daughter that she wished she'd had for herself?

As sure as I had been that I had fucked up my older children and that I was doomed to repeat it with Cleo, I was suddenly sure that I wasn't. I could be those things she asked. For our daughter. Because Celia believed I could be. Because she demanded it of me. Because I wouldn't be the man who repeated the sins of her father.

I once again brought my hand up to her cheek. Her face was wet with tears, her eyes full of more that had yet to be shed. Yet she was, at that moment, the strongest person I had ever known.

"I will," I said hoarsely, a ball stuck at the back of my throat. I cleared my throat. "I promise. I will. For both of you."

A tear leaked down my cheek as I kissed her forehead. Another fell as I bent to kiss Cleo. She stirred, her eyes squinting and relaxing several times, as though she were trying to open them. Then she gave up and gave her energy instead to suckling at her mother's breast.

"Good," Celia said, her own voice tight. "Thank you, that's...good."

We settled into silence, heavy but not burdensome. As

though I was carrying a load that I very much wanted to be carrying. My emotions were a knot inside me, too tangled to pick out all of them individually.

One, though, stood out from the rest, one I was quite familiar with—the "almost" feeling. The one I'd experienced most frequently after Celia had come into my life. Before her, I'd always been insufferably far away from whatever it was that was the goal, the abstract completion that I longed for and could never actually achieve.

Then she'd appeared, and that "will-never-reach" feeling had grown more and more possible, and now it felt so close. Like trying to catch a string of a helium balloon just as it drifts out of my grasp. Like closing my hand around a fistful of fog or smoke and opening it again to find a bare palm.

I closed my hands now, one around Celia's shoulder and another around Cleo's tiny foot. I lay there, as long as I could, until a nurse came in to tend to my women, way beyond when my limbs had fallen asleep and my neck had got a crick, afraid if I opened my hands again I'd find them both empty.

EIGHT

CELIA

I gasped and brought my hand to my chest, a cliched gesture that was both authentic and fitting for the moment. "Oh my, that's spectacular!"

Spectacular was actually an understatement. The Edwardian style jewel on Genevieve's finger, with its bead of diamonds around a larger stone, was genuinely one of the most gorgeous engagement rings I'd ever seen.

Also, possibly one of the most expensive. The center stone had to be at least two carats, and if I had to guess, I'd say the whole thing probably cost a hundred grand.

I supposed that was the kind of bauble you got when you hooked up with a Pierce. Once upon a time, I would have been seething with jealousy, despite having not an ounce of attraction for Chandler. It was his last name that I'd coveted. I could barely remember feeling that way now, as content as I was with a sleeping four-month-old baby in the next room and a husband that I loved madly at my side.

A husband who hadn't said a word since his older daughter stuck out her hand to share the good news.

"Daddy?" Her voice was cautious but hopeful. Understandably so. She was only twenty-four, and last she'd told us, she'd indicated marriage wasn't anywhere on their radar. She and Chandler hadn't even been together quite a year yet. Not to mention the bit about him being a Pierce. It was natural to assume that her overprotective father might have some reservations about their union.

I bit my lip as Edward remained silent, feeling the tension thickening around us. Just as I was about to put my hand out to touch his thigh so I could nudge him out of his stupor, he stood and without a word, walked out of the room.

Genevieve and I exchanged a glance then she exchanged one with Chandler who had her ringless hand clenched tight in his. The expression on her face was one of bewilderment. His, on the other hand, was tightening with what I could only imagine was rage.

Heat rushed up my neck in mortification. It was one thing to be skeptical about their relationship. It was quite another to be an ass about it.

I stretched my neck so I could look through one of the openings in the bookcase that separated the living room of our suite from the next. Edward hadn't gone far, apparently. He was in the dining room leaning over the wet bar.

"Edward? What are you doing?" Admittedly, there was a sharpness to my tone. Things had been so good between us, and I didn't want to start a fight, but I would if he didn't get his act together. She was still his daughter, and she deserved his support no matter what her choices. Weren't those words that had come out of his own mouth when she'd first decided to work for a company he abhorred after graduation?

And what was there not to support, anyway? He'd said he'd been happy when she'd taken the job at Pierce Industries. He already knew she wasn't returning to London anytime soon. She'd been dating Chandler for months. The only thing that had changed was she was now engaged to one of the wealthiest men in America. There was no way he could justify the cold shoulder.

"Coming." The clinking sound accompanied his response. A second later he was back in the room carrying four glass flutes and a bottle of Dom Perignon that had been put in the fridge a couple of days before in preparation for a celebration of our own that we had yet to make time for. "I thought the occasion called for champagne," he said, distributing the glasses. "It's not every day that your child gets engaged."

The rest of us sighed in unison, the tension immediately evaporated and replaced with smiles and hugs and congratulations.

Then Edward popped the champagne. "Shall I pour one for you, love?"

I mentally calculated how much breast milk I had stored in the fridge. Enough to get through the night, I was sure. Which meant I could express and dump if I had any alcohol now.

Still, I hesitated. Nursing was one of my greatest joys, a special time for me and Cleo to bond with each other. With Edward too, who was often at my side for feedings when he was home.

Seeming to read my mind, he said, "Let me feed her

when she wakes. I rarely get the opportunity."

My devil had grown awfully princely over the years. It made my chest tight to think about. "In that case, fill mine to the top."

Everyone laughed as Edward poured each of us a full glass. When he'd finished serving, he set the bottle down and lifted his flute. "To a long and happy union. May you continue to love and bring out the best in each other for the rest of your days."

Simple, but sincere. Genevieve wiped her eye as she raised her glass to clink against each of ours.

"Honestly, Dad," she said when we'd all taken our first swallows and remarked on the quality. "I was scared there for a moment."

Edward arched a brow. "You were? Whatever for?"

She stared at him like the question was ludicrous. "You didn't say anything. Then you got up and Left. The. Room. That's not the behavior of a father who is about to give his blessing."

"Genny had already been nervous you wouldn't approve." Chandler gazed adoringly at his fiancée. "I'd even prepared a speech defending our decision in case…" His brows knit, and I could tell he was imagining himself standing up to Edward. "Well, thank God it didn't go that way."

I smiled to myself, feeling lucky that I was married to such an intimidating specimen.

An intimidating specimen who was at that very moment being especially intimidating. "You thought I wouldn't approve? Because you're both so young or because you've known each other less than ten months or because you're a Pierce?"

"Most people think the name is an advantage." Chandler, poor thing, managed to sound brave despite himself.

"Indeed, I'm sure they do."

"Dad," Genevieve chided. "You are being awfully *you* right now when I was just praising you for *not* being you."

My husband smirked, which his daughter responded to with an equally childish sigh.

"Fine, let's discuss this then." Edward crossed one arm over his chest, his flute held up with the other. "How could I possibly argue about your age? I married Genevieve's mother when I was younger than you both by a few years even, though perhaps that isn't a good example since we ended in divorce. On the other hand, Celia and I had known each other far less time than you when we got engaged, and whether she likes it or not, she's stuck with me."

His glance at me was playful with the hint of a wink without actually moving his eyelid. "As for the name..." Here Edward grew eerily sober. "Chandler knows full well it won't stop me from killing him with my bare hands if he ever hurts you. Don't you, Chandler?"

Chandler swallowed. "Uh. I do now."

A chill ran down my spine. Edward was considered formidable for a reason—he was as much bite as he was bark. Even now when I suspected he was pulling the kid's leg, I couldn't help remembering Camilla and her abusive husband. Edward had killed Frank, I was sure of it, and maybe it was justified, but was murder ever really justified

I wished I knew the story. It was a secret he refused to tell since I had a secret of my own, and I'd gotten used to ignoring the burning want to know for the most part, but today, I desperately wished I had answers. It might calm the terrifying certainty that, though I was sure Edward meant for his words to be taken in jest, he was actually being quite sincere.

"Dad!" Genevieve said with a laugh, breaking the tension knotting in my belly. "Stop it. Please. You're scaring my fiancé.

Finally, Edward caved, a grin breaking out on his face. "In all seriousness, blessings to you both. I'm very happy for you. And maybe sometime Chandler can tell me how he gets away with calling you Genny."

She nuzzled into Chandler. "It doesn't sound the same when he says it as when you do. Out of your lips, it makes me feel like I'm seven years old. Out of his…" She blushed, making it apparent the nickname had become special between them.

"It's very exciting," I said, stepping in so she wouldn't have to say more in front of her father. "And I'm so thrilled for both of you. Truly. Now tell us everything about how it happened. I'm dying to hear the details."

An hour later, after we'd finished the champagne and heard the story twice—once from Genevieve then almost entirely again from Chandler with Genevieve frequently interjecting to comment, the conversation began to die down and the couple made innuendos about calling it a night.

"Thanks again for the bubbles," Chandler said, setting down his empty glass. "They really stock the good stuff here, don't they?"

"No, actually, they don't," Edward laughed. "I'd purchased it Friday for other celebratory reasons."

"Oh. Did we…?" Chandler's ears went red, obviously afraid he'd made some gaffe. "I feel bad about taking your champagne. Not if you were saving it for something important."

"Stop it," I said, feeling pleasantly tipsy. "We'd rather share it with family. We can get another bottle, or better yet, we'll wrap that celebration into this one and call it good."

Genevieve was the one who thought to ask. "What was the occasion?"

Edward looked to me, giving me the opportunity to decide what I wanted said. I appreciated it. And I also didn't. There had been a time when he would have made these decisions for me, when he would have taken more of a dominant role in our relationship. He still cared for me in all the ways he once had, choosing my clothes and helping me with my agenda, just now he deferred more to me for my opinion. He didn't command anymore, he suggested.

Maybe he thought he was being a better man by giving me more space of my own. It was true that I'd grown stronger and more capable since the days after he'd broken me down. This might very well be the next step in building me up again, and I was forever grateful for that. But I missed the way we used to be and desperately hoped we would find our way back to some form of that eventuall .

Meanwhile, it was up to me to answer. "My uncle's trial is over. Or, it's almost over. The Crown Court found him guilty on several charges on Friday. Now we're just waiting for sentencing."

God, it felt better to say than I'd realized it would. I hadn't had a reason to verbalize it since I'd found out since Edward had been with me when the verdict had come through. He'd been the only person I'd discussed it with at all so far, partially because I couldn't imagine who else I would talk to about it. I'd avoided my parents, not wanting to hear my father lament about injustice that I related to far better than he ever could. Edward had called Camilla, but I had let them talk alone rather than jumping in.

Beyond not having anyone to speak to about it, I hadn't quite known how it would come out if I did. It felt like a weight had been removed that I hadn't realized I was still carrying. I'd thought that I had unloaded everything Ron-related by now, so it was surprising to feel I still had more to set down. And as good as it felt to finally be free of that, it also made me strangely sad. I'd spent the better part of Saturday crying off and on about it, and Edward had been a saint, taking care of Cleo by himself since it was Elsa's day off, bringing her only when she needed to nurse, and I needed to cuddle.

Today, I felt much better. The grieving was over, and now there was only release in its place. It sort of felt like floating, like a feather in the wind, rising and falling with each gust, never touching the ground.

"Will the US extradite him?" Genevieve asked. We hadn't told her much about my past with Ron, but she was a smart cookie. She knew.

"Not unless the sentence he gets is minimal. Which it could be, and that would be a whole other nightmare, but there's also a real good chance it will be severe."

"Oh, Celia. What a relief!"

Chandler seemed still in the dark, but he was gracious all the same. "You must be grateful to have that media circus finally done with.

"I am. I am." Tears pricked at my eyes, much different than the ones that had overtook me the day before. I blinked them away. "But I'd much rather focus on your celebration instead. Have you picked a date yet? Please, say it isn't too soon. You have to leave time to let me throw an engagement party in your honor."

Her eyes widened in surprise. "You don't have to do that."

"Of course I don't have to. I *want* to."

"I'm so flattered." Her own eyes looked glossy. "And after the amazing event you threw for my graduation, I would be a fool to turn you down. But don't you want to be getting back to London now that the trial is done? I don't want to keep you here any longer than need be. I know you've been quite homesick."

"It's true, I want to get home, and we will. Soon." I felt Edward's eyes on me, but I couldn't look at him without giving myself away, and I wasn't quite ready for that. "There's some other things we're tying up here first, and neither of us want to miss out on the fun surrounding a wedding. Please let me plan something. It would be my honor."

Another quarter of an hour later, with permission granted to throw a dinner party in their honor, the couple made their goodbyes. I slipped away to check on Cleo in the adjoining suite, then, finding her still asleep, I returned to the living room where Edward was settled on the couch, his legs crossed and his arm draped across the back of the sofa, waiting for me. "Would you come sit with me, bird?"

A sharp ache pierced between my ribs, a longing for the order rather than the request. The dominance had even been toned down in our sex after we'd come to our truce. I'd hoped it might spice up again after Cleo, but the handful of occasions we'd found time and energy to make love since her birth we'd done exactly that—made love. I wasn't complaining, I really wasn't. I enjoyed what we had, and if we kept the status quo for the rest of our lives,

I would die a happy woman.

Still, I knew we could be more. That we *were* more. That the absence of his command was really an absence of my submission. I'd walled off a part of me from him and so he'd walled off a part of himself from me. Intentional or not, I wasn't sure, though I suspected it was the latter. Maybe he noticed it too, but I doubted he'd done it purposefully. And now that this was how we were with each other, perhaps he was as uncertain as I was how to return to what we'd been.

"If you'd rather not…" he said when I hadn't moved or responded.

I shook my head from my thoughts. "No, I want to. Sorry. I guess the champagne gave me a little bit of a buzz." I sat next to him on the sofa, curling my feet up underneath me as I burrowed into his side.

"Are you too buzzed for a serious discussion?"

"Nope. Just buzzed enough to feel good. Are you going to kill it?"

"I don't plan on it." He drew me tighter to him, stroking his fingers down my arm. "I'm only wondering why you want to delay going back to London. Have you changed your mind about living there?"

"I haven't. I'm dying to take Cleo home and settle in where there's more space. Even with the additional suite, this place is rather small and stifling.

He was silent a beat, and I sensed he was trying to fi - ure me out. I liked his curiosity enough to not rush to giving him answers. It was rare that I had an upper hand with him, and I wanted to relish it a little longer before laying down my cards.

"I hope you didn't offer to throw the engagement party

on my account," he said after a time. "I'm very appreciative, but it wasn't necessary."

I sat up so I could look at him. "Yes, it was for you, you
silly. And for her. I'm not that close to Genevieve, but I do
love her and want to be part of her life."

"I love that about you."

His declaration gave me the confidence to reveal more.
"But also it was for me. It will give me something to do
besides be cooped up in here all the time while we go after
Werner."

The air turned electric. I could feel the charge emanating off his body as he studied me. "What are you saying?"

"I'm saying, I think it should stay in the family."

"And you have a plan for that? I doubt you would bring
this up if you didn't."

It wasn't quite a plan that I had, but rather a desire.
A desire to give my husband what he needed. A desire to
lay my heart at his feet. A desire to show him that I was
a strong woman, but not so strong that I couldn't also be
sometimes mastered.

Just, how to turn that desire into action?

I turned my body so I was facing him completely. "I've
been so stuck on making sure you didn't go head-to-head
with Hudson, and I still feel that's the right choice, but I
was too preoccupied to realize there are other ways to get
what it is you're after. Not the CEO position—even if we
could manage that, this isn't the time. Cleo needs a father
who isn't working all the time, and that would definitely
keep us in the States, which is not where I want to be in
the long run.

"But majority shares—or at least equal shares with

Hudson. That could be doable."

His eyes narrowed, considering. "You think Hudson might be amenable to selling us one percent now that Genevieve is marrying his brother?"

"Possibly. I think it's worth trying. But if he won't, there could be another way." I ran my teeth across my bottom lip. "I want to help you find a wa ."

"Go on." I could practically hear his pulse tick up.

My own heart was racing. "Hudson owns forty-two percent. We own forty percent. There are still those other eighteen percent shares."

It wasn't news to him how the shares had been distributed. Werner Media was still privately-owned—*family*-owned for the most part. The company had been started years ago by my grandfather and his brother, Chester. When Uncle Chester had died, his fifty percent had been distributed among his children, just as Grandpa Werner's shares had been passed to my father and Uncle Ron, but no one had had the ambition to run the company like my father had. So little by little, he'd bought family members out of most of their shares. A few relatives had since sold their remaining shares to outside parties who were unwilling to sell again, but there were four cousins that still owned two percent each.

Edward guessed where I was going and shook his head. "I've already approached the other shareholders. They've all said no to selling."

"You approached them when you were still an enemy of my father. Now you're part of an alliance with him. You'll have been validated in their eyes. Also, since the values of those shares have dropped recently with Ron's trial, some may be more interested in bailing now."

"Possibly." He wasn't convinced, but I hadn't expected he would be.

The real benefit of my involvement came with what I offered next. "If none of the outsiders are interested, I could talk to my cousins. None of us are particularly close, but I'm pretty sure I have some sway with two or three of them, especially if I leveraged some family secrets here and there. Buying out any one of them would make us equal with Hudson. Buying one percent off two of them would do the trick too."

His eyes sparked with something I hadn't seen in months. "Buying them all out would put us ahead of Hudson."

For half a second, I worried I'd made a mistake bringing this up. I didn't want to hold him back, but his ambition scared me at times. It was too monstrous. Too much a life of its own.

Instead of pulling back, though, as I would have done in the past, I gave him the chance to step up to the common ground as I had. "I don't think we need to be greedy. He still has power in unexpected ways. I'd prefer to strive for equality. For now."

Again he considered. Seconds passed, long and thick, until he reached his hand up to caress my cheek. "This isn't for you. This is for me, isn't it? You'd really help me go after those shares?"

"If it's still what you want, yes. I will."

In one swift move, he lifted me from his side, brought me to straddle his lap, and kissed me. Kissed me hard. Kissed me like he hadn't in months, with hunger and desperation and worship and control. His cock pressed intently at the space between my legs and my pussy wept with eagerness as finall , *finally*, his mouth took mine with rough authority, a reminder of how he'd fucked me once upon a time. A promise of how he planned to fuck me again.

And then the urgent wail of a hungry baby burst through the monitor. My breasts leaked in response, my nipples aching with the need to express.

Reluctantly we broke apart. "I'll heat her bottle," I offered.

He shook his head. "Go pump," he said, and I shivered at the emphatic tone in his voice. "I'll bring her to you when she's been fed."

I walked to the bedroom, wet and unsatisfied, but a smile curved boastfully on my lips. We'd had our bumps, but I could see a path for us now, a path that might not be easy, but one that I was confident we could walk togethe .

NINE

EDWARD

" '"The market's reaction to the alliance between Werner Media, Accelecom'—that's daddy's company, Cleo-Leo—'and Pierce Industries has been strong, despite the recent drama surrounding former Werner CEO Warren Werner's brother Ron. This support is likely due to the manufacturing giant Pierce Industries and their contribution of tech components enabling the partners to, not only make plans to lay cable networks in the near future, but also to dominate the field.'" I frowned at the words I'd just read. "Well, that's bloody rubbish. As if Pierce is the reason for anything that's successful."

"You've bored her to sleep."

I peered up at the soft voice to see Celia standing in the doorway between our suite and the adjoining bedroom we'd been using for a nursery. She nodded toward the bundle in my left arm, and I looked down to find the baby that had been wriggling only a moment before was now fast asleep.

I chuckled. "I don't blame you, kiddo. Talk of Pierce Industries bores me too."

"I know they encourage reading to your child from an early age, but do you really think business magazines are the most appropriate choice of material?"

I shrugged. "She was fussy, and it needed to be read. Seemed like a two birds with one stone sort of situation."

Celia's smile was filled with adoration, and it warmed my chest recognizing it was meant for me as much as our daughter. "Better be careful. I'm at risk of being charmed."

"Oh, you're charmed all right." I tossed the iPad onto the ground so I could cradle Cleo with both arms as I stood from the rocking chair. We'd had it brought in only a few weeks before, and I couldn't for the life of me figure out how we'd got on without it. "She's charmed too, as you can tell."

Celia laughed, a sound that turned into a yawn as she stretched her arms overhead. "You should have woken me. I would have taken her." She glanced at the clock on the bedside table. "Oh, it's not even six. Where's Elsa?"

I set the baby down in her crib, careful not to disturb her slumber. "I sent her home early. And why would I wake you? You don't get nearly the amount of sleep as you should, and caring for our child isn't a job designated strictly to you and our nanny."

"Look at you win bonus points. You've been so good about being here for her, but I also appreciate that you have a full-time job on top of it."

I turned to study her, suspecting she needed validation for expecting me to participate in raising our baby.

She wanted my involvement as much as I needed to be involved, but neither of us had experience with a household where the father shared in the child-rearing duties. It was new ground for both of us, and though it was often bumpy, I was grateful to be walking it with her at my side.

"It's hardly a hardship to cuddle with Cleo," I assured in a hushed voice, picking up the baby monitor as I crossed to my wife. "But it's also nice to have a break, so if we want her to stay sleeping, we best get out of here."

Once the door was closed behind us and Celia had taken the monitor so she could check the volume, I pulled her into my arms and kissed her. "Should we start thinking about dinner?"

She cocked her head, exposing her neck, and I suddenly regretted making our kiss so brief. Dinner, it seemed, was not what I was hungry for.

"I need a shower first," she said, pulling away. "I changed before I fell asleep on the couch, and I still smell like spit-up."

She smelled perfectly fine to me. I was tempted to tell her so or to offer to help her smell like something else, but I was conscientious of making sure my wife had time for the pleasures of ordinary things like bathing that were often foregone in the hustle and bustle of motherhood.

Recognizing that didn't mean I was noble enough to resist imposing. "I'll join you."

"Good." She threw a saucy look over her shoulder as I followed her through the bedroom into the bathroom where she set the monitor on the counter. "I can tell you about the phone call I had this morning."

I would have frowned if she hadn't chosen that moment to peel her shirt over her head. Men could say what they would about children killing all desire—they hadn't seen my wife in a nursing bra. Her breasts pushing full and plump against the lace cups turned my cock to stone.

"Talking wasn't exactly what I had in mind," I said, tossing my tie on the floor then quickly undoing my cufflinks

"I think you'll be interested in this particular conversation." She shimmied out of her yoga pants, leaving them in a heap with the discarded top before reaching in the shower to turn on the water.

"Nothing is as interesting to me right now as you taking off your clothes. But go ahead and try to prove me wrong. Who was this phone call from?"

"Hudson." The name echoed against the tile, giving it more emphasis than it would have had if she'd said it while facing me instead of the faucet.

It was a suburb effect, intended or not.

I froze mid-unbuttoning my dress shirt. She was right—I *was* interested in this conversation. "Go on."

Seemingly happy with the water temperature, she turned back toward me. "He wanted to talk about the engagement party we're throwing for Chandler and Genevieve."

"News travels fast." I continued the task of loosening my shirt, my pace slower than it was a moment before, distracted by the change in conversation as much as I was by the damp spot at the front of Celia's panties.

"It does always seem like Hudson is the first to know most everything." She stepped into me and grabbed my shirt, tugging it out of my pants as I finished unbuttoning, then helping me discard it.

I slipped my hand inside her panties to cup her cunt while the other played with the strap of her bra. "This needs to go."

She tried not to react, but I saw the flash of lust in her eyes at the command. Or perhaps she was merely responding to my fingers skating along her seam. Her breath caught when I skimmed higher, against the bud under the hood of skin. She clutched onto me, her eyes closed, as she shivered.

I loved her like this—playing strong while falling apart. A beautiful dichotomy orchestrated with the touch of my hand.

"You're distracting me," she moaned.

"That's the point."

"Two can play this game." She stroked her hand up the length of my cock, still buried inside my trousers. "Now that I have your attention, I can go on. Hudson is concerned about everyone's 'comfort'—his word, not mine. Wants to be sure there won't be much reason for me to interact with his precious wife."

The scratch of her nails up my length made me hiss. "He really is scared of you, isn't he?"

"Eh, he's protective. His efforts to look after his own would rival yours."

"I doubt it." I tugged again at her bra, reminding her she was not as naked as I wanted her then shooed her hand away so I could be rid of my own clothes. Talking was fine and I appreciated the tales of her days, but if all her Pierce news amounted to was talk of upcoming nuptials, I was of the mind to postpone it.

Celia, though she got the hint about stripping, wasn't ready to give up the conversation. "Anyway, I agreed to let him approve the seating chart—"

"—That was generous—"

"—and then I told him we weren't leaving the States without a bigger share in Werner."

Nearly completely undressed, I paused in the midst of tugging off my sock. While I normally didn't find talk of business very erotic, I was suddenly extremely aroused. "And what did he say?"

"That he wouldn't sell, of course." She stepped out of her panties and tossed them aside with her toe. "But I also reminded him there were other ways for us to get what we wanted, that we were serious about going after them, and that the only way we could ever truly move on from this outdated feud was to give us equal stakes in the company."

As much as I loved Celia shattering because of me, I equally loved her dominating others. Especially when it was on my behalf.

I prowled toward her, backing her into the walk-in shower. "I don't think I've ever been more attracted to you than I am right now."

She smiled coyly but with pride. "He said he'd think about it."

"He won't."

"He might."

Her back hit the wall, and I caged her in with my forearms pressed against the tile on either side of her head. I stared at her lips, plump and inviting. "Bloody greedy." I didn't know anymore if I was speaking about Pierce or myself.

"I don't think this is about money."

I forced myself to focus, lifting my eyes up to meet

hers. This really was a significant turn of events. It had been one day since she'd told me she would join me in the pursuit of Werner, and if there had been any question as to whether or not it was simply lip service, I couldn't doubt her now. She'd thrown the gauntlet.

And Pierce had stood his ground.

It was such a ridiculous business move. He had no reason to keep that controlling interest when he didn't ever exercise any authority in the company. With our alliance, it was possible he could face monopoly accusations if his investment ever became public, a risk that didn't concern me since Accelecom was foreign owned. Pierce knew I'd pay well over the market value. So why was he so obstinate?

"He *is* scared of you," I said, finally seeing the situation with clarity. My wife hadn't just been a nuisance to him as I'd previously suspected—she'd been an outright threat.

Fuck, that was hot.

I cupped my hand over her breast, letting the weight of it settle in my hand. "To think you're a dragon after all."

"You've reminded me plenty of times that I'm not."

"That's how a man dominates a woman, don't you know?" She gasped as I pinched her nipple, rivulets of milk running down her skin as it mixed with the streaming water. "Tells her she's something other than she is enough times that eventually she believes it."

"You mean they gaslight? Who knew?"

I bent to tug at her peaked nipple with my teeth, despite knowing it would cause more letdown. Her breasts had been more or less off-limits because of the mess it made, a mess only she cared about. In the shower, though, she didn't have that excuse, and I took full advantage, expecting still to be scolded.

When she pushed me off of her a second later, however, it wasn't the nipple play that earned the scolding. "Are you admitting you gaslit me? I was a dragon this whole time and you made me believe I was only a little bird?"

"You'll always be my little bird, bird," I said, chuckling. I ran my knuckles down the side of her cheek, my smile fading. "But you were also always a dragon."

"You *did* gaslight me!" Rather than being angry, her expression seemed victorious.

It was a victory that I wasn't ready to let her have. "Perhaps it wasn't about you. Did you think of that? It was about *me* not wanting to believe you were a dragon. For my own sake."

"As if I scared you." It was bravado, though.

"Are you sure you didn't?" I fisted my cock, stroking it up and down once, twice before rubbing the tip against her seam.

"*You* scared *me*."

"You liked being scared."

"I still do."

I let a beat pass, let my head dip between her folds, then let myself say the thing that had been between us for weeks now. For months, even. "You like being loved more."

It shouldn't have been such a pronouncement, but it was. The shift that had occurred when she'd stood up to me had been named. She was no longer afraid of me like she had been, and fear was what had brought us together. It had been our glue, hadn't it?

Then I'd fallen in love with her, and that was what she required now from me. My love. And that should have been better. That should have been more than enough. It shouldn't matter that she no longer bowed to me, that I could no longer bend her to my will. At my side was what I'd wanted, too.

Or so I'd thought.

Celia understood the significance of the statement. Her brow cinched. "Can't I like both?"

I flipped her around to face the wall, unable to look at her while she asked for what I didn't know how to give. Lifting her thigh so her foot rested on the bench, I spread her open and notched my crown at her entrance.

My method of distraction wasn't working. She twisted her head over her shoulder. "Can't I *have* both?"

For a split second, it seemed possible, and I tried to imagine myself in that role—the husband that both ruled and equaled. A man who could let his wife win and still be in charge. How did that work?

Even if I thought I could fill that position, Celia would have to yield, and she didn't do that now. She stood her ground. She fought like a dragon, and a dragon didn't need a master.

As the possibility flickered away, I shoved into her with one blunt stroke. "I don't scare you anymore."

"You still have secrets." Her words came out choppy as I drove into her with staccato jabs.

Fucking her should have taken my mind off the rest. It didn't. "Is that why you insist we keep them secret? So that we can have something mysterious between us?"

"I shouldn't have brought it up."

No, she shouldn't have. Because now I was mad, and it was stupid and petty to feel so, and also it wasn't. The truce between us had calmed the conflict but it hadn't erased it. The secrets still stood between us like a clear barricade of teflon. There was no getting through them no matter how transparent they appeared, and still the illusion that it was possible kept me beating my hands against the walls.

"There's good reasoning to it," I said, pushing her with my words as well as my brutal thrusts. "Because if you don't know, you can always assume the worst. Then you can still pretend I scare you whenever you want." I reached around her body to pinch her clit. "Or is it not my secrets that scare you the most, but what I'd do with yours?"

She cried out, on the verge of orgasm, I suspected, but she managed to hang on, and a moment later she was collected enough to speak. "Even without the secrets, you scare me." It was quiet, a confession of sorts. "You're the only person who has ever loved me exactly like I am. The only person I've ever trusted entirely. That means you are more capable of hurting me than anyone who has hurt me before, and that's the most frightening thing I've ever imagined."

My tempo stuttered as I digested her words. Knowing everyone who had hurt her, knowing the *ways* they'd hurt her—that was a mighty declaration. It rocked me at my core. Made me off balance. That was a form of sub-mission, wasn't it? Being vulnerable like that. Making me aware of my power.

Then if the problem between us wasn't her inability to submit to her equal then it was me who couldn't dominate mine. All that time ago when she'd said I always had to win? She'd been more right than either of us had known. Because when I'd given in, when I'd dropped my pursuit of her past, and committed to loving our child as she'd demanded, I lost hold of something I'd taken for granted as permanently mine. I'd lost hold of my authority, and I didn't know how to get it back.

Taking advantage of my slowed pace, she turned around again to face me. She cupped my cheek with her palm and wrapped her leg around my hip, guiding me back into her heat. I pressed into her, all the way, as far as she could take me.

Sighing, she pressed her forehead against mine. "So good," she said. "You feel so good." Then, "We're good too, aren't we?"

Once again, I turned her around, this time pivoting so I could bend her, and she could brace herself against the bench. I shoved inside her, moving in and out with increasing speed.

"How can you ask that?" I gritted out. "How can you even ask?"

Then I fucked her with savage stabs, over and over and over, until her question was long lost to the friction and the frenzy and the orgasms that shuddered through us both. Until even I could believe that I'd ignored responding because the answer should have been obvious and not because I didn't know what it was.

TEN

CELIA

I **need to see you.**

The text popped up at the top of the Atlantic article I was reading while feeding Cleo. It was early, still. Just after six, and it was a Saturday. But Hudson was always up at the crack of dawn so that wasn't the surprising part of the message. The surprising part was that he'd sent it at all.

Of course I'd see him. I'd told him what we wanted, and if he was reaching out, it meant he wanted to negotiate. What else could he want? And he wouldn't want Edward there. I knew that as sure as anything, so meeting when Edward was at work was my best option.

Before I could overthink it, I typed a one-handed response. **My Monday is open. Where?**

His next text came almost immediately. **It needs to be sooner. Today. At my office.**

"He thinks he's out of The Game, but he still tries to control every situation," I said, mostly to myself, though Cleo looked up at me with her bright blue eyes and smiled around my nipple. "Right? We won't let him do that, will we?"

Tomorrow, I typed, just to hold some ground. **In the restaurant at my hotel. Five pm.** The baby was usually sleeping then. A good time to slip away.

The Sky Launch. At six.

"Oh, please." I was not meeting at his nightclub. I didn't usually care about his turf or mine, but since it so obviously mattered to him, I was reluctant to give in. Though, maybe being amiable was the way to go. I was the one who wasn't in the position that he was. He was the one with the stocks we wanted, not the other way around.

But if I'd learned anything from the men in my life— my father, Edward, Hudson himself—it was to never take the weaker stance. If anything, that was when to be even more firm. Besides, Hudson didn't hold all the cards here. I'd meant it when I told him we'd pursue purchasing stocks elsewhere. I didn't have to be as amiable as he demanded.

I pulled up WhatsHalfway, an app that found a middle location between two spots, and entered in the hotel and Hudson's office address

Randall's, I texted back. **It's a bar halfway between you and me. Six pm will be fine.**

His response didn't come as quickly, which meant he was thinking it through. And if he was thinking it through, it meant he'd come to the same conclusion as I did—we'd have to compromise.

Sure enough, his next text settled the matter. **See you then.**

I dropped my phone in my lap with a sigh. It had been almost two weeks since I'd talked to him about letting Edward and me buy those stocks. Hudson did like to think things through, and it had been enough time for him to have done that, but it wasn't like him to have a total one-eighty without much prodding. Had something—or someone—changed his mind?

Or was this meeting about something else entirely?

No. It had to be about the shares. I wouldn't know any more than that until we talked. But there was still one issue I had to deal with before then. I rubbed my hand over Cleo's fuzzy head. "Now we just have to figure out what we're going to tell Daddy."

She broke away from my breast so she could smile again. "You're not really interested in eating anymore, are you?" I pulled her away and reattached the cup on my bra then sat her up on my lap. She was getting strong. Soon she'd be sitting on her own. It felt suddenly like it was all moving too fast, that any second she'd be asking for her own phone and locking herself in her room with her music blaring. I hugged her to me, as though that could somehow hold the moment, as though it might slow time down and keep her *mine* for longer.

The door between our two suites creaked open, pulling my focus.

"If that's not an adorable sight," Edward said from the doorway, wearing nothing but his pajama bottoms. "We need to get a photographer in here. Before she's too wiggly to pose."

"I was just thinking she was growing up too fast." I brushed my lips across her forehead, making her grunt with frustration since the action had blocked her from tugging at the open drawstring on my nursing nightgown.

"That's how it happens. One minute they're crawling, the next they're engaged and moving permanently to the States."

It was the first time he'd said something suggesting any melancholy at all about his older daughter's upcoming nuptials, but I'd suspected he felt it. "Good thing you have this one to help lessen the blow of losing that one."

He came toward me with a smirk. "Yes. Good thing." He reached for Cleo, and I passed her over, then had to take a second to catch my breath. The sight of a bare-chested man holding a baby had never done things to my insides until it was *my* bare-chested man holding *my* baby.

Whoa. It was the definition of breathtaking

Edward rocked her as he stepped away, running his nose along her forehead. "Good morning, birdie," he said, the variation on my nickname one he'd adopted for her recently. "It's too bad you can't talk yet. You could tell me what it is that Mommy's trying to hide from Daddy."

I froze midway from standing up from the rocker, color draining from my face. How did he know?

Dammit, I was an idiot. "The baby monitor," I said as it dawned on me.

"The baby monitor," he repeated.

He held out his hand to help me up the rest of the way then used it to pull me into him, wrapping his arm around my waist when I was there. I didn't mistake it for affection, though it was clearly that too. No, this move was about asserting himself on me. "Do you have something you'd like to tell me?" he asked, pressing his lips to my temple.

I didn't even consider lying. We were on the same side when it came to the Werner shares, even if we weren't on the same side when it came to Hudson, but there was no reason for that to be an issue, as far as I could tell. "Hudson wants to meet up. He texted a little bit ago."

"That's great," he said, surprising me. "Did you tell him yes?"

"I did."

"Good. When are we seeing him?"

I pushed gently out of his arms. "Well. Tomorrow night. But he didn't invite *us*. He invited *me*."

"I'm okay with showing up without an invitation." He said it casually, his focus seemingly on Cleo who was suddenly very interested in his beard.

"Edward…" I tried to decide if this was worth battling.

Yes, it was. For several reasons, not the least of which was that the fewer personal interactions that occurred between my husband and Hudson, the more likely I was to keep my secret about him.

Not that I could tell that to Edward.

"If we both show up, then he'll feel outnumbered," I said instead. "He won't likely be willing to negotiate if he doesn't feel like we're coming to this on equal ground."

He knew I was right, but he still considered. "I could go in your place."

"If he wanted to talk to you he would have reached out to you." I forced myself not to take a defensive posture. "Look. He didn't have to ask to meet at all, and he did. I don't think this is the time to try to turn the tables. I should go and see what he has to say, and if that doesn't turn out to our benefit, we can change the game plan."

A beat passed. Then two. I was just preparing to double down on my argument when he surprised me once again. "I suppose I can agree to that."

"Really? Awesome." I stood up on my tiptoes and gave him a chaste kiss. "Now, since you're up...want to make the coffee or change the diaper?"

He pretended to think about it. "Hazelnut or Colombian blend?"

Turned out Edward's agreement had caveats—he wouldn't come in with me, but he insisted on waiting in the car.

"It's not like there's any parking here," I said as the driver neared Randall's bar. "Are you just going to have Bert circle the block until I text you, or what?"

"Works for me." He called to the front seat. "How about you, Bert?"

Bert shrugged. "Whatever you want, Mr. Fasbender. Doesn't matter to me."

I folded my arms over my chest knowing anything I said would be dismissed. We'd already argued about it all afternoon as I'd gotten ready, donning a fitted red dress that I only just barely fit into post-pregnancy and taking extra care with my makeup. All I'd accomplished with the bickering was that I was arriving for my meeting almost fifteen minutes late. Edward wasn t budging.

Still, I couldn't drop it. "What's even the point? I'd call you and tell you everything just as easily."

"Call me eager," he said as the car pulled up in front of the bar.

If it were only that, I wouldn't be concerned. The problem was that I didn't trust him. There was one reason he'd insist on coming with and one reason only.

I hesitated before opening the door. "Give me at least half an hour before showing up, if that's what you're planning. Please?"

The driver behind us laid on his horn, but Edward took his time answering. "Fine. Half an hour." He looked at his watch. "Starting now."

I couldn't decide if I should take that as a victory or a loss. Since I was on the clock, I didn't have time to ruminate. I opened the door and began to step out when Edward grabbed my arm to halt me.

"You're a dragon, Celia. Go in breathing fire.

It shouldn't have boosted my confidence as much as it did, but I walked into the bar with courage and composure, my spine straight, my wits together.

Until I realized Hudson wasn't alone—his wife was with him.

I knew right then, whatever I'd thought this meeting was about, I'd been wrong. This was something else entirely. Something I had not been prepared for. Hudson saw me as a threat to his marriage, to his wife. It was why he still held those shares over me. He'd never put us in the same room without good reason.

Unless I was wrong. Unless her presence signaled things had changed.

It was too much to hope for, and a knot tightened in my belly, weighing me down. To counter it, I rounded my shoulders. Lifted my chin. Put on my mask.

My eyes met Alayna's before I got to the table, and I saw a flicker of insecurity. Should I take that as some sort of victory? Or should I admit that it hurt that she still didn't trust me?

I stuffed the competing emotions down inside me and activated the safety switch, the one Hudson had shown me—I went numb.

"Hudson, Laynie," I said, injecting a smile into my tone. They sat at a circular booth, Hudson on one end, his wife pressed so closely to him it was almost as though they were one person. Without being invited, I scooted in at the opposite end and addressed Hudson, mostly because he was the only one of the two of them I really knew how to talk to. I'd only ever been fake with Laynie. Attempting to be genuine now seemed futile.

But also, he'd been the one who set me up in this arrangement, and my complaint was meant specifically for him. "I didn't know we were bringing our significant others," I said curtly. "Should I call Edward? He doesn't have any plans."

He's just down the block, I added, silently wondering now if that was a good thing or an even worse thing than I'd originally thought.

"That won't be necessary." Hudson was cool, his words clipped. "This conversation doesn't involve him. It does, however, involve Alayna."

The hair raised at the back of my neck, some strange sense of foreboding that I couldn't shake.

It was silly, honestly. Probably just PTSD from the last time I'd seen Alayna, when she was still Withers instead of Pierce. When she'd broken my nose with one jab of her fist

I'd deserved it. But that was ages ago. Why were we all together now?

"I'm intrigued," I said, studying the woman who had

once been my foe. She still hated me. It was evident in her expression, and a few recent remarks from Genevieve had indicated the same. "How are you, Laynie? It's been so long since we've seen each other face-to-face. You look…" Like a woman with one-year-old twins. *"Tired."*

It was childish and petty. Mean, even, and I wasn't quite sure exactly what I meant by saying it when, honestly, I could relate. Maybe that's what I resented most about our relationship—there could be so much to like about the woman, so much to bond over. I could imagine the friendship that would never be, and it made me ache in strange places. Made me more bitter than I should have been.

Because wasn't all of this supposed to be over? For me, it was. I thought it was for Hudson too.

His face gave nothing away, his expression stone, still I could feel the glare behind the facade. "What can we get you to drink, Celia?" A tumbler of scotch already sat in front of him, but he raised his hand to signal the waiter.

"Nothing. Water, I suppose." I crossed one leg over the other.

"Really?" He sounded irritated, which meant the situation was getting to him too. "You were the one who suggested we meet at a bar, and you're not even having a drink?"

I hadn't chosen it, the app had.

But I was irritated with his irritation. And with being set up. And with all the distrust around me, whether I'd earned it or not. "I'm nursing. I can't drink, unless I'm going to dump it all after, and I'm not." I nudged his drink closer to him. "But we all know you're in a much more agreeable mood when you've had one of these. Hence, the bar."

Yeah, again it was petty, suggesting he might have an alcohol problem. I couldn't help myself. He'd ganged up on me. Ironically, I realized I was probably reacting exactly the same way I'd told Edward that Hudson would react if we'd ganged up on him.

"I changed my mind," Hudson said abruptly. "We don't need to meet with you. This isn't going to get us anywhere. Alayna, grab your purse. We are leaving." He pulled out his wallet and began flipping through the bills inside

"Hudson," his wife said, placing her hand on his arm. "We should stay."

He hesitated then threw some money on the table, but when he pocketed his wallet, he didn't stand to leave.

I had to concentrate to keep my jaw from dropping. Whatever they needed to discuss with me had to be important. Important to *them,* anyway. Which meant it could be useful to me.

For the first time since I walked in, I felt a flicker of hope.

"Thank you," I said. "I would hate to have wasted this trip." Conscious that the clock was ticking, I pressed the conversation. "Now, since Edward is not involved in this matter and Alayna is, I am assuming that we are not here to speak about the three-point alliance?"

"That is—"

Alayna interrupted her husband. "Like Pierce Industries is going to sell you shares. Did you forget that we have the majority for a reason? Hudson needed to have something to hold—ow!"

She cut off sharply, throwing a scowl in Hudson's direction.

146 | LAURELIN PAIGE

"That is correct," he finished, his teeth gritted. "We are here to ask you for..." He paused. "*Assistance.*"

I tilted my head, evaluating. "This is interesting. You must be mighty desperate if you're asking me for help. You have to know that's going to indenture you to me."

"Why don't you hear the situation out before you start bartering about payment? At one time, you and I helped each other with no strings attached. Especially when we found the outcome benefitted both of us. You might find this is one of those times."

A welcome stab of warmth penetrated my numb cocoon. Whether he meant it to be manipulative or not, his words acknowledged the friendship we once had. That friendship had been real. With all the poison we created in the world, we'd also soothed each other's aches. For a time, anyway. And even if he wanted to use that against me, he couldn't deny that we'd been what we were.

That cost him to admit that. I could set down my weapons for a moment, though I kept my shield up as I gestured for him to continue. "Go on then. I'm listening."

He glanced at Alayna, to assure her or be reassured, I didn't know. Then his focus came back to me. "We have received a series of threats recently. Letters, addressed to me, containing menacing language toward my family."

The momentary warmth vanished. "And you think I did it?" Of course they did. Of course the past could never be forgotten. Of course I would live with my sins for the rest of my life. How had Hudson managed to escape the same curse?

"No, we didn't—" he began.

"Well..." Alayna said softly.

Hudson shut her up with a glare. "We didn't come here

to accuse you. But the threats reference the past. The time when you and I were…" Another glance toward his wife, and I realized that he was as uncomfortable about who he'd been as I ever was.

"Playing together," I finished for him. His gaze dropped, weighted with guilt. "I see."

I also saw I'd been wrong with my earlier assessment—Hudson *hadn't* escaped his past, though there was every chance the worst was just now catching up to him.

I could empathize with that. More than I wanted to admit. In fact, with my husband currently circling the block with every intention of busting in soon, I understood Hudson completely.

"Do you have these letters with you?" I asked, despite feeling the pressure of time. "May I read them?"

He reached into his jacket pocket and pulled out a stack of photocopied papers then slid them across the table toward me. Then he threw back the rest of his drink, finis - ing it in one swallow.

It had taken all my courage to go to him that day in his office, to ask him to help keep my father in the dark about the ownership of his company. I'd had to set down a lot of anger and shame and regret in order to walk through his door. It was evident that he was now doing the same.

I know, Hudson. I fucking know.

I blinked away the sting in my eyes and focused on the papers in front of me. Quickly, the words I read replaced any notion toward sentimentality with something else— fear. The letters were clearly threats, the most haunting phrases sticking out as though they'd been written in bold.

"…should have counted on your past coming back to haunt you."

"You can't buy your way out of paying for your sins."

"...don't deserve your happy life."

"The safety of your tower is an illusion."

"You weren't always perfect. Your past is filled with misdeeds."

"The people you hurt remember."

I tried to ignore the sick feeling in my stomach to see the clues peppered in, references, as Hudson had said, to games we'd played. A mention of an affair. Of a marriage charade. "This reference about the mask you wear," I said, thinking out loud, "could be referring to that masquerade party we went to." Whom had we messed with that time? Whomever it was, it was a different game than the one with the fake marriage license that was mentioned in the next letter. And another game entirely from the one with the sick dog.

I shook my head, confused. "But none of the rest fits." I flipped to the last page of the five he'd handed m

"That one contained a picture of Alayna in the park with the twins. She hadn't known she'd been photographed."

A chill ran down my spine. If I'd discovered that Cleo and I had been secretly followed...

Then a more chilling thought—had Edward found out about Hudson? Was this his doing?

I swallowed down another wave of nausea with a, "Hm."

I didn't want to think about it, but I forced myself to really consider. It wasn't impossible that this was Edward. He had access to my journals. He could have made these references based on what he'd read there.

But was this really Edward's M.O.? Threatening children? And why would he keep trying to press me for my secrets if he already knew?

Maybe I was jumping to conclusions. Please, God, let me be jumping to conclusions.

But a glance at my watch said more than twenty minutes had passed since I'd sat down, and if I didn't get out of there soon, Edward would walk in and discover who Hudson really was, whether he already knew or not, and then Hudson would have a whole hell of a lot more trouble than just a stalker.

I gathered all the letters together and passed them back to Hudson. "I do think you're right, that it's someone from the past," I said, throwing the suspicion off of Edward for myself if not for anyone else. "But it's like a scavenger hunt. You have to do a lot of digging before you can figure out what these vague clues mean."

Hudson didn't take the letters. "We were hoping that you would help us put those clues together."

If I helped them, I'd be able to rule out Edward for sure.

And if it wasn't Edward, would that be better or worse? Knowing that there was a real threat to Hudson and his family. Or, rather, an *unknown* threat, because Edward was as real a danger as any.

But if it wasn't Edward, he'd find out about Hudson and all the time I'd spent protecting him would be in vain.

And if it was Edward…

I wasn't sure I wanted to know.

"I can't do that. I can't take these." He still refused to take the letters so I set them down on the table. "I'm sorry that I can't be more helpful, I just can't."

Alayna leaned desperately toward me. "You can't? Or you won't?"

I wanted to help her then, genuinely. From one mother to another, I wanted to figure out who was behind the threats to her family. Threats that I'd helped cause, one way or another.

"We don't have to take up much of your time, Ceeley," Hudson said. "If you even just allowed us access to the journals so we could piece together—"

"The journals?" It shouldn't have startled me that he would remember the journals or even that he'd ask for them, but it did, only because, I realized then, how easy it would be for Hudson to put things together and suspect Edward might be involved.

And now twenty-five minutes had passed. "I don't have them here. They're in London. I'm sorry. It's not going to work. I can't help you. Now, if you'll excuse me, I really must be going." I grabbed my purse, slid out of the booth, and without looking back, headed swiftly toward the exit.

"Celia, wait."

Against my better judgement, I stopped just feet away from the door and turned back toward Hudson.

"This person could come after you, too," he said. "I might only be victim number one. You aren't innocent here. Your past is as tainted as mine."

If it wasn't Edward sending these letters, having Hudson on my side would be a real benefit.

But getting involved wasn't worth the risk. The risk to *him*.

"And I understand I'll be on my own if and when that happens. I can't help you, Hudson."

He looked at me incredulously. And with utter disappointment, like I'd let him down more now than at any other time in the course of our relationship.

"I really thought you'd softened," he said, and the words hurt most because I had and because he couldn't understand how much I'd fought to protect him.

"You know nothing about me, Hudson," I said as Alayna walked up to us. "Not anymore." I was out the door before he could say anything more.

...and three steps later I plowed right into Edward. "What's going on? The meeting's over already?"

Fuck.

"There was no meeting," I said, then realizing that Hudson and Alayna might be seconds from leaving the bar themselves, I corrected myself. "It was a bust. Nothing useful."

I started walking down the block, wanting distance from Randall's, but Edward snatched my elbow, stopping me. "What does that mean? He refused to sell again? Why did he want to meet?"

His questions sounded genuine, not like the kind meant to throw a woman off his tracks. But was I blinding myself about Edward?

Suddenly, I felt like crying.

All of it was too much. Either my husband was an unhinged psychopath or there was someone with a real grudge going after Hudson, and whichever it was, I couldn't explain it to Edward without making matters worse.

Which meant I needed to lie, and I didn't want to lie to the man I loved.

So I stuck as much to the truth as possible. "It was a

setup," I said. "Hudson brought his wife. They have no intention of selling. They made that very clear."

Edward's brows furrowed. "Then why did they call this meeting? Just to rile you up?"

I shrugged, a tear escaping despite my attempts to hold it back. "Yeah. Something like that."

Immediately, he was fuming. "He brought you here to bloody bully you? Fuck that. Fuck that man. I'm going in there and telling him exactly what I think about that."

He'd already turned toward the bar so I had to quicken my steps to grab him. "You can't!"

"I'm not letting him get away with this, Celia. We've been reasonable. Terrorizing you is indecent and uncalled for and like hell will he do that to my wife without paying."

"He didn't terrorize me! I promise. He didn't. Can you please let it go?"

He calmed down, but only slightly. "Obviously he did *something*. Tell me what happened."

I shook my head, at a loss for what to say.

He turned toward the bar door again, and once more I pulled him back. "Please, Edward. Please, let it go. I'm upset because he reminded me of who I'd been in the past. That's all. There's nothing you need to say to him. I promise. Please, just take me home."

He looked unconvinced, his body still slightly poised in the direction I'd just come from.

"Please!" I begged, more desperate than I'd ever remembered being with him, and it felt like I was pleading for so much more than just to stop him from going in that bar. I was pleading for him to choose me, for once, instead of his wrath. For him to listen to what I needed and not what he thought I needed, a battle I'd lost over and over and over in our marriage. "Please, Edward! Please!"

He paused.

With a labored sigh, he put one arm around me and pulled out his phone from his pocket with the other. "Bert, we're ready," he said.

He held me until Bert came, neither of us speaking, and even when we got into the car, I clung to him, grateful that he'd listened, relieved that he'd chosen me.

But also fully aware that the clock was still ticking, and that eventually—soon, even—the time bomb would explode.

ELEVEN

EDWARD

"Second quarter reports aren't ready yet, but I guarantee you the earnings are well above predicted. Now is the time to double down on investment, not back out."

I tapped my pen against my chin and stared out the suite's living room window at the sun setting over the park. The rep from Sonovision continued his spiel through my mobile, but I was barely paying attention. The phone call had been on my agenda for days, and as it was Sunday evening (after nine in the morning in Tokyo), I hadn't thought to cancel it until it had been upon me.

I had no real cause to cancel, anyway, except that I was distracted. Celia's reaction to her meeting with Pierce unnerved me for several reasons. I very much wanted to hang up on Sonovision and call him instead. Whatever he'd said or done to cause my wife's distress deserved following up, and I was eager to do so for her sake.

And I was still very much interested in negotiating for the Werner shares. That battle wasn't anywhere near over, and if Pierce had expected his little scene tonight to dissuade me, he obviously didn't know who he was dealing with.

But as much as I was ready and willing to attack Pierce, I was very aware that Celia was keeping me in the dark. She'd shut down entirely on the ride back to the hotel. Once in our suite, she'd occupied herself with the baby and ordering dinner. When the meal arrived, I'd hoped to have a chance to talk with her, but she'd spent the entire time on a phone call with her mother who was lamenting about the likelihood that Ron's sentence would be announced the following day. The bits and pieces I'd gleaned from that conversation riled me up in their own way. How the woman's concerns about her brother-in-law could still be so self-centered and trivial with no regard to Celia baffled me. Though Madge's ignorance to what happened to her daughter might have been understandable before Ron's arrest, it certainly seemed she should ask the question after his past was revealed. Her husband, for sure, was practicing willful denial, and so I spent my own dinner alternating between fantasies of putting Pierce in his place and fantasies of putting the Werners in theirs.

As soon as Celia hung up with her parents, my alarm went off reminding me of my scheduled phone call with Sonovision, forcing any discussion to wait even longer. All that to say, negotiating a new anime streaming service for distribution in the UK was the least of my current concerns.

"We could be ready to send a contract over in an hour," Toshiro said, calling my attention back to him. "You could be ready to stream by August."

He allowed me to consider. In the silence, I realized the water had stopped running in the next room, which meant Celia was done with her shower, and frankly she was the only situation I could truly invest in at the moment.

"I'm going to need to discuss this more with my team, Toshiro," I said, hoping he wouldn't realize the conversation had been the waste of time that it had. "And we'll want to wait for your second quarter reports before deciding anything. Get those sent over when you have them, and we'll talk again."

I hung up before he had a chance to refute, just in time for Celia to come out of the bedroom to grab something from the kitchen fridge.

"Feel better?" I called from my desk. It took all I had not to jump up and corner her, demand answers, force her into breaking down her walls and telling me everything.

We weren't like that anymore, though. We hadn't been for quite some time.

She crossed to stand by the bookcase, a bottled water in her hand. "A bit," she said, unscrewing the cap and bringing it up to her lips. When she lowered it, she kept her eyes out the window. "I'm sorry tonight wasn't more helpful. We just need to change our course of action, is all. I'll start reaching out to my cousins with shares available to sell tomorrow."

"Mm," I said, taking a deep breath before commenting with something more substantial. "You realize that it would be helpful if you talked about what happened tonight. Not just for me, but for you."

"I'm not so sure about that."

"I am. Sit down. Let's talk."

Her gaze swung to meet mine, and I caught a flash of panic in her eyes. "Are you suggesting a session?"

"Why not?" Immediately, I chastised myself for not being more commanding about it. "Yes, I am suggesting a session."

She swallowed, then ran her tongue tentatively across her bottom lip as she looked toward the couch then me at the desk. I could sense her thoughts whirring as she contemplated giving in.

Once upon a time, she wouldn't have deliberated at all.

Once upon a time before that, I wouldn't have given her a choice.

Eventually, she shook her head. "It's really not necessary. Nothing needs to be rehashed. I just…" She trailed off, her brow creasing deeply.

Whatever was bothering her, it was pressing at her. I could feel her anxiety in the air, like it was a live thing with energy. It ripped at my insides, making me feel both like fire and mush. I burned to do something for her, to fix it, to figure it out, and I ached that she wouldn't allow it, that she stood so far out of reach.

"What is it?" I asked, standing from the desk. My mobile buzzed with a call, but I ignored it and took a step toward Celia, stopping when she shook her head.

"Go ahead. Take your call."

I silenced it. "It's not important. What are you worrying about? Tell me."

"Nothing," she said too quickly. She paused. "Just… you haven't done anything…have you? With Hudson?"

"I don't know what you're asking."

"Like…you haven't tried to bully him or, I don't know.

Terrorize him? In some way?"

"No." It rankled that she had to ask, despite knowing that I wasn't forthcoming about a good deal of my agendas. "I'm trying to earn his trust right now, not destroy it. Why? Did he suggest that I had?"

My mobile started to ring again. A quick glance said it was Hagan, likely wanting to know if he needed to follow up on my call with Sonovision.

At the same time, the bell to the suite rang. "Take it," Celia said, nodding to my phone. "I'll get the door. It's probably turndown service." She headed down the hall.

Cursing under my breath, I answered the call without saying hello. "There's nothing to follow up on. I postponed negotiations until their next quarter reports come in."

"I heard. Toshiro's assistant pinged me. They're threatening to try to sell elsewhere."

"Fuck." The deal was a good one, not one I wanted to lose.

But the heated conversation that drifted from the front of the suite suggested it had not been turndown service.

"Do you want me to call them back?" Hagan pressed.

I tried to concentrate on the question. "They aren't going to attract other buyers without the latest quarter re-ports," I reasoned. "If they're pushing so hard, especially. It looks like they're hiding numbers."

"I can arrange some sort of temporary agreement based on quarter finals," Hagan suggested.

The tone of the voices in the background escalated.

"Do that," I said, knowing the decision was rushed. "I have to go." I had already started toward the door, pocket-ing my mobile as soon as I hung up.

I hadn't expected the sight I came across when I turned the corner into the entry hall. Hudson Pierce holding back an angry brunette who was screaming at my wife and looking like she would tear out Celia's throat if let to do so. "It was you!" she shouted. "You're so fucking sick. Hudson said you'd changed, but you will never change. You have no heart. Manipulating and conniving. Does your husband know what...what a...*dragon* he married?"

Celia protested defiantl , and knowing her as I did, I was positive that whatever she'd been accused of, she was innocent.

False accusations thrown at *my* wife? In *my* hotel suite?

I was immediately livid.

"What the hell is going on here?" I roared, not so loudly that the baby would hear me in the next room, but forceful enough to be given notice.

The room went abruptly silent, all eyes turned to me. Hudson loosened his grip on the rabid woman who I could only assume was his wife.

And Celia, the woman who had been only strong and defiant in her interactions with me for more than a year now, went white, her eyes wide with fear.

It would have been one thing if it seemed that her fear was directed at our guests. It was quite a different thing realizing that her fear was directed at *me*.

"Edward," she said, taking a cautious step toward me. "It's nothing. Hudson and Alayna are...old friends."

"Old friends, my ass," the woman blurted out.

I knew the relationship between these women was rocky at best. Pierce's insistence that he needed insurance against Celia from going after his wife was proof that their past had been highly complicated.

But except for Celia's apprehension toward me, it seemed more like she was the one needing protection. Mrs. Pierce had both her claws and teeth out.

I felt suddenly feral, ready to take her on. "Is there a problem?" I asked, coming further into the space.

Of course, the other issue was that my wife very obviously wanted me calm. "I didn't realize that you and Hudson Pierce had been *friends*, darling," I said, because why the fuck was she using that term to describe him now?

Celia's shoulders sagged, her eyes lowering to the ground, an act of submission I hadn't seen from her in months.

"Actually, there *is* a problem," Hudson's wife said defiantl .

"Alayna," Hudson hissed, seeming to want her tempered. Cordially he addressed me. "Edward, you haven't met my wife."

"No, I haven't. And I hear we are about to be family." I studied her in a way meant to put her in her place. "It's a pleasure to meet you, Alayna."

"It's really just a misunderstanding," Celia said quickly, her eyes imploring.

I knew what she wanted from me. She wanted me to turn around, let it go, walk away, the same way she'd wanted me to do so at Randall's earlier in the night.

I'd walked away then, against my better judgment. Because I loved her, and she'd begged, and I was trying to be the man she wanted me to be, one who listened and respected and yielded.

I couldn't be that man now.

Not when it was clear that there was a battle that Celia was fighting alone. Not when I had every reason to doubt she was leaving me out of it for motives other than my own good.

"I'd like to hear what Alayna has to say, if you don't mind?" I stared at Celia intensely, willing her to defy me. As often as she'd fought me in our marriage, she'd always obeyed my demand to heed me in public. For half a second, I wondered if that would change now.

Then her eyes lowered, giving in, which was both a relief and emboldening. "Alayna?" I said, encouraging her to speak.

She lifted her chin like a star student proud to have been called. "Hudson and I are being terrorized. We have reason to suspect the threats may be coming from your wife."

"That's not necessarily true," Hudson said immediately.

Simultaneously, Celia piled on. "I haven't done anything to you. I didn't send a single one of those threats."

I put my hand up to silence her, noting her choice of words. *Threats.* She'd asked if I'd threatened Hudson. What the fuck was going on?

"If she didn't do it," Alayna continued, "She could prove it, and help us find out who is threatening us, at the same time. It would be easy, if she'd let us see the journals that she kept from the time that she and Hudson..." She trailed off, but she'd said enough to start the pieces coming together.

Celia's journals documented the "games" she'd played on other people. With her partner. Did that mean her partner was—?

Alayna plowed ahead suddenly, answering my unspoken question. "Hudson and Celia had a working relationship in the past. I don't mean to butt into your marriage. It would be truly cruel and devious to interfere with your relationship." She threw a glare toward Celia. "And so I apologize if this is the first you are hearing about their former partnership. But my family's safety is on the line, and this is truly important."

The picture locked in place, a second's worth of time sharpening the image until it was crystal clear —Hudson Pierce was the man who taught her. Hudson Pierce was the man she'd been protecting. Hudson bloody Pierce.

My mind wanted to follow each of the threads this dis-covery highlighted all at once, wanted to try to analyze whether I felt victorious or validated or irate or goddamned relieved, but of course, I couldn't react at all. I had to keep it together for the moment. Protect my family. Stand up for my wife.

"I see," I said, careful to hide any trace of surprise. "I *do* know about Hudson and Celia's working relationship, of course."

"You do?" Alayna sagged with disappointment, as though she'd hoped the news would put a riff in my relationship with my wife.

She had no idea.

"I do. Celia tells me everything. Don't you, darling?" I sidled up to my wife, putting my arm around her. Protec-tively? Threateningly? "Well, almost everything." Admit-tedly, my clutch around her waist might have been tighter than necessary.

Celia's head lowered with guilt.

Or fear.

Fear that I now understood.

Fear that was justifiable

First, there was the matter of threats that the Pierces had been receiving, not altogether surprising considering the shit I'd read they'd done. I could imagine there were plenty of people who wanted to see him hurting. Celia, too, which was why it was important to help find the bugge .

"I can guarantee you that Celia is not behind this," I said, intent on clearing up any thoughts to the contrary. "And to prove it, we will have the journals flown here from London. They can arrive here by Tuesday. You may come back then. Now, if you don't mind, Celia needs to get some sleep. Our baby will be waking up in about five hours for her feeding, and you are correct, Celia really is a dragon when she hasn't gotten enough sleep."

Alayna appeared both shocked and relieved as I ushered her out the door. Hudson managed to hide any emotion, but I sensed his gratitude.

Good. He'd best remember that feeling when I talked to him next, and I would talk to him again. Soon, in fact. Very soon.

Tonight, though, I had my wife to deal with.

TWELVE

CELIA

I'd been afraid of my husband on many occasions. Many times it was even a turn-on, as he'd so often pointed out.

Tonight, though, as he closed the door behind Hudson and Alayna, the quiet that filled the space between us was thick with dread that I'd never felt before. A kind of foreboding that made my bones feel cold and my stomach feel like it was carrying a cannonball.

After the door had shut all the way he still didn't turn around. He just stood there, one hand braced firmly against the wall, the other on the knob of the door.

"Edward…" I said tentatively.

"Don't." His voice was tight but controlled.

I gave it a beat, watching the muscles in his back expand as he breathed in deep then let it out. Then breathed in deep again.

Apprehension got the best of me. "What are you go-ing—?"

He whipped around to face me, his eyes blazing. "I mean it, Celia. I'm not ready for you to talk yet."

I clammed up. While I was desperate to know what he planned to do to Hudson now that he knew who he was, I sensed it was probably best not to push him right now. I had no doubt I'd find out soon enough anywa .

I just had to hope that, whatever he planned, it wouldn't be devastating. Or that I'd be able to talk him down.

My silence seemed to settle him somewhat. His next breath came easier. Then he said, "Living room. I need you to be sitting down for this conversation."

He also appeared to need a drink for it because he stopped at the minibar on the way and filled a tumbler of cognac before following into the living space where I'd perched myself on the edge of the couch.

I'd left plenty of room on both sides of me, thinking he'd sit as well or take the armchair or his desk, but instead he stayed standing. It made me feel small, and perhaps that was his intention. It also made me irritated because it was obvious he was going to handle this with a heavy hand instead of like a reasonable adult.

That meant I had to be the grown-up. "Look," I said as soothingly as possible, "I can imagine what you're think-ing—"

"You cannot possibly imagine what I'm thinking. If you could, you would be scared to utter a single word until I asked you to."

A chill ran down my spine. I shut up and waited as he paced the room, back and forth, taking small sips of his brandy, each second adding to my growing apprehension.

He's processing, I told myself. Instead of acting rashly, he was actually thinking it through. That was a good thing.

Wasn't it?

"I think it's safe to say we're clear now about who A was," he said, finall . "Who A is. Is that correct?"

"That's correct." I added "Sir" as an afterthought, hoping a show of deference would help my cause.

"Oh, that's cute. Thinking you can earn points now with subservience. It's too little too late, I think, don't you?"

So much for that idea.

I thought the question was rhetorical, but when he waited, his eyes stabbing into me, I felt compelled to respond. "I'm not sure if you want me to actually answer that or not."

"No. I don't." He took one more swallow of his drink before setting it on the desk. He clapped his hands together. "So. Hudson Pierce."

I nodded once.

"Hudson bloody Pierce." His fist pounded against the desk, causing me and the liquid left in the tumbler to jump.

Automatically, my mouth opened in an anxious need to try to clear up whatever needed clearing, but the warning look he gave me caused it to close again just as fast.

I wasn't just scared of him, though. My irritation had escalated to pissed. Because shouldn't he be happy now? He'd finally gotten what he wanted. Finally discovered my secret. Shouldn't he be gloating? Why was *he* angry?

Yet he definitely was. I could feel the anger radiating off him hotter than the fireplace burning in winte .

"Let's go through this," he said curtly. "If you don't mind, just so I can have a clear picture."

"Sure."

He glared at me, as though my speaking had been out of turn.

"You asked if I minded," I said with hostile bravado. "If you expect to get anything from me at all, you better treat this like a civil conversation, Edward. I am not your property. I am a human being, and whether you feel like I deserve it or not, I will not sit here if you're going to do nothing but belittle and terrorize me."

His gaze narrowed. "If you'd rather be treated like I would treat any rival who had crossed me, then I can do that. Granted, I don't think you realize the privileges you gain from your status as my wife."

You're being an asshole right now.

It was what I wanted to say, but his threat reminded me that although I knew without a doubt that Edward would never do anything to really harm me, that wasn't the case with someone he wasn't married to. Someone like Hudson.

And so my capitulation was about protecting my one-time friend, nothing else. I lowered my eyes to my lap, signaling my submission.

"Good. We're on the same page here, at least. How about you help me confirm the rest." It wasn't a question. "You grew up with Hudson, your mothers were friends. You developed a bit of a crush on him that he proceeded to take advantage of. Correct so far?"

It had been more than a crush but less romantic than he

suggested. I'd been in the aftermath of Uncle Ron, need-ing some assurance of my value as a woman. As a person. Hudson had been the one I'd turned to.

But Edward wasn't interested in any of that right now, and honestly, he already knew. And the ending was ac-curate. Hudson *had* taken advantage of my feelings. So I answered simply. "Yes."

"He played you, then you took the betrayal badly—"

"Is that really necessary?"

He ignored my interruption. "—and got back at him by sleeping with his father. Honestly, did you need Pierce to teach you anything? You seemed to already have retribu-tion down pat."

He was being mean, and it hurt.

But I could handle betrayal better these days, and I knew how to be mean back. "If you're going to look at it that way, then the person I didn't need to teach me was you. Hudson never aimed for retribution. That was always your angle."

He smirked, as though I'd shot him with an arrow that had long missed its mark. "Right. Because the people Hud-son taught you to manipulate were innocent whereas the ones I've encouraged you to go after were not."

"This is pointless." I stood up, ready to walk out of the room when his sharp tone cut through the air like a whip.

"Sit. Back. Down."

That rage would have to find an outlet somewhere. I'd come this far making sure Hudson didn't receive it. I couldn't stop now.

I sat back down.

"So. The score was settled." Was that what he was doing? Keeping tally, back and forth? Trying to decide who deserved to punish whom? "Until you got pregnant with a child that, had the true father been implicated, would have potentially destroyed Pierce's family."

"I didn't get pregnant on purpose," I said when I could see him mentally adding that as a point against me. Though, after I said it, I realized it was helpful to Hudson if the marks weighed in my favor.

His expression grew colder. "Forgive me for not jumping to believe that's true. You should understand why I might have trouble believing your conception had been unintentional."

My anger heated like molten lava nearing eruption. "I didn't try to get pregnant. Believe it or not, it's the truth. And fuck you for comparing that situation to Cleo who was very much wanted and conceived in a marriage after my husband had outright said that we could have a child together at some point."

The mention of Cleo, whom I knew full well that he loved, did nothing to settle him. "Regardless, you got pregnant. Then you bullied Hudson into taking responsibility? Showed up and threatened to disrupt his life unless he did?"

"He offered! I hadn't expected anything." I was mad enough at the insinuation, madder still when I realized it might not just be something he was considering now. "Have you thought that all along?"

"He clearly despises you, as does his wife. I'm trying to understand his motivation. Why did you even go to him first if you didn t want him to fix it?

"Oh. Because you assume I always need someone to fix things for me. That I can't take care of anything myself."

He didn't deny it.

My hands clenched into fists in my lap. "I'm so fucking mad at you right now, I can't even begin to express it."

"That makes two of us."

We'd been mad at each other before and worked it out through some rough sex, but this was different. This couldn't be solved by his cock.

I wasn't even sure it could be solved by words, and yet, I took a deep breath, and tried. "I went to Hudson because he'd been my friend. And after I'd involved his family like I had in our fucked-up battle, it seemed only fair that he be the person who knew first."

"So it was out of compassion that you went to him. Not exploitation."

He was taking my confessions, things he'd suggested he thought I should put behind me, and using them against me. Spinning my words to show me in my worst light.

My chest ached, like my heart was splitting in two.

But maybe this was my due. We'd never fully addressed The Games with Hudson. Maybe there were still demons for me to exorcise here, and maybe these were things Edward needed cleared up too.

I sighed. "Compassion is probably giving me too much credit. I went to him because I needed him. And I think it was because of his own guilt about the situation, that he stepped up and offered to claim it as his."

"Not because he cared for you."

This was harder to admit for some reason. "Maybe that, too."

"He would have married you?"

"I don't know. It was assumed that we would."

Edward's jaw tensed. He picked up his drink again and threw the rest back. "But he was looking for a different kind of partner. Not a wife. One who would participate in his cruel games."

"He wasn't looking for a partner at all," I insisted. "He hadn't even told me about his experiments. I had to guess. And none of that came up until I lost the baby. He never intended to invite me into that, whether we'd gotten married or not. Whether I'd had the baby or not."

"Except that he *did* invite you into it."

"I invited myself. You know this. I've told you this." My frustration was growing, despite my best intentions. "I was sad and distraught and tired of feeling things, tired of not knowing how to cope, and I just wanted it all to end. Can you try to understand that? And there was Hudson, stone cold and stoic, and I desperately wanted to be like that. So I asked him to teach me. I *begged* him! It wasn't him at all. It was me. All me."

"Was it *all* you? You're sure he didn't manipulate you into that position?"

I hadn't ever considered that before, and the question gave me pause. When I thought about it, though, I was certain I knew the truth. "I'm sure."

Edward was determined to see the worst. "But he knew you were hurting. Agreeing to anything with a woman who is in that state of mind is irresponsible."

"Seriously?" I stared at him incredulously. "Because a woman can't know what she wants for herself? I knew, and I went after it, and we became a team, and those terrible things we did? They made me better."

"They made you an emotionless dragon."

"Is that any worse than being a vengeful devil?"

My words hung in the air, and I regretted them almost immediately. They were honest, but they weren't productive, and I didn't want to be fighting, I wanted to be fixing.

"You're right that it didn't help long-term," I conceded, not entirely withholding my anger from my tone. "I get that now. It was a survival technique, and you already knew this about me when you decided to love me, so don't act like I'm suddenly not good enough because I had a rocky past."

"I never said that." It was the softest he'd spoken since the discussion began.

I matched his mild tone. "It feels like you're saying that."

For a moment, he looked like he might yield. Like he might set down his fury and wrap me in his arms instead.

Then the moment was over, and he went hard again. "You're displacing. That's how you feel about yourself, not me. I don't have a problem with your past. My problem is with your present."

The accusation surprised me. "What bothers you specifically? That I don't want my husband to go to war with someone who got me through a terrible time? That I want to put the bad parts of my life behind me?"

Without answering, he changed gears. "Why did you and Pierce fall out?"

I looked away and shook my head, frustrated that this whole conversation, like every conversation, was on Edward's terms.

But I'd known who he was when I'd fallen in love with

him, too. "He didn't want to play anymore. And I did."

"He quit his own game?"

"His sister intervened, I think. Because he had someone who could see he had fallen down a hole, someone who loved him, and she pulled him back out. I didn't have that someone, though Hudson tried to get me to quit too, but I couldn't. It was all I had. I didn't know how to *be* without it."

I looked back at Edward, the man who had been my confessor through so much of my past sins. Once again, I confided my wrong-doings. "I was lonely without him. I tried to rope him back in a few times. He'd taught me well, you see, and I used it against him. Or I tried. Nothing worked until Alayna. I was there when he first saw her, and I'd never seen him like that—lit up and interested. Over someone that wasn't a potential pawn. He'd gotten better enough to be able to start feeling like that, which I couldn't understand, but I could observe.

"I took advantage of that." My voice cracked suddenly, the gravity of what I'd put Hudson through hitting me squarely. "It makes me sick, what I did. Makes me literally taste bile. I used his attraction to Laynie to bring him back into The Game. I coerced him into hurting her. And when that wasn't enough, I tried to unravel them in other ways, and part of it was simply because I didn't know how to give up on an objective. Hudson had taught me that too. But a bigger part of it was me trying to hold onto something that had never really been mine. Had never really been real, even."

I swiped at the tear on my cheek with the back of my hand. Crying always had an effect on Edward, which made me more conscientious of trying to hold the tears back. I didn't want to manipulate him. I wanted to come together honestly.

Turned out I needn't have worried. My tears didn't faze him in the slightest. "So you kept at him, kept pecking away at their relationship, and in order to get you to stop, he got Glamplay to sell him their Werner shares."

There was no amusement in my chuckle. "It's funny, isn't it? I got his father involved when I slept with him. He got mine involved when he bought those shares. Karma, man."

Edward's brows raised as I stood slightly in order to reach the tissue box on the ottoman then settled when I was back in place. After dabbing my eyes, I went on. "It worked, of course. Not just because I didn't want my family's business to fall apart, but because that was when I finally got it. Hudson had gone to extremes to put me in my place, and from everything I'd learned from human behavior in our years together, I realized he'd done it. He'd truly fallen in love.

"That was a big deal, you see. I'd wanted in on The Game because Hudson didn't have feelings about anyone. When he fell in love, it made everything that we did seem futile."

Whoa.

I huffed out a long breath. I'd never articulated that before, not out loud. Not in my head. But that had truly been what had ended us, hadn't it? Hudson had shown me that The Game didn't work. It was still possible to feel things while playing them, and so what was even the point?

Still, like a hamster on a wheel, I'd kept on, praying he was wrong, hoping to one day play my way out of feeling any guilt for everything I'd done.

It had all been in vain.

The only reason I eventually changed and rebuilt and learned to accept myself was because I'd met Edward.

I wanted to tell him that, and I started to, but he spoke first. "He fell in love with Alayna and that was devastating. Because you were in love with him."

"What? No." I was appalled. "Where did you get that? Are you actually listening to me?"

"I am. Very intently, and what I hear is that you were so in love with him, this man that was all you had, that you tried to break up his relationship, and when that didn't work, when he went to extremes to get rid of you, you still held onto him by continuing with his games."

"*The Game* was all I had. Not *him*. I still played because it was all I was good at. It was all I knew."

"And then, years later, when you're supposedly in love with me, you still choose him. Choose to protect *him* instead of opening up to *me*."

I shot up off the couch. "Because you said you were going to go after him! I didn't choose him over you."

"Choose to keep me in the dark about someone who might be after both of you because of things you'd done," he continued, his tone rising. "Someone who might be a threat to the mother of my daughter, because you still are more concerned about his safety than our family."

The lightbulb finally went on. "Is that what this is? You're jealous?" In another situation I might have been flattered. Right now, I was livid. "Are you fucking kidding me?"

"This isn't jealousy, Celia. This is rage. This is betrayal. This is me questioning every vow we made to each other and doubting the very foundation of our marriage. It was one thing when A was a distant ghost in your past. To discover he is in your life now, that you are still interacting with him, that you are continually choosing him—"

Cleo's wail broke Edward off mid-sentence. Honestly, I was surprised she hadn't woken up sooner. Our voices had certainly risen in volume. It was a good thing that it was only her wall against ours, or we might have had man-agement knocking as well.

"I'll get her," I said, unsure if it was the worst or the best time to put the conversation on pause. On the one hand, there was so much left to be worked through. On the other hand, upset as we both were, it was probably a good idea to take a breather.

I left the door slightly ajar when I went to Cleo's room, hoping Edward might follow. Her presence was always calming. Even when she was upset, she put things in per-spective. Forced us to recognize what really mattered.

But Edward didn't follow.

I wiped my own tears before I picked Cleo up and hugged her to me, tight. "I'm sorry, baby," I said, kissing her head. "Mommy and Daddy just got a little mad at each other. It's going to be all right."

I didn't know that, though. I doubted things would be all right tonight, anyway. And when I heard the heavy slam of the door in the suite next door, and I realized that Ed-ward had left, I worried it might never be all right between us again.

THIRTEEN

EDWARD

I left because I needed to think.

Problem with thinking was that it meant feeling as well. The hotel bartender was helping with that.

Or, he was until he announced last call and left me with a tab that could have bought an entire bottle of cognac.

"One more," I said, handing him back the bill so he could adjust the total. "And I'll charge it to my room. Twenty-seven-oh-five."

"Got it, Mr. Fasbender."

I threw back the remains of the glass he'd poured the last time he'd been by, and tried once more to organize my thoughts.

Hudson Pierce was the enemy.

Hudson Pierce had been the enemy all along.

What should I do about Hudson bloody Pierce?

Ruin him, was the usual answer to questions like these, and it did keep returning as an option, but I could never hold onto the thought long enough to conceive of a viable plan because every time I tried to imagine what he *deserved*, I had to consider, not only what he'd done, but what had been done to him, and that brought me time and time again back to focusing on Celia.

And with Celia came the emotions, bleak and drenching like a torrential downpour. She'd deserved what he'd done to her, hadn't she? Why did that make me so enraged?

I'd known about her past. I'd overlooked her sins even if I hadn't forgiven them. I'd destroyed the woman she'd once been and had paved the way for her rebirth. Her history hadn't mattered.

It still didn't.

So why was I so utterly shattered?

Nothing had changed, really. Hudson owned as many shares of Werner now as he had yesterday. He still owned them for the same reason. Celia had still had a partner in her crimes. The anger I'd felt about her secrecy regarding that partner had already been dealt with. It shouldn't matter that the man she'd protected had a name that I already knew or that it had been a man who shared such an extensive history with her. It shouldn't matter that the man had been the first that she'd loved

Except that it did matter.

It mattered very much.

Because, as I'd said so blatantly to her before I'd left the room, she'd chosen to honor her bond with that arsehole above the bond she had with me. Because not only had she once had feelings for Hudson, but it was also quite evident that she still felt something for him, be it romantic in nature or something more complex, and that feeling had obviously meant more to her than complete transparency in our marriage.

Because no matter what I did to Hudson, even if I ruined him completely, it wouldn't make Celia any more *mine*. Which was what I wanted more than anything, if I was honest—to own her heart completely. To be her one and only master, the man she not only loved above all others but at all.

That felt outrageously juvenile to admit.

I drowned the emotion with a long swallow from my newly filled glass. Then, I pushed it away and signed the tab before standing. Too quickly, it seemed, since the floor teetered as I did.

"You need help to your suite, Mr. Fasbender?"

The bartender was trying to be helpful, but it took all I had not to snap his head off for the inquiry. "I'm fine," I said tightly.

Besides, I wasn't going to my suite. Too much alcohol had left my head—and my heart—more muddled than when I'd first come down. When the room finally stopped spinning, I headed instead to the front desk.

"Do you have any rooms available?" I asked.

"We do. How long will you be needing it, sir?"

I gave him the most honest answer I could. "I don't know."

I woke to my mobile ringing, the volume seeming much louder than usual as the normally gentle chirp sounded like a gunshot next to my head. With bleary eyes, I looked at the screen, half expecting to see Celia's name before I silenced it. She'd texted the evening before, several times, and each one I'd ignored. The only reason I even looked was to be sure it wasn't Jeremy asking questions about her journals since I'd texted him last night to have them shipped overnight.

It wasn't his name on the ID, though, or Celia's. I glanced at the time before I answered. Why the hell was Leroy Jones calling me at eight in the blasted morning?

"It's early," I said instead of hello. It was even earlier in Albuquerque where Leroy worked for the FBI.

"It's not early in London," he said, decidedly more chipper than I was. "From the tone of your voice I'm guessing you've forgotten what day it is?"

It was Monday. Beyond that I was having a hard time even remembering where I was. A few more blinks, and my head cleared although the pounding throb at my temple remained.

I sat upright, regretting it as soon as I did. "Ron's sentence has been announced?"

"Yep. Ready for this? Twenty-six years."

"Twenty-six years," I repeated, dumbfounded.

"Twenty-six years. It's more than we'd hoped for."

"What does that mean as far as the US is concerned?" There'd been talk of extradition to face charges in the States, but that decision had been put on hold until the trial in the UK was over.

"It's more than we could get on the evidence we have

here," Leroy said. "Statute of limitations has long passed for Celia, and the couple of leads we have with recent victims don't hold a lot of weight."

"So it's a closed case."

Leroy misread my subtext. "He's going to be locked up for the rest of his life," he said. "Does it matter if it's in your jails or in ours?"

"No, it's good," I said, meaning it. "Celia will be happy about this. I'd be happier if he'd gotten life, but I'm not displeased with the outcome."

"Think you can put this behind you now?"

"Not sure I'm good at putting anything behind me." It was a little more honest than I'd meant to be. "As for Celia, I'm not sure this is something you ever get over, whether justice is served or not."

"No, I'm sure that's true. I'm not going to hear some mysterious account of the douchewad hanging himself in prison, am I, or getting taken out with a shiv?"

I chuckled, then winced as the sound echoed too loudly through my skull. "If you do, I won't be behind it. Man deserves to spend the rest of his years suffering. Death would be too merciful."

"Tell you what, Fasbender. You ever want a side job taking down motherfuckers like Werner on the down low—aka, outside government jurisdiction—let's just say I can make that happen."

I managed to smile. "Good to know I have the right kind of friends. I'll even honestly consider it before telling you no. Thank you for the news."

I hung up just as my mobile beeped with a low battery warning. Tossing it down, I lay back down and covered my face with my arm. I hadn't bothered to close the curtains before falling asleep—I hadn't even made it under the covers—and the sunlight streaming in felt like shards of glass in my eyes. It had been quite a many years since I'd had a hangover, and now I remembered why I was very strict about limiting my drinking. I needed a bottle of water and two Advil, but both required getting out of bed and one possibly required leaving my hotel room.

I sat for a few minutes contemplating going back to sleep, but despite my misery, my head was awake now and that meant the thoughts were back, a tangled web of what to do and how to feel. I'd never understood Celia's desire to escape her emotions so distinctly as I did right then.

And now there wasn't just The Problem with Pierce on my mind, but the news about Ron. I should be there for Celia when she found out. We'd done our celebrating when he was found guilty and the sentencing was a relief, but every announcement about the man stirred her up in some way or another, as was to be expected.

News of Ron stirred me up as well. He was one of the sources of my anger. He was such a vile, despicable excuse for a human being. He was Satan himself, as far as I was concerned. What he'd done to Celia was unfathomable and unforgivable. If I'd been around when it was happening, if I'd known, I would have murdered him on the spot.

And her father!

Warren had been around, had known and he'd turned a blind eye. He'd chosen the easy path instead of the right one. He'd ignored the signs and her confession and chose to stand by his brother...for what? For the sake of his company? For the sake of convenience? Was that where Celia learned to protect her tormentors? From the man who'd chosen Ron over her?

I sat up again, ignoring the pounding in my head as I swung my feet over the side of the bed and stood up. I couldn't be there for Celia right now—I wasn't up for it physically or in the right frame of mind—but my temper raged on through the repercussions of last night's over-drinking, strong and bold and unrelenting.

And while I had yet to decide what to do with Hudson Pierce, I now, at least, had somewhere to focus my anger.

Thirty minutes later, still wearing the clothes I'd slept in, Madge Werner opened the door of her penthouse apartment to greet me. "Edward, what a surprise to see you so early." Then, she got a good look at me. "Oh, goodness, you look terrible. What's wrong? Is it the baby?"

"Cleo's fine. Where's your husband?" I pushed past her, leaving the foyer in pursuit of the son of a bitch. "Warren?"

I found him in the hall wearing a robe and pajama bottoms. "Morning, Ed." If he was startled to see me, he didn't show it, barely giving me a nod before heading toward his office. "Phone's ringing off the hook, people wanting a statement. We'll want to coordinate with Murphy on the company's official stance, but my lawyer's already on it. Nothing to worry about on this end." He paused at the door so he could give me his full attention. "And we can still appeal, you know. Be sure we'll appeal."

"You most certainly will *not* appeal," I snapped.

Madge gasped behind me.

Warren frowned slightly, his expression perplexed, as

though he hadn't heard me right. "What was that?"

I pinched the bridge of my nose. The two Advil I'd found in the hotel minibar were not working as well as I would have liked, the terribleness of my headache adding fuel to the volcano churning inside me.

There were things I needed to say. Important things that needed to be heard. While I was desperately close to just "blowing," it wouldn't be productive.

I took a breath to calm myself. "Warren, sit down." I nodded at the couch in his office

His frown became more severe. "Can this wait? I know you have concerns about this whole Ron debacle, but—"

"Sit. The fuck. Down." So much for being calm.

He was so stunned, he did without further objection. I pivoted to find his wife sneaking o f toward the kitchen.

She gave a fake smile. "I figured I'd just leave you two to—"

"You should sit down as well, Madge, since this also involves you." I managed to be softer with her, but only barely.

"Oh. Okay." She went dutifully to the couch, folding her hands in her lap. Celia had definitely not inherited her need to buck authority from her mother. Her father then?

Actually, she'd probably developed it as a survival technique since Warren wasn't really an authoritarian either. He was entitled, which was entirely different and more annoying as far as I was concerned.

I moved to lean my backside against Warren's desk, taking the place of command in the room. By that time, Warren's irritation at being ordered around in his own office caught up with him, and he stood back up. "What's going on with you, Edward? Whatever this is, it can't be so important that it needs to happen now. In case you haven't heard the news from London, I have things I need to be doing."

I gave him an intense glare that sent him sinking back into his seat. "Yes. You do have things you need to do. Defending your good-for-nothing brother is not one of them."

His irritation escalated to frustration. "Hey, now, that's uncalled for."

"Is it, Warren?" I folded my arms across my chest, my gaze piercing into him. I'd come here with an agenda, but I hadn't quite worked out this part of the confrontation. Despite the current disagreement with my wife, spilling the details of her abuse felt disloyal. But I didn't need to spill anything, did I? Warren already knew. "Think about it before you answer because you know exactly what I'm talking about."

Madge looked from me to her husband. "What's going on?"

"I think you should leave," he said coldly, his eyes pinned on me.

I gave him a quick smile that held no warmth. "I bet you do. But I'll assure you that I am not leaving. It's past time that we had this conversation. The only reason I didn't confront you sooner was out of courtesy to Celia, hoping she'd eventually deal with you herself, or that, miracle of miracles, you'd behave like a decent father and reach out to her on your own, but you aren't a decent father, are you, Warren? And it isn't really fair to expect her to approach you considering the reaction she got from you the last time."

His jaw tightened. "I don't have to listen to this. In my

own home. Madge, call security."

She stood immediately, as though it were a habit to do as her husband bid, but she stopped just as quickly when I said, "Madge, you need to hear this, and I believe, you are ready to hear it."

"Leave her out of this," Warren said with as much hostility as fear in his tone.

It was understandable, really. I couldn't imagine the terror of having to admit how he'd betrayed Celia to anyone, let alone her mother.

Madge hesitated, deliberating. When she spoke, she looked at me. "Is this about Ron? Ron and...Celia?"

"No," Warren said.

"Yes," I said simultaneously.

She swung to face her husband. "Warren, you told me that nothing happened. You promised me that nothing happened."

So she'd guessed. It was reassuring, at least, to find out the woman wasn't as clueless as she'd seemed. Though she should have had the balls to ask her daughter about it, not her worthless, cowardly husband.

"I said...well." Warren was flustered. "I'm sure I didn't promise anything."

"You did," she insisted, her tone growing shrill. "When I asked you if it was possible if anything happened, you said there was no way. That all of the charges were a fabricated lie from a money-grabbing ex-girlfriend. And when I brought up how odd it was that Celia had wanted to stop seeing him so abruptly as a teen, when I said I had a bad feeling about it, you said..."

She trailed off, but I didn't have to hear the rest of the

conversation recapped to know the basic premise. "He lied."

"I didn't lie," Warren barked. "I didn't know anything, honey. I still don't."

Lying piece of dirt. "You did. He did, Madge. He knew because Celia came to him as a teenager and told him that her uncle, a man she had trusted and looked up to, had been grooming and abusing her for years."

"No," Madge half gasped, half cried. "Oh God. No." She sank back to the couch, her face ashen.

"And then," I continued, "after all the courage it took to tell her father, the man who was supposed to love and protect her above all else, he accused her of lying."

"She told you?" she asked, incredulous and horrified

Warren shifted toward his wife. "It was so long ago now. I can't remember exactly what she said. You know how kids are. The things they say to get out of spending time with family."

Madge heard past the bullshit. "Why didn't you tell me? Why didn't *she* tell me?"

"Would you have let yourself hear her?" I asked, happy to stir the pot. "Your husband certainly couldn't be bothered."

"That's not how it happened. She came to—"

I stood up straight, cutting him off. "You know what, Warren? I don't fucking care about your side of the story. The only version of events that matters to me is Celia's, and thank God after more than twenty years, she's finally seeing justice and that shitty piece of human garbage is behind bars. Countless lives that man destroyed, and you could have prevented all of it."

I was well aware that Ron had ruined my family long before he'd ever set a finger on Celia, but it still felt good to pin it on Warren. If he had been more involved in his brother's hand in his business back in those days, he could have prevented what happened to my father's company too, though I suspected he would have turned the same blind eye to his business practices as he had to Celia's confession.

Strangely, after all the years I'd wanted to destroy Warren for the demise of my family, it was only anger for Celia that incited me today. "Your brother is in jail for the rest of his life, but you still have amends to make. I came here today to be sure that happens."

Warren stood, his full height still several inches below mine. "I don't owe anyone anything, and I'm not giving out explanations or apologies for something that happened—"

I took a threatening step toward him. "You don't want to finish that sentence. Because if it ends with you dismissing all of this as something that's ancient history, then I will not be responsible for my actions, and I promise you, you do not want to find out what happens when I'm this mad."

I let that sink in, not just to menace him, but also because I needed some composure before going on. As much as I wanted to break every bone in his body, it wasn't the goal.

"I already think your daughter is too good for you," I said when I was the tiniest bit calmer, "and if she walked away from you completely, I would be elated. But she loves you, both of you, for some unimaginable reason, and because I'm devoted to that woman with my entire being, you *will* fix this. You *will* do right by her. You *will* step up—years too fucking late, mind you—but you will finally step up and show her that she is more important to you than you've ever led her to believe. Do you understand?"

Madge shook her head. "I don't feel well. I need to lie down."

I watched her leave the room with disappointment. From what I knew about my mother-in-law, I expected she would spend the next week in bed. No wonder Celia hadn't gone to her as a child. She would have had to coddle and soothe her mother when it should have been the other way around.

Madge was a lost cause.

Warren, though, the man whose amends mattered most, still stood in front of me, silent, half cowering, half ready to do combat. I watched the bob of his Adam's apple as he swallowed and the way his eyes darted, calculating his next move.

I could have punched him in the throat for even considering anything other than what I demanded. "Do you understand?" I asked again, my voice practically a growl.

His shoulders sank then, as though he finally felt the weight of his betrayal. "I'm not sure how to do that."

I nodded, because I'd assumed a response like that, an unwillingness to even try to figure out what his daughter might want or need from him. Even knowing it was coming, it made me want to remove his balls with my bare hands.

With gritted teeth, I forced myself not to launch myself on him. "Good thing I figured it out for you already." I pulled my mobile from my jacket pocket, opened up my email app and hit send on the message I'd drafted on the ride over, the device plugged into the car charger as I'd typed. "I've sent you a statement. I recommend releasing it word for word since I don't trust any of your alterations would be suitable. Of course it's your decision whether you decide to release it or not, and if you can find a better way to make amends with Celia, then go ahead. If you can't, I recommend you stick to this script."

He scowled as he circled around me to his desk. A few clicks later, I watched his eyes scan the screen as he read what I'd sent, his skin going pale. "I can't just release this. Not without coordinating with Murphy and the board. There could be financial repercussions from saying something like this. It isn't just about our family here."

"Atonement isn't supposed to be easy," I said, coldly. "In my experience, it only means something when it comes at a price."

"I don't know," he said, rubbing his fingers over his brow.

I'd had enough, my patience completely worn out. "Take the time you need to make it real, Warren," I said, putting the discussion to a close. "Difficult as this may be, you and I both know this is the least you can do to make things right."

I left without a glance back, and only when I was in the lift did I finally sigh with relief. I felt good. Well, better than I had. Adrenaline surged through my veins and for the first time in the last twenty-four hours, I remembered an emotion that wasn't based solely in rage.

But I was still angry. And still a wreck. Still not in any sort to be around my wife, so when I got back to the hotel, I grabbed the dry cleaning waiting for me at the front desk and changed for my work day in my new hotel room instead of going back to the one I shared with Celia.

FOURTEEN

CELIA

As soon as Elsa arrived in the morning, I handed off Cleo and set off for Midtown. I was frustrated and paranoid, worried Edward would follow me and think the worst so I took a cab instead of calling for Bert, and I left my cell at the hotel.

The phone was a source of distress, anyway, and it felt good to be unleashed from it. I'd spent most of the night texting and checking for replies from my husband. He didn't answer any. He hadn't even read any after midnight, which increased both my anxiety and my anger.

Because what was he planning to do?

What had he already done?

Was Edward the one harassing Hudson? It was still possible. Based on his reaction, I was certain that Edward hadn't known Hudson had been the man I'd been protecting before last night, but that didn't mean Edward hadn't gone after him for another reason.

I comforted myself with the fact that the threats I'd read hadn't been in Edward's handwriting. That got him off the hook, didn't it?

Whether it did or not, I clung to it as truth.

But then I couldn't stop playing out other worst-case scenarios in my head, imagining what Edward would do to Hudson if he hadn't done this. Imagining what he'd do in return. God, it was awful. They were both so powerful and while I'd seen the best of each of them, I also knew how diabolical they could be at their worst.

It made my stomach hurt to think about.

When I could distract myself from ruminating, I didn't feel any better. In some ways, I felt worse. Fuck Edward for putting me through this. Fuck him for disappearing on me. Fuck him for being so rigid and domineering and manipulative.

And fuck me for loving him as desperately as I did.

Needless to say, I probably wasn't in the most ideal frame of mind when I showed up at Pierce Industries just before nine in the morning, but there I was, pissed and ready to lash out.

"He's on his way up," Trish said when I demanded to see Hudson.

Not bothering to sit down, I waited, my stare pinned on the elevator across the hall.

He saw me immediately. Our eyes met, and whatever spark of life had been in his before he'd seen me vanished, leaving his gaze cold and stony.

Without saying anything, he unlocked his office and

gestured for me to go in. He followed closely, shutting the door behind him.

I'd told myself on the ride over I'd be civil. I'd told myself I'd be restrained.

Both promises went up in smoke as soon as I was alone with him in the office. "You really fucked up, Hudson," I said before he'd even made it to his desk. "And you can't blame that on me. This was your doing. *You're* the one who brought this to my house."

I hadn't realized how much guilt I was feeling until the words came out. I didn't want to be the person harassing Hudson and his family. I didn't like that version of me. I was a different person now, but if Edward wreaked havoc on his life, it would be my fault. Hudson would point the finger at me

But I'd tried to prevent it! I'd tried and risked my relationship doing so. It was Hudson and his busybody wife that had fucked everything up, and I was here to make sure he got the record straight.

Unfortunately, Hudson wasn't in a mood to listen, which probably stemmed in part from my hostile approach. He slammed his fist down on his desk. "Did you do it? Are you behind this? Yes or no? Once and for all."

I flinched, the accusation hurting more coming from Hudson than when his wife had only alluded to it. "No! I told you, I didn't—"

He cut me off. "Then I *didn't* fuck up. We need those journals. We need them to solve this. Whatever it took to get them, I don't regret it."

He was curt and dismissive, and I knew in my bones that this entire interaction was unproductive, but I was now not just angry and worked up and worried but also I was goddamned hurt. By both Hudson and Edward. And while I was still learning how to deal with strong emotions, these were some of the most potent I'd had in a long time. They spun in my belly and pressed upward, demanding to be let out. They ruled me.

So instead of leaving, I spewed on. "I have *always* been real with you," I told him with raw sincerity. "No matter what I've done, what schemes I've pulled. I have still always been honest with you, when we were face-to-face. So when I say I didn't do this, you should know I'm telling the truth."

Hudson sank into his chair and looked up at me with disdain. "How could I know anything?" he asked with feigned innocence. "I don't know you anymore. Remember?"

The sharp pain in my chest made it impossible to speak, impossible to even breathe. All I could do was nod and stare and nod some more. What had I even expected? That Hudson would just intuitively understand all I'd done to protect him? That he would apologize or acquiesce or that he'd console me and tell me not to worry about a thing?

Even if it were possible for him to set aside everything that had happened after he met Alayna, even if he knew that I'd tried my damndest to keep him out of this, he was still going through a crisis of his own. Someone was threatening his family. His focus was there, as it should be, on the drama that was already happening to him. He couldn't be expected to be concerned about drama that was yet to come. He couldn't be expected to be concerned about me.

Then why was *I* concerned about *him*?

Without another word, I spun around and left Hudson's office. It was time I got my own priorities straight. Hopefully both of those priorities would be waiting for me when

I got back to our suite.

———————————

Edward wasn't at the hotel when I got back. He didn't return that evening either. My messages remained unanswered, as did my calls. By bedtime I'd stopped reaching out all together. He'd come back when he was ready, no sooner, and that was that.

I'd done this to him once. I'd taken off from London and hid away at my parents', refusing to talk to my husband except for short yes or no texts.

Reminding myself of that fact did nothing to calm the intense storm inside me, but at least it helped my head keep it together.

Thankfully, once I put away my phone, I had a task to keep me preoccupied. The diaries had arrived in a box from London by special delivery just after eight pm. While Cleo gnashed at baby cereal in her high chair, I spread out the books across the dining table, eleven black leather-bound journals containing the record of my cruel past.

I picked one up and leafed through it, my stomach churning as my eyes scanned familiar names and places. There was a lot written in them that I'd forgotten. Much more that I didn't want to remember. Going through them with Hudson was going to be tough, and for the first time since he'd disappeared, I wished Edward was back specifically to guide me through the task. I still wanted to fight with him, but I wanted him to comfort me, too. Wanted him to wrap me in his arms and let me feel my feelings and tell me what to do.

I can take care of myself.

With a sigh, I put the book back down and worked out a plan for how to get through them. Then I put in an order for breakfast room service and left the journals for the next day.

When I woke up the following morning, my priority was firm in my mind—put our differences aside and find the person who was terrorizing Hudson and Alayna. I'd been too wrapped up in myself to realize how serious the situation was. There was someone angry with things Hudson and I had done in the past. Someone who very much wanted to even the score. His family's lives were in jeopardy. If it wasn't Edward behind it, there was a very good chance that my family would be threatened next.

And if it was Edward...well, I needed to know that too.

"Come on in," I said cheerfully when the Pierces appeared at my door. I nodded to the room service cart that had arrived only minutes before they had. "I've already ordered tea and coffee." I assumed Hudson still drank black coffee, but his wife...? I directed my next words to her. "I didn't know which you preferred in the morning. I also have an assortment of fruits and breakfast pastries, in case you haven't eaten yet. I know sometimes it's hard to remember to take care of yourself in times of stress."

"I've already eaten," Alayna said without feeling. Then, warmer, she added, "Thank you."

I refused to be anything but a perfect host. "They're here if you change your mind."

"How about we just get started?" Hudson said, as efficient as eve . "Where are the journals?"

"Since you're obviously not hungry either, Hudson, they're in here. Follow me." I walked them down the hall and around the corner to the dining room.

"Is Edward working with us as well?" Hudson asked as they followed behind.

I was glad I wasn't facing them when I answered. "No. He went into work." It could have been true for all I knew. Point was, my marital troubles were not of interest to Hudson, nor were they important today. "It's just us and the nanny."

When we reached the table, I turned to face them. As composed as Hudson usually was, I was surprised to see him viscerally react to the sight of the journals, as if their mere existence churned his stomach.

I know the feeling, bud.

It felt oddly reassuring to have that in common.

"I don't know if you had a plan about how to attack this," I said, suddenly nervous. I tucked a stray hair behind my ear. "But I was thinking that you and I, Hudson, could each grab a journal and start reading through it. When we come to a name of someone involved in an experiment, we could record the name as well as any other details that may be important regarding the subject. Such as whether or not we believe they might still have hostile feelings toward you or me. Most of those references in the letters seemed vague, but if we come across anything that seems to possibly be referenced, then we can note that as well."

It was a pretty straight-forward plan, one that removed Alayna from reading the journals, which was selfish on my part.

But they were, in fact, journals. They were private and terrible and not the kind of thing I ever wanted anyone reading. It had been bad enough when Edward had read them. He'd been enraged and disgusted. I couldn't imagine the contempt Alayna would feel reading them, especially when she already hated me so intensely.

I would have thought Hudson would feel the same way, but when no one spoke, I wondered if I'd thought wrong. "If you have another plan…"

"No," Hudson said. "This is good." He removed his jacket and sat down to work.

I followed suit, taking a chair across from him.

"What should I do?" Alayna asked.

It wasn't my place to keep her away from the journals. I looked to Hudson for that.

Thankfully, he seemed to be on the same page. "You can do the recording, Alayna. As Celia and I read, we will call out information. If you could track it and sort it, I think that would be the best use of your time."

I worried momentarily that she might object to being kept on the sidelines. From what I knew of Alayna, she had always been headstrong and ready to buck against anyone who tried to hold her down.

But she surprised me, taking to the job enthusiastically and even setting up a shared spreadsheet on the laptop she'd brought.

We dug in then, working throughout the morning. It was difficult reading, as I'd expected it would be, but I concentrated on detaching myself from the stories I read, and that helped the process go smoother. We developed a sort of rhythm between the three of us, Hudson and I shouting out details, Alayna confirming them before entering them into her computer. It was a good process.

That wasn't to say there wasn't tension amongst us because there definitely was. It wove around us like the tight weave of a spiderweb, keeping us trapped in its sticky silk-like thread. The only time it broke was when Elsa brought Cleo. Alayna was a sucker for a baby, it turned out, and no one could remain somber around mine.

It was only a momentary reprieve. As soon as Cleo was burped and back with the nanny, the contention was back, worse than before. It didn't just surround me, either. Alayna and Hudson bickered as well and eventually they excused themselves to take their clipped conversation to the hall.

Admittedly, I was pleased that, for once, their argument couldn't be blamed on me since I'd been on my best behavior, which was probably petty, but also it was a big thing. I hadn't ever spent time in a room with the two of them without scheming and plotting to turn them against one another. It was new for me, and as silly as it was, I took it as evidence of how far I'd come.

When Hudson returned, he came back alone. "It's a little much for Alayna," he said, vaguely. "We're on our own for the afternoon."

I held back a dozen snarky comments that came to mind. "Probably for the best. No one should have to deal with our shit except us."

"Amen."

If only my husband felt the same.

Reminding myself of my agenda for the day, I pushed the thought away. "I'll call down and tell room service one less dish for lunch."

When that was done, we resumed working, only breaking when our food arrived then quickly resuming when we'd finished. Our process had altered with Alayna's absence. Now we took turns reading, the other recording on

Hudson's laptop. It was easier than it had been, despite being down one person. We both knew our stories so well that we could fill in the details that the other had read almost at the same time as they were recited out loud.

The tension was far less noticeable as well. In fact, there was almost a sense of camaraderie. Whatever our past sins, Hudson and I had committed them together. That created a bond between us that could never be broken, no matter what changed about us as individuals.

Maybe that's why I'd been so quick to keep Hudson a secret, because we'd been linked like that. I was bound to protect him. Whatever Edward thought, he was wrong—I hadn't chosen Hudson over him. I hadn't made a choice at all.

Eventually, Hudson closed his laptop. "I think that's enough for today."

I looked at my phone. Almost five o'clock. Where had the time gone? "Did we figure anything out?"

He hesitated. "Not really. Did you?"

"No," I answered honestly. Nothing we'd read connected to any of the letters Hudson had received, and I still was no closer to figuring out if Edward was involved. "We still have a few journals to go through."

"Back at it tomorrow?"

"Of course." He was about to stand when I stopped him. "Are you scared?"

"Of the person sending the letters?" He settled back in his chair. "Yes. I am. Someone is very angry, rightly so, I presume. Valid anger is one of the most dangerous weapons I've encountered."

I'd seen my husband use valid anger as a weapon. It

had almost gotten me killed. I'd lived, but what about Camilla's husband? I was sure Edward had killed him. Would he go that far with Hudson?

A chill ran down my spine. "I feel like I should tell you I'm sorry."

Hudson seemed to assume my apology was for the past since his eyes scanned the journals laid out in front of us. "I was as much a part of this as you were." He waited a beat. "Sometimes I'm not so sure I shouldn't be apologizing to you."

It was peculiar how the cold I'd felt a second ago could so quickly turn to warmth. I didn't want an apology from Hudson, never had, but he'd considered it, and that meant something. Small that it might be, it was still something.

I flashed a brief smile. "It won't do any good, for either of us, at this point."

"No, I don't believe it will."

I stood as he did, planning to walk him to the door, but my thoughts were still tied up in the journals. "Should we be doing something? For all those people that we..." I couldn't find the right words

Hudson didn't have that problem. "For our victims?"

"Yeah."

He sighed, a heavy sigh that practically thudded with its weight. "I've tried, you know. I still try, when I find the opportunity. Try to make it up. Try to pay it back. Every token of retribution is selfishly a way to ease my own heart. It's impossible to make up for those kinds of hurts. There's no price that can be paid to fix someone that you've so utterly broken."

An immense grief wrapped around me. Not just for my

own wrongs that could never be fixed, but also for all the wrongs Edward felt had been done to him. He sought justice at every turn, trying to mend wounds that would never close.

"How are we ever supposed to move on?" I asked, my voice small.

Hudson shook his head, as though he didn't have that answer, but his words said differently. "We do just that. We move on. If we can't fix it, it doesn't do any good to dwell on the guilt. All we can do is forgive ourselves, try to be better in the future. And we can love the people in our lives wholly. We can believe in and fight for their goodness as strongly as we once worked to tear people apart."

"Use our powers for good." I'd said it once before to Edward when he'd wanted me to go after everyone who'd hurt me in the past. I'd hated the idea then, but now, framed like this, I could envision it as something different. Something beautiful and kind and right.

"Use our powers for good," Hudson agreed. "I like that."

Yeah. I really liked it too.

Suddenly I knew exactly what to say to Edward and what needed to be done in order to heal the rift between us.

Now he just needed to come home.

Fifteen

Edward

The incoming notification sounded on my mobile, a different tone than a normal call indicating it was FaceTime. Only one person communicated with me through this app, and only for one reason.

I glanced at the time then lowered my cigarette out of screen's view before I answered. Freddie's face filled the screen. "It's nearly eleven there. Isn't it past your bed-time?"

My sister leaned into the screen. "He had a nightmare about you. Couldn't go to sleep until he made sure you were alive and well."

"There was a monster with fire coming out of its mouth and a big swamp thing, too," my nephew said excitedly. "And both of them were trying to eat you and I couldn't see your eyes and I thought you were gone forever!"

Freddie's dream felt eerily like a metaphor for my current life.

"No monsters here," I said, twisting my phone so he could see the expanse of the hotel room balcony. "No swamp things either. And if you can see, I still have my eyes."

He laughed as I brought the phone up close to one eye then the other.

"See?" Camilla said from the sideline. "Uncle's fine. You're probably just having dreams because you miss him."

"Will you come home soon?" he asked me.

He wasn't the only one wanting an answer to that question. Though the texts from Celia the day before had referred to our shared hotel suite as home and not London as Freddie meant.

I didn't have an answer for either of them, unfortunately.

"You'll be the first one I tell as soon as I know," I promised.

"I hope it's soon," the six-year-old said with a yawn.

Camilla kissed Freddie on the forehead. "Think you can sleep now?"

"I'll try."

Camilla took the mobile. "Hold on for a second while I tuck him in?"

"Sure." It wasn't like I was doing anything other than brooding.

The screen went dark as she held her mobile against her body, the sounds of good night and the shifting of bed blankets coming through muffled. I took the opportunity to flick the growing ash of my cigarette into the glass I'd brought out with me to use as a makeshift ashtray, then brought it up to my lips for a drag.

Just in time for Camilla to return to the screen. "Please tell me that's a joint and not a cigarette."

I blew out a stream of smoke. "I could tell you that, but I'd be lying."

"What the hell, Eddie?" The image bobbed as she walked down the hall to another part of her house. "You haven't smoked in years. Have you taken it up again?"

Her concern was both annoying and oddly comforting. "It's the first one of the pack so I can't say that I've taken it up again. I suppose that's something I won't really know until I do or don't buy a second pack."

She frowned, a frown that grew deeper when I took another drag. "I kept you on because I wanted to ask how Celia was doing after Ron's sentencing, but now I wonder if I should be asking after you instead."

I ignored the inquiry about me, which was an answer in itself. "I couldn't tell you how Celia is doing. I haven't seen her in two days."

The bouncing image subsided as Camilla settled into her bed. "Ah. Must be quite a row if you're both avoiding her *and* smoking."

"I'm not avoiding her, exactly." I took another puff then crushed the butt into the glass. "I'm relieving her of having to spend time with my temper. It's a courtesy, re-ally."

"Yes, that is a courtesy. The Edward Fasbender Temper is quite terrifying, speaking from experience. Congratulations on having the sense of mind to stay away."

I let out a humorless chuckle. "It would be funny if it weren't so true."

"Perhaps."

A beat passed, and I thought seriously about lighting another cigarette.

"You know, Eddie, speaking again from experience, when you sent me away to school, I would rather have had your rage than your distance. Your anger blazes like an inferno, but your silence is colder than any winter I've known. Personally, I'd rather be warm."

"Thank you for that, Camilla. I didn't feel bad enough already." I pulled another cigarette from the pack.

"It wasn't said to make you feel bad. It was said to give you some perspective."

I tapped the unlit fag on my knee. "Should we talk about you now? I think that will be a lot more productive."

She sighed. Then she launched eagerly into telling me about the new man that she was seeing, and I lit the cigarette and listened and was happy for her, but also I thought about what she'd said, really thought about it, and by the time we hung up, I'd decided.

It was time to go home.

***

I found Celia bent over the desk in the living room, scrawling something onto a piece of hotel stationery. She must not have heard me come in because when she looked up, she startled.

The flash of surprise on her face quickly vanished,

though, and was replaced with a genuine smile. "You're here."

"I'm here."

"Thank God." She ran to me, throwing her arms around my neck.

Without hesitation, I hugged her tightly, burying my head in her hair. There were so many ways she could have greeted me—with accusations or resentment or the silent treatment—and she'd chosen joy. I couldn't have felt more cherished. I couldn't have been more relieved.

We held each other like that, neither of us willing to let go. I could have done without words for longer, content to be wrapped in Celia's warmth, except that there was something missing. Some*one* missing. "Is Cleo sleeping?"

I felt her head shake against my shoulder. She leaned back so she could look up at me. "She's with Genevieve and Chandler. They picked her up a few minutes ago. I'm surprised you didn't see them in the hall."

"I didn't. Are they sitting for us?"

"I asked them to take her for the night." Celia's expression grew serious. "So I could go look for you. I was just writing you a note."

The mention of my disappearance brought our argument back into view. We couldn't ignore the elephant. Might as well address it straight on.

I pulled away, slowly. Reluctantly. "Probably wouldn't have found me. I booked another room."

"You've been in the hotel all this time?" She tried to sound like it was funny but failed.

"Most of it." I took her hand in mine, running my thumb across the knuckle above her wedding ring. I'd never get tired of seeing it on her finge . "Can we talk?"

"I'd like that." She let me lead her to the sofa and set her down. As soon as I sat next to her, she turned her body toward mine. "I'm sure you have plenty to say, and I want to hear all of it, but I have something I need to say to you first."

Before I could respond, she'd moved to kneel on the floor at my feet.

My suit suddenly felt too warm. "Well, this is an interesting way to open up a dialogue."

"Does it get your attention?" She waggled her eyebrows as she nudged my knees apart so she could crawl between my legs.

"You definitely have my attention, though you had it when you were sitting at my side as well."

"Good." She flattened her hands and ran them up my thighs.

Naturally, my cock reacted. God, I loved her on her knees. I especially loved her on her knees for me.

The timing, however, was not necessarily appropriate. "Conversation is becoming less and less appealing, bird. I'm not complaining, but I think you'll agree that there is a lot that should be said between us, and my rehearsed script is suddenly leaving my mind."

"Then you can just listen because this has to be said before anything else." With her hands still on my thighs, she sat back on her haunches and peered up at me. "I choose you, Edward."

I didn't think I could breathe. I didn't dare.

Celia's hands slid so they were closer to my knees. "Above everything, Edward, I choose you and Cleo and what the three of us have together. There isn't anything else that matters. I trust you to love us and care for us. I trust you to keep us safe and protected. And I trust you to consult with and treat me as a partner on the matters that affect us all.

"I've said most of this before, I know, and I meant it when I did. But I realize now that it wasn't fair to say that and then keep parts of me from you. I've been entirely focused on what I needed—a say in the big decisions. But why should you give me what I need when I haven't given you what you need? So here I am giving you what you need—trust and honesty. Take it from me. It's yours. No strings. I know you'll give me everything I need in return."

Something dislodged in my chest, a loosening of something I didn't realize had been tight. Had I never believed that before? That she'd chosen me?

I *hadn't* believed it.

I'd chosen *her*. I'd gone after her for my own reasons, and when I fell in love with her, it was me who decided I'd keep her. She was with me because I'd made her mine, the same way that Marion had been with me because I'd made her mine. And when I'd lost Marion it had been because I'd lost interest in keeping her. There had never been any need for or benefit to being chosen. I'd believed with all my heart it hadn't mattered.

Yet, hearing Celia declare it now, I realized how very wrong I'd been. Being chosen made all the difference. It mattered more than her love. More than her submission. It was the greatest gift anyone had ever given me, and while I'd never worried about my merit, I suddenly felt very unworthy.

I cradled her face in my hand. She leaned into my touch, her gaze still on mine, her blue eyes intense as she waited for me to speak.

But what could I say after that? Everything in my head felt small and banal. And what was in my heart couldn't be expressed. There was no sequence of words that could relay the mass of emotions within me. I felt unleashed. Reborn. Aroused.

I moved my hand from her cheek to the back of her neck where her blonde locks were gathered in a low bun. Gripping my fingers through the hair underneath, I tilted her head toward mine as I leaned in. "I hope you understand that I'm going to have to fuck you now."

"Do what you want with me," she said just before my mouth crashed with hers. "I'm yours."

My teeth nipped on her upper lip, and she opened up to me, her mouth taking my tongue as it licked and stroked and tasted and devoured. Kissing her felt as intimate as fucking, and I kissed her for long, heavy minutes before the throbbing of my cock forced my attention elsewhere.

"Take me out," I said when I broke away. I bit the shell of her ear before leaning back to give her room. "Hurry up about it. My cock is lead."

I shimmied out of my jacket while she made quick work of my belt. Next it was the button, then the zipper. I was so hard that my crown popped over the band of my boxer briefs, red and leaking. I lifted my hips so she could pull my clothing down, but as soon as my erection sprung free, I sat back down.

My hand returned to grip her neck, messing up what was left of her bun. "Do you choose me even like this?" I asked, pulling her face toward my aching cock.

She couldn't answer since, the moment she opened her mouth, I thrust inside.

I plunged inside, over and over, deeper, until my head tickled the back of her throat and made her gag. When I pulled out, it was only meant to give her some air but she took the brief reprieve to cry out, "God, yes."

I'd made her choose like this before, but then I was asking her to choose the things I liked doing to her. It was so much different hearing her choose the man who did them.

I pushed her head back over my cock and held her down, her nose pressed up against my skin so tight there was no way she could breathe. "Do you choose me, angry and possessive and mean? Do you still choose me?"

This time when I let her up, she was gasping, tears running from the corners of her eyes. "Yes," she said, her voice raw. "I still choose you."

Her mouth was suddenly not enough.

I stood, pulling her up roughly with me. After a vicious kiss, I tore open her blouse, sending buttons flying through the air. Then I took advantage of her nursing bra, pulling down one of the cups so I could fondle her breast with my bare hand.

She whimpered when I squeezed her nipple causing me to tighten my pinch. "And now? When I hurt you and make you cry, do you still choose me?"

"Always. I choose you always."

My need was a living beast. With a roar, I swept the accessory tray off the ottoman and shoved her down in its place. I wasn't gentle as I peeled down her knickers and trousers, grateful they were wide-leg so I didn't have to remove her shoes to get them off of her. Just as roughly, I hitched one of her legs over my shoulder and stretched out over her, pushing her thigh flat against her chest so she was open wide.

I grunted as I shoved inside her. "You choose me, good or bad, whatever I've done, whomever I've hurt. Whatever my sins, you choose me."

"Yes, yes, yes," she panted in rhythm to my thrusts.

Whether she was agreeing with me or begging for more, I didn't know, but I chose to believe it was the former while also giving her the latter. I continued my assault with one driving effort—in, in, in, in, knocking against her clit with each thrust. In, in, in. As far inside her as I could go. As far inside her as I could be. Until we were no longer she and I, each with our own history and baggage, but one entity, our pasts both part of the same story, one with a complicated but very happy ending.

She climaxed first, her cunt clenching tight like it didn't bear to let me go. I pressed through her snug opening, meaning to just stay inside her while she came. But she felt too good, and she was too beautiful beneath me, all wrung out and tortured, and I came too, the pleasure starting at the base of my spine and igniting every neural pathway as fast as a lightning strike.

I hovered over her, spent and unmoored. It felt like I'd released much more than my cum inside her. Like I'd been relieved of the weight of something much heavier and burdensome.

Fuck. She wasn't supposed to be like this.

But she was, and I loved her, and I would do everything in my power to keep her mine. Even if it meant setting down my ego and trying something new. Like partnership. Without resentment. Without any barriers between us.

I pushed off her, tucked myself away, then dropped onto the couch behind me and watched Celia's chest rise and fall as her breaths slowed and she pulled herself together. When she was steady, she propped herself up on her elbows and looked at me.

She was a mess—her hair all over the place, her mascara smudged, her lipstick smeared. She was gorgeous.

"It wasn't fair to expect your trust when I have betrayed it on more than one occasion." I was the one wearing the most clothing, but I felt strangely the more naked of us both.

She nodded once, taking it in. Accepting.

Then she peeled herself off the ottoman and climbed on top of me, straddling my lap. "So now we try to do better," she said. Plain and simple. So easy it would be impossible to screw up.

I grabbed her face with both hands and pressed my mouth to hers. It wasn't as erotic as our earlier kisses had been, but it was somehow just as intense.

The sun was streaking its last rays across the sky when our lips finally parted. "You taste tobacco-y," she said. "Have you been puffing cigars?

"I took up smoking, actually. Don't worry, I've already quit." I'd tossed the pack as soon as I'd hung up with Camilla.

"Damn right you've already quit."

I smiled at her reprimand. "Oh, but I do happen to have two cigars in the inside pocket of my jacket for later. I bought some high-quality Cubans today thinking we might celebrate Ron's sentencing. I should have been here when you got the news. Are you happy?"

"Happy is a strange word for it." She shifted from my lap to sit beside me, leaning back into my arms when I angled toward her. "I'm glad, yes, but I don't know that his sentencing changes where I am with what he did to me. I'm only better because of you."

"I'm not taking all of that credit. It was you, too." I stroked my hand up and down her bare arm, enjoying the weight of her at my side so much that I hesitated before bringing up the delicate subject. "How did today go? With the journals."

She tensed, sitting up more. "It went okay. It was probably best you weren't around, even though I could have used your support."

"I'm here now."

"You are, and I have to ask...You knew I would eventually."

"What am I going to do about Pierce?" I was sure that was the question without confirming, but I needed her to know I was on the same page.

Being on the same page didn't make the question any easier to answer. I felt oddly less concerned with Hudson Pierce than I had in days, but he was still there at the back of my mind, waiting to be dealt with.

Right now, though, I was still more concerned about Celia's part in the equation. "Well," I removed my arm from around her. "Since we're trying to be better about discussing these things, what are you afraid that I'll do?"

I studied her profile as she took a deep breath in, then let it out. She kept her eyes straight ahead, not looking at me as she spoke. "You could try to ruin his business, which scares me because of what he might do to you in return. Or you could try to go after his family, and that scares me for the same reasons. But also it scares me because I don't want you to be the type of man who would do that. I'm afraid you already have done that."

I reached out and turned her face toward me so she could see my eyes. "I'm not the person who's terrorizing the Pierces. I promise on Cleo's life."

"I'm sorry," she said.

"Don't." I shook my head, not wanting her to feel guilty no matter how much the accusation stung. "I hate that you had to ask. But I also understand why you did."

"That makes me feel a lot better."

"Good." I swept my thumb across her bottom lip before I let her face go. "Do you believe me?"

"I do." And I believed her. She kept her gaze on mine. "I'm also scared of what you might do to Hudson personally."

"You mean you're worried I might hurt him physically."

Her nod was barely perceptible. "You told me you had those men beat up, the ones who scammed Hagan when he was a teenager."

"I did do that. That was a unique situation." Violence was generally not my preferred method. It was too easy. Over too quickly. It didn't hurt the way real ruin did.

"Okay," she said, and I could feel her gathering courage, could see the steely resolve in her eyes when she finally had as much as she needed. "But you killed Camilla's husband. Didn't you?"

We were in this now, both of us, honest and open and trusting, no more secrets, no more lies.

So I answered with the truth. "Yes. I did."

SIXTEEN

CELIA

I tried to swallow and couldn't.

I tried again as I wiped my clammy hands on my open shirt. "Okay," I finally managed to say.

And then nothing because what was there to say after that? I was still grappling with what to *feel*. On the one hand, Edward had shared something with me that I thought he never would share. On the other hand, what he'd shared wasn't something I necessarily wanted to know.

But I wanted to know all of Edward, didn't I?

Then why did I have the sudden urge to run? It warred with my instinct to stay.

"Hey," he said, taking my hand in his. I watched as he ran his thumb over my knuckles, his touch both warm and heavy despite the light strokes. If he knew the battle going on in my head, he didn't address it. "If I'm going to tell you this—and I am—we're going to need a drink."

"Like a session, but for you? That's serious." As if the fact he'd murdered his brother-in-law wasn't serious enough.

"More like it's a story that's hard to tell and alcohol makes things easier."

"Exactly. A session."

He stood, and somehow I stood with him. My legs still worked even though they felt numb. I was able to walk, one step in front of the other, like I always did, but I didn't follow him to the minibar. Instead I went to the bathroom to get cleaned up. I washed quickly at the sink then threw the tattered blouse in the trash, took off my bra, and put on a robe. Routine, normal things. Everything was good. Everything was fine

In the bedroom, I paused to catch my breath.

My husband was about to tell me how he killed a man. A terrible man, perhaps, but did that justify murder?

This wasn't exactly new information. I'd guessed that Edward had a hand in Frank's death before now, but not knowing the details, I'd been able to push it away and ignore it. Once he told me this story, I wouldn't be able to pretend anymore. I'd have to decide if it mattered. I'd chosen Edward, but I'd have to choose again. Could I stand behind a cold-blooded killer?

I shouldn't have brought it up.

"Am I pouring you a glass?" Edward called from the other room.

Too late for regrets. For better or worse, I needed to know. Edward needed to tell me. And I needed to be there for him as he did, the same way he'd been by me when I'd confessed my worst sins.

Besides, against all reason, I wasn't really all that worried about it. Whatever he said, it wasn't going to change who he was, and I already knew who that was. I already loved him.

Nevertheless, wine would help.

"Sure," I said, meeting him in the dining room. "I have to pump later anyway since Cleo isn't here. I'll just throw it out instead of storing it."

He handed me a glass filled with some dark red with a bitter bouquet. *Fitting.* "The cabernet franc," I said, after I tasted it. "You'd bought that for a special occasion."

"Special doesn't always mean celebratory." He took a sip from his own glass, his mouth puckering as the flavor hit his tongue. "I think this will do just fine. Shall we?

I walked with him back to the living room and took a place on the couch, curling my feet up under me. Edward looked from the chair to the bench. It was our pattern to sit apart during sessions, and I was sure he was deciding which he would find most comfortable

"If this is your session, that means I'm in charge, right?"

He laughed. "Whatever you say."

I glowered momentarily then relaxed into a smile. Edward's way through these was to be stoic and controlled, which I appreciated, because I needed that from him. But he didn't need rigidity and distance from me. He needed warmth.

"Then, since I'm in charge, I say we change things up." I patted a spot on the sofa next to me. "Come sit by me."

His lips twitched with what might have been disapproval, but after a slight pause, he strolled over. "You know why I required the space between us in your sessions?"

I peered up at him standing above me. "Because you're cruel and cold and you like to be able to watch while I squirm?"

He scowled at my response. "Because I thought it would help me not accidentally fuck you."

Huh. It was odd how an unknown detail like that from our past could make me swoony, even under the circumstances. "Funny then how all of your responses involved fucking me on purpose."

"Funny indeed."

I grinned. "Well, I can't guarantee you won't accidentally fuck me if you sit by me. But since you've already just had your way with me, you might be safe for a bit."

"I suppose I'll have to take my chances." He sat down, not close enough so that we touched, but close enough to be cozy. "Whenever I'm ready?" he said, making fun of himself since those were the words he always said to start my sessions.

It struck me as surreal—the wine, the intimacy, the lighthearted vibe between us. It felt as though he were preparing to tell a story about "that one time" he went fishing or some other jovial reminiscence. Did that make him a worse person? To not only be capable of murder but to also behave like it was no big deal?

Or was the carefree act for me? His way of making his tale easier to hear.

Both thoughts sobered me. I took a long sip of my wine.

Then, I buckled in for the ride. "Yes. Whenever you're ready."

"Very well." He cleared his throat and began. "I've told you before that Frank Dougherty wasn't a good guy. I should have known it from the start because Camilla only ever found herself with the worst of men—a pattern, I'm told, that stems from the abuse at the hands of her foster father. But Frank wasn't like the others. He was from a good family, and though he was privileged and reckless as many trust-fund heirs are, he was the first man to make my sister happy.

"Or, he did in the beginning, anyway. By the time he stopped making her happy, she was too involved with him to let on. And when they married, which was a little after a year of dating, they moved to Berkshire where Frank's family house was located, and though I bought a country house near Bray to be near her, I didn't see her as often as I would have liked. I was busy with work and kids and. Well. I was preoccupied.

"So I'm not sure exactly when it was that he started hitting her. Let alone when hitting turned to full-on beatings." He paused to drink some of his wine, medication to follow the wounding words. "She had bruises when I'd see her, but I didn't come to the country enough to notice the frequency, and she always had an excuse. Fell while hiking. Tripped over the dog. Everyday injuries. Red flags, but she never made a big deal and so I didn't either. I believed the perfect marriage image was real. He worshipped her in my presence, and at a time when I was very uninterested in my own marriage, I envied what they had."

He finished off the rest of his glass in several gulps, and I was grateful for the break, brief as it was. It gave me a moment to absorb what he'd said. Gave me a moment to feel for the sister-in-law that I'd begun to feel close to during the effort to snare Ron. I'd known she'd suffered abuse in the past. Beyond what Edward had told me, it was evident in her carriage, in the way she dressed, in the reclusive manner in which she lived.

Hearing her abuse confirmed, though, made it real, as real as the ending we were heading toward. The words that my husband had used to explain that reality took up the space of a minute when the acts they conveyed had taken far more of Camilla's life.

I hurt for that life she'd led. The ache burrowed in between my ribs, a twisting constant sort of pain. I imagined those years she'd spent in secret, enduring abuse she most likely thought she deserved, walking on eggshells all the time in order to not incur more. Ron had hurt me too, similarly and not at all the same, and there was an intense part of me that felt her pain like it was a memory, yet I was sure I understood only a fraction of what she'd gone through.

More important at the moment was Edward's pain. His love for his sister was very fatherly. It was evident he felt responsible for what she'd gone through, so much so that years later the telling of her story still required a good amount of alcoholic lubrication.

When he set his glass down on the nearby stand, I passed him the rest of my wine. He smiled appreciatively. "Needless to say—" he swirled the liquid, watching it coat the sides of the glass "—I had no idea what was wrong when she called one day at the office and begged me to come to Berkshire to get her. Said she needed to leave and that she'd explain when I got there. Very vague. I tried to get more information from her on the phone, but she insisted it wait and that it was urgent. Camilla wasn't one to cry wolf. I dropped everything and went."

I smiled. "Of course you did."

He shrugged like it was no big deal, but it was. He wasn't a knight in shining armor, perhaps, but he was a hero all the same, and I loved him for that, even when his methods of protection were on the dark side.

My smile faded as I remembered we were headed to a grim ending. "Then what?"

"Not knowing what I was walking into, I drove myself instead of taking a driver. It was late afternoon when I got to her house. She was waiting at the gates with an overnight bag, wouldn't even let me pull into the driveway. She got in, urged me to drive, and refused to say anything more until we were somewhere 'safe.' I didn't know what safe meant, of course. I should have taken her to London, and I would have if I'd understood, but I didn't. So I took her to Brayhill, which was nearby, and flat out told her I'd take her nowhere else until she explained."

He took a sip of my wine then set the unfinished glass down beside him. Sitting forward, he rested his elbows on his thighs and clasped his hands together in front of his face. "I didn't believe her at first. Which I regret very much. But she'd put on that show for so long. They'd been married for ten years, and I'd never had any clue. I'd even forgotten about the times I'd seen bruises until I really thought about it later on. In the end, she had to peel off her shirt and show me the scars. Camilla's always stayed covered up. She's self-conscious about the marks her foster father left, and I'd known about those, of course, as well as other scars, but I hadn't seen so much of her skin in nearly a decade."

His torso expanded as he took a long breath in. "It's not my place or my story to comment much on what I saw," he said, breathing out. "Let's just say it convinced me."

I ran my hand up and down his back, not sure if it was meant to comfort him or me. He accepted it for longer than I thought he would. Then, when he glanced over his shoulder at me, I pulled my hand back into my lap.

"What happened that finally pushed her to call you? Something worse than usual?" It probably wasn't relevant, but the question came out anyway. A sick sort of curiosity, and I braced myself for details of an altercation that had to be horrendous. Being beaten at all was appalling. Yet my mind ran away with all the possibilities that would make it worse—did he burn her like her foster father had? Cut her? Break her bones?

In the profiled position, I could easily see Edward's jaw tense, mirroring the dread that I imagined. "She'd tried to leave him before, apparently. Without success. He always tracked her down, made her feel like it was impossible to get away. She'd been too embarrassed to involve me, she said. Can you believe that? Embarrassed."

Yes, I could believe that. I'd felt the same about Ron.

"As for the fight that day, she didn't say much about the details except that it had been a typical row. Apparently his violent streaks came in cycles, and there'd been a fairly good reprieve before that morning. The reprieves always ended eventually, according to what she told me, and she'd been half prepared for it this time, but was hoping beyond hope that he'd meant it this time when he'd said he'd changed. She thought if there was any chance that he would, this would be it."

Putting together what I already knew about Camilla at the time of her husband's death, I realized why she'd put so much stock in him. She'd been six months pregnant. "She wanted to protect Freddie."

"She did." Retrieving the glass of wine, he stood and

paced over to the window. "Freddie was the only reason she called me," he said, looking out into the night. "She didn't care enough about herself on her own, but for him…"

He washed the thought away with a swallow of wine, then turned back to me. "To be fair, Frank had really made it difficult for her to see any other path. He'd ostracized her from her friends. He'd taken complete control of her life—her accounts, her daily schedule. She couldn't even get access to her car without going to him, which was why she'd needed me that day. She had no money, no vehicle. She'd only been able to phone because he'd been in the shower. She managed to call me and take her bag down to hide by the side of the road during that time. Then she spent the next hour placating his every whim and praying he wouldn't check her call log, which he often did. She got away to meet me by telling him she was going for the mail."

It sounded similar to every account of domestic abuse I'd ever heard, which made it no less horrifying. I pulled my feet up to the sofa and hugged my knees to my chest, needing the support to hear more.

Edward's support was the wine. He finished it off and set it down on the side table. "Obviously, once I was convinced, I was ready to tear the man apart with my bare hands. I fantasized doing so for much of the evening, in fact. Planning all the ways I'd destroy him when we should have been headed back to London. They were brutal, believe me. Ways in which he truly suffered. Who knows what I would have done. I would have started legally, though. I called my lawyer that night to request a meeting the next day when we got into town. I believed we had time, see. I didn't think that he would come after her so quickly or know to come looking for her at Brayhill. Stupid, right? Where else would she go? I suspect things would have gone quite differently if I hadn't thought I was so invincible."

He sank down in the armchair. "I never did figure out how he got past security. She'd left her mobile behind. My best guess is that he found where she kept the system code saved in her contacts, but he may also have lured her to let him in some other way. I'd given her my laptop when she'd gone to bed. He might have emailed her there or messaged her through a social app. I didn't want her to ever think I blamed her, so I never asked. All I knew was that, in the middle of the night, I was woken with shouting from the guest wing. I didn't even think about it—I grabbed my gun."

My skin prickled with foreboding, but I tried to remain expressionless as he went on, the way he always was when he listened in my sessions. It was harder than I'd imagined.

Whatever my face said, he went on. "Camilla and I were the only ones in the house. I was ninety-nine percent sure that Frank was our intruder, but I had no plan. I just went to the safe, took it out, loaded it with a full cartridge, and went to her room. The door was open when I got there, and I must have arrived just after it happened because they were both by the fireplace, Camilla standing with the poker in her hand, Frank swaggering as blood gushed from a wound at his head. Whatever threat he'd been, he was outnumbered now. We could have dialed 111, had him arrested and taken to hospital. He may have survived. Though she'd hit him pretty hard. There was a good chance the injury was fatal on its own. Either way, I didn't let us find out. As soon as I registered what I was seeing, I aimed my gun and shot. Three times, to be sure."

There it was. The terrible truth, not quite as terrible as I'd imagined, gruesome as it was. No premeditation. Self-defense, most likely, according to the law. Potentially hard to prove, but with Edward being who he was...

Except.

"Frank died in a fire," I said, remembering the accounts I'd read. The entire estate had burned down.

Though, of course that had been a cover, I realized now. As likely as it was that he could have walked away unscathed, there was also the chance that he wouldn't. It was only Camilla's word that her husband was a danger. If Frank had entered without breaking in, it made it harder to claim self-defense. It might have been different if it were only himself, but since Camilla had hit Frank first with the poker, Edward would never have risked going to the authorities. His only choice was to cover up what happened, which had to have involved a whole new level of risk.

Confirming my thoughts, Edward leveled his gaze on me. "Do not underestimate the power of a rich white man, Celia. It was nothing to get his body taken back to the Dougherty home, to have the estate burned to ashes, to have the fire service call it an accident, to have the coroner cite asphyxiation as the cause of death."

It was Ron's similar position that had kept him from being arrested for years. It was how so many men got away with evil deeds.

I rubbed my palm across my forehead. "That's terrifying," I said without thinking.

"Which part?" Edward asked sharply. "Because all of it terrified me. I'd killed a man in cold blood. I covered it up without any inquiries from authorities. I got away with it scot-free. It disturbed me so much that, needing comfort, I ended up calling the one person I knew that wouldn't care what I'd done."

"Marion." She'd referenced the last time they'd been together when she'd seen him that day in the office. This had to be the time she'd been talking about.

"She came straight away," he said, though I hadn't needed the confirmation to know I was right. "She let me take out my horror on her. When she left, she was as black and blue as Camilla ever was, I guarantee it."

Edward was a sadist, but he tended to prefer psychological pain to physical. For him to lean on the latter said what sort of place his head had been in.

I rubbed both hands over my face. There was a lot to process. It was outright murder. No denying that. But if he'd lived, it was unlikely he would have gone to jail for any real time. Frank had money on his side too, and rich men rarely got punished for their sins. He might always have been after Camilla. They'd definitely have always been connected through their child. What worse things could Frank have done to Camilla and Freddie if Edward hadn't done what he had?

It was complicated, and I would probably need to take some time before I completely understood what I thought about it.

None of that mattered right now. Strangely, my concerns at the moment were less about what Edward had done in the past and more about how he viewed himself now because of them. From his bitter tone, it was evident he was carrying a shit load of blame for things that, in my humble opinion, he didn't deserve to be blamed for.

Especially when the only one blaming him was himself.

I dropped my hands from my face, set my feet on the floo , and leaned toward him. "Okay, hold up. This is a terrible story—I'm not going to deny that at all—but there are a number of things you've said that seem to lack perspective."

"Oh, really," he said patronizingly.

"Yes, really. Number one—" I held up my index fi - ger "—the things you did to Marion within a consensual sexual relationship are nothing at all like what Frank did to Camilla. You know that. My God, out of everyone in the world *you* know that. You were the one who forced me to see that the relationship I had with Ron was different from the relationship I had with you. You not seeing it now is shortsighted and frankly, it's martyrdom. You are neither short-sighted nor a martyr, so what the fuck?"

His frown eased ever so slightly. "I didn't feel good about it, regardless."

"Of course you didn't. You were dealing with other shit, and you weren't behaving like yourself, but was Marion upset?"

He paused before he shook his head. "She was not. In fact, she was rather into all of it."

I held my hand up in the air to stop him. "More than I need to know, thank you, and let's just be clear that I'm not ever going to be into the pain stuff no matter what shit you're dealing with."

"Duly noted." This time his frown was almost a smile.

Feeling bolder, I moved to the ottoman in front of him and put up two fingers. "Number two, it was not your fault that you didn't take Camilla to London. It was not your fault that you didn't know what Frank was doing to Camilla all those years. Is it my mother's fault that she didn't know what Ron was doing to me?"

"Yes, actually, I think it really is."

I shook my head. "You're wrong, but bad example. The point is, you couldn't have known because she didn't want you to know. And I think, deep down, you know that. You know it, and you hate it, because it means you don't have control. It's probably one of the reasons you push so hard to maintain truth in your relationships now, because you don't ever want to be blindsided like that again. I understand, and I'm going to try to be better about meeting that need with you, but you also need to let yourself off that hook. It was not your fault."

His expression had grown unreadable, and I had no way to know if I was reaching him, but I sure liked what I was saying. It was making sense as I spoke it, and I was seeing him clearer than I ever had.

He must not have thought I was too far off base, because he was still sitting there, and he still appeared to be listening and he hadn't tried to win the conversation for himself, which was surprising. And validating. I knew what I was talking about, and he couldn't deny it.

Now for the most complicated part. "Number three." I put up three fingers then waited a beat to be sure I had his full attention. "You shot Frank to protect your sister and her unborn child. It was clearly self-defense. Was it lawful? No. Was it ethical? I think philosophers might argue about that one. Whatever. You may not have even been the reason he died."

He interrupted me. "Oh, no. I killed Frank Dougherty. It will never be thought for one moment that it was at Camilla's hands. I will not let that be on her shoulders."

And yet another reason why I loved him. Even at his darkest, he was always motivated by the ones he cared for.

"Okay. It was definitely you," I granted. "You killed a man. In cold blood. And you covered it up. I get it. It's not pretty. I'm not going to lie and say it is. It happened, you can't change it, and you probably should feel...I don't know, *something* about that for the rest of your life."

"I don't regret it, Celia. At all. And if I'd have been around when Ron..." He didn't have to finish that sentence. We both knew what Ron had done. "I wouldn't have waited for him to come into my house. I would have gone after him. I would have done worse."

"I know." I'd already had a feeling he'd only gone after my uncle legally because he'd wanted me on his side. "And maybe you would have done worse to Frank, too, if that night hadn't happened like it had. Maybe it would have made you hard and terrible. Maybe it would have turned you down a dark road that you could never come back from.

"But it did happen like it did. And you obviously do feel something about it. Whatever that feeling is, it's not a feeling that you like, and you can't let that go. So listen to me now—don't believe that this is your one and only defining act. It's not even in the top five. You are a man who took on the care of his sister as soon as he could when they'd both been orphaned. A man who gave his sister a job and a home again when she was pregnant and alone and needed it most. A man who rebuilt his father's business into something bigger than it had been before. A man who raised two children, a good portion of which he did alone, into two amazing, brilliant adults. A man who gave an entire family a job and a place to live on his paradise island. A man who spent more than a year of his life trying to put a predator behind bars.

"And you're a man who would kill for the ones he loves most. Not just a man who will say the words, but a man who will go the distance if need be. There's no one else I'd rather have my life in his care. There's no one else I'd rather have my heart."

I'd rushed through my declaration to be sure he wouldn't interrupt, and now my heart beat so fast it felt like I'd been running. I took a breath, waiting for him to speak.

In a flash, I was pushed on my back on the ottoman for a second time. Edward hovered over me, his mouth inches from mine. "How is it you see so much good in a man who is clearly a devil?"

"Oh, I see the devil, too," I assured him. "I like him just as much."

"Are you sure I haven't just groomed you to respond this way?"

"I might be who I am right now because of you, but it's exactly who I want to be."

He kissed me at that, a long, luxurious kind of kiss that ended with him sweeping me in his arms and carrying me to the bedroom where he peeled off my robe and kissed my entire body, taking his time to be sure there wasn't an inch of me that hadn't been covered with his lips.

Then, with his clothes deserted on the floo , he covered my naked body with his and made love to me with a sweet attentiveness that I'd never seen from him before. I loved this side of him, like I loved all his sides, like I loved the man who controlled and the man who would kill. I espe-cially loved that, for the first time ever, I was pretty sure I was seeing all the sides of him there was. No holds barred. Bare and vulnerable and mine.

After, he held me tight around the waist as we lay fac-ing each other, our eyes level. We didn't talk for a long time. We'd said so much already, and there was a lot that could be said like this—silent, our gazes locked as we stroked each other's skin.

But there was still something unresolved, and eventually he addressed it. "You have to let me do what I need to do with Pierce. It's my war now. I can't let it go unsettled."

My muscles tensed automatically. Then I took a breath in, and relaxed as I blew it out. This was what all of this had been coming to. If I'd thought it was going anywhere else, I was fooling myself. I'd told him I trusted him, and now I had to prove it.

"Okay," I said.

It was his chance, too, to prove what he would do when it wasn't a gun in his hand in the middle of the night. When the threat wasn't imminent. When there wasn't so much to lose. When it was only his pride versus his foe.

"Let me just ask you one thing," I added, careful not to undo all the progress we'd made. "With what happened with Frank, with what happened with Ron—which situation feels more resolved to you now that they're both said and done?"

He didn't get a chance to answer before the buzzer rang. It was late. I didn't know what time exactly, but it had to be late.

"I put the do not disturb up when I came in," Edward said, erasing any chance that it might be turndown service.

The buzzer rang again. I jumped out of bed and grabbed my robe, tying it as I rushed to the door in case it was Genevieve and the baby. The buzzer rang once again before I got there, followed by heavy pounding.

I didn't even bother looking through the peephole before opening the door, and was thoroughly surprised to see it wasn't my stepdaughter, but Hudson, alone, exasperation written all over his face.

Without an invitation, he pushed inside, clinging to me so desperately as he did, we almost both tipped over. "Find her," he begged, his voice threadbare. "Find my wife."

SEVENTEEN

EDWARD

Celia greeted me at the door as soon as I came up from work the next day. "They found Alayna," she said. "She's fine. A bit bruised up, but overall fine."

My wife was relieved, and so I was too. It had been Celia I'd been most concerned about when Hudson had shown up at our room the night before. His wife was missing. Presumably, she'd been taken by the person who'd been threatening them, and since all signs pointed to that person being someone from Hudson and Celia's past, I was rightfully worried that Celia was next.

Not one of us had gotten any sleep. While the two of them had stayed up scouring the journals for clues, I'd been on the phone arranging bodyguards and extra security for Celia as well as her parents, my children, and Camilla. When the sun came up, I showered and dressed and left for my makeshift office on the conference level of the hotel, but I cancelled all my appointments for the day and spent it instead investigating Pierce. He'd been looking for the perpetrator from the inside out. I thought there was benefit from changing the angle and searching from the outside in. Even after Celia called to tell me it looked like the abductor hadn't been someone they'd played at all, I kept on with my mission. Just in case.

"And the man who took her?" I barely dared to breathe.

"He's in jail. And anyway, he wouldn't have come after me, so don't be worrying about him making bail." It was like she could read my mind.

Still, I was wary. "You're absolutely sure? He acted alone? There's no one else in on the scheme?"

She wrapped her arms around my waist. "It was just him, and yes. I'm sure. Hudson and I never played him. His motives had nothing to do with me."

"Good." I kissed her before I released her. "I might just keep the bodyguards for a little while, though."

"If it makes you feel better, I understand. Besides, if you're going to tangle with Hudson, you'll need them."

"Celia," I warned. I knew what she was doing—trying to bait me into discussing my plans with Pierce.

She put her hands up in the air in surrender position. "I'm not interfering. Doesn't mean I can't still have opinions."

If I hadn't been so tired, I'd likely have spanked her ass red for her opinion. It would have been for fun, though. Not punishment.

"Are you hungry?" she asked, changing gears as she helped me out of my suit jacket. "There's a sandwich in the fridge, if you are. Otherwise, I'm ordering you to bed.

I slept most of the day, so I can handle Cleo. You, on the other hand, haven't slept since yesterday, so don't try to tell me you aren't exhausted."

I peered at her over my shoulder. "Ordering me?"

She handed me my jacket with a sigh then dropped to her knees to bow dramatically at my feet. "Oh, master," she teased, "I know I am not worthy to command you. I beg of you to please have favor on me and allow me to care for you for once by feeding you and sending you to bed."

I laughed. "Get up, you temptress."

She took my hand as I bent to help her up. "Am I turning you on?"

"Always." I kissed her again, because she was there and because I wanted her. But she was right that I needed sleep, so I cut it off before it went anywhere interesting. "No food, thank you. And I'll sleep. Shortly." Now that I knew the Pierce threat wasn't a danger to my own family, there were other things that needed to be sorted out.

Cleo's cry came over the baby monitor, waking up from her late afternoon nap on schedule. "I'll feed her in her room so she won't be a distraction. Get to bed, soon."

She crossed toward the adjoining suite, and I headed to the desk.

"I mean it, Edward," she scolded.

"I will. I promise. Give me ten minutes." I smiled at her until she'd disappeared into the next room, the door shut behind her.

Then I hung my jacket on the back of the chair and sat down at the desk. I pulled the pad of hotel stationery from the top drawer, centered it in front of me, and stared at the blank page.

The day spent researching Hudson Pierce hadn't been a waste. I'd learned a lot about the man in relatively few hours, quite a bit I'd already known from previous investigations—I never did business with anyone without a thorough background check. Still, a good deal of what I'd discovered had been new, details that shed new light on the man I very much wanted to confront.

So much had changed in the past few days. New information had been revealed. My beliefs had been challenged. It was a different man who sat in my skin today than the one who'd worn it a week before. I wasn't even the same man as the one I'd been the night I'd learned Hudson's real role in my wife's life.

Change was inevitable. Of course it was. I expected it. I took pride in being someone who could pivot when needed, and I'd done it successfully in both my business life and personal life on many occasions. But through the years, as far back as I could remember, my core had been rooted in a well-proven tradition of eye for an eye, tooth for a tooth. Entire civilizations had thrived on that principal. It was simple. Justice in the most base form.

For me, it had been a compass as well as an anchor. Vengeance had dictated my direction and had held me together through the roughest of storms. Who would I have been without a place to put the mass of rage and spite and jealousy that lived inside of me? How could I have functioned? How could I have built my business or provided for my loved ones or even gotten out of bed day after day after day without the inspiration of a mission that I believed in?

But I'd heard Celia as she'd questioned me the night before. With what happened with Frank, with what happened with Ron—which situation feels more resolved to you now that they're both said and done?

All day it had been in the back of my mind, popping to the front whenever I let it. I wished it had been harder to answer. I wished it had been easier to dismiss with excuses. I wished it wasn't so obvious what I had to do next.

Wishing did nothing for progress. Only action mattered, and stalling wouldn't get me what I wanted or what my family needed.

Now was the time.

With my decision made, I reached into the inside pocket of my jacket hanging behind me and retrieved my pen, then scrawled out a note on the paper in front of me.

I'm grateful to hear your wife is back in your arms.

You and I have unfinished business.

Edward Fasbender

I tore the sheet from the pad, folded it in thirds, and tucked it in an envelope that I addressed with Hudson's name. In the morning, it would go out in the post and be received in the coming days. Then we'd officially be in the endgame. There would be a winner, and one or both of us could move on.

Now, though, with the course finally settled, I did as my wife commanded and went to bed.

A little more than a week later, I met with Hudson at an investor appreciation dinner that both Accelecom and Pierce Industries had been invited to. "Neutral territory," he'd said, which wasn't quite true since the whole of New York City seemed to belong to the man.

To be honest, whose territory was whose didn't concern me, as long as we had the opportunity to speak in private and at length. Hudson had assured me he could make that happen, even though the event had a forecasted attendance of two-hundred-fifty people

It wasn't until we were at the top of the stairs to the roof and Hudson pulled out a personal set of keys that I understood how he could make the guarantee.

"You own the building," I said as we walked away from the door out onto the private terrace. "Seems like that should have been disclosed beforehand." I reached inside my tuxedo and pulled a lighter and the two cigars I'd bought the week before from my inside pocket. They'd been meant for me and Celia, but this felt more apropos.

Hudson took the cigar I offered and shrugged. "My building, your cigar. Seems an equal amount of trust is required from both of us."

"Are you so sure about that? Seems a lot easier to lace an item with poison than to push another man off a building."

He studied me, as though trying to discern how much of a threat I posed. While I'd told him on more than one occasion that I wanted Werner Media, I'd given him no reason to believe I felt any real loathing toward him.

After a beat, he bit the cap off his cigar and spit it on the ground. "Lucky for both of us, neither of us stands to gain by the demise of the other."

"Perhaps not." I held my lighter out to him. "Though

that theorizing underestimates the value of pure satisfaction."

He laughed. "Touché." He toasted the foot, then lit the fille , puffing a bit before drawing the cigar away to study the label. "Gurka? These are high quality. Nice flavo . What'd they run? Twelve k a box?"

"Fifteen."

"Impressive." He handed me back the lighter.

I prepared my own cigar, making sure I had a strong cherry before pocketing my lighter. We puffed in silence, both of us looking out over the New York City skyline, the summer night bright with artificial light. It was astonishing how calm I felt. In my head—as I'd planned this approach, what I'd say, what I'd do—I'd expected more adrenaline. Instead, there was a quiet peace, so foreign to my nature it would have alarmed me if I let it.

Instead, I embraced it. Held it like it was my wife. Let it be my foundation, a firmer bedrock than any I'd planted on before.

I wondered in those moments what Hudson must think about this meeting I'd called. He hadn't asked its purpose, clearly believing my goal was the shares, a natural assumption. Would he bring it up? Or would he wait for me? It was a fun little game trying to guess.

But I wasn't here for games. The time for those was long over, for both of us.

The past seemed to be on his mind as well, because, after a long brooding silence, it was he who brought it up. "Did you read them?"

I didn't have to ask to know he meant the journals. "I did. Cover to cover. Every one."

He tried to hide his wince, but I saw it. "I didn't want Alayna reading them. I've tried to keep her from that as much as I could."

"Oh, Celia would have liked to keep me from them as well, I'm sure." I drew again on my cigar, letting him make of that what he would.

He considered. "While I'd like to say that I respect my wife's privacy, I'm not so sure I wouldn't have done the same thing in your position."

I didn't know enough about Hudson Pierce to make any assumptions, so I asked outright. "And had you been in my position, if you'd read that log of cruel manipulation, what would have been your reaction?"

He answered quickly. "I would have run. As far as possible."

"But Alayna knows, however much you've tried to spare her, and she's still with you."

"Alayna's a better person than I am."

"Mm." I didn't doubt that. I did, however, doubt his perspective. "And if it had been Alayna who had done those things, you still would have run?"

"She wouldn't have. She isn't capable." But he'd paused, and while I imagined he was right about what his wife was or wasn't capable of, I also sensed that he'd realized there was nothing he wouldn't have forgiven her if she were.

The point was made, anyway.

And it created a convenient segue to my next point. "There was one victim those journals never detailed. A game played on a naive young girl who never considered her childhood friend would betray her."

He remained stoic, but the accusation hit its mark. "It's true that I hurt Celia first. I don t deny that."

"And do you regret it?"

"Some days more than others." To his credit, he looked guilty. "Less so when I remember what she's done to me. What she's done to Alayna."

The reminder of Celia's sins felt pale next to all that I knew were Hudson's. The all too familiar call to vengeance beckoned at my ear. "I know all too well how easy it is to hold a grudge."

"Calling it a grudge is simplifying the matter. She caused real harm to people I love."

"Just like you caused real harm to people that others loved." I matched his defensiveness with my own. "To someone that I love."

For a moment, he held his stance. Then his shoulders relaxed. "It's different when you're on the other side," he admitted.

"That it is." I held up my cigar, non-verbally questioning what he'd prefer I do with the growing ash.

He nodded to a gold cylinder bin that I only realized was an ashtray when I crossed to it and saw the basin of sand at the top. I set the cigar down to allow the excess ash to shed naturally and turned back to face the man I'd considered my rival. "I investigated you, you know. Looked into more than just your business background. Dug into the charities you support—autism, mental health, addiction treatment. Plus there are a great deal of college and business grants you fund, most started in recent years. A few of those recipients seem to have familiar profiles." Having read those journals gave me an advantage. No one else would have connected Hudson's benefactors to the wrongdoings of his past.

His face turned to stone, but the slightest shade of color topped his cheeks. "Celia isn't the only game I regret."

"Right. You've changed. From what I can see, it seems genuine. Though, one might argue that guilt doesn't make for noble motivation."

"I never claimed I was noble."

"I find that respectable. You don't flaunt your philanthropic acts. There's actually a lot about you that reminds me of myself. I go out of my way to contribute to causes that represent what I consider to be my greatest failings. I also believe firmly that karma doesn't happen on its own. It requires time and attention that must be carried out by those with the ability to dedicate themselves to the cause.

"You are exactly the kind of cause I find myself most drawn to." I let that sink in, let the threat penetrate, let him understand precisely what I was implying before I went on. "Even if I hadn't known Celia, I would have wanted to ruin you after reading those journals. You think I should have wanted to run? No, I wanted a reckoning. You were a powerful man who took advantage of people who were vulnerable. For your entertainment. You preyed on the weak. You deserve to pay retribution for every heart you broke, every marriage you destroyed, every dream you crushed, every soul you wrecked. You deserve to have everything taken from you."

He turned to face me head-on, but while his posture was offensive, his words were not. "I'm not going to defend myself. I can't."

I hadn't realized how much I'd hoped he'd try until that moment. If he had, I might not have been able to go through with this. My anger would have been too fueled to smother.

But his refusal to fight made it impossible to change my course. Which was for the best.

"You don't have to defend yourself," I told him. "You already have a defendant. Celia has done nothing but defend you since the first time you came up. She's protected your name. She's justified your actions. She's stood by you. She's pleaded your case. At first, I thought you had her brainwashed. I've since learned that she's a smart, sane woman who is more than capable of thinking for herself, and she does. All the time. Sometimes to my detriment, which I admire more than I care to admit. So then I thought she was in love with you."

He perked up at that insinuation.

"She's not," I said quickly, unwilling to let him consider the notion for any length of time. "She never really was, from what I gather. You made her think maybe she could be once upon a time, but I'm sure you know as well as anyone the quality of manipulated emotions."

"Unfortunately, I do."

"The reason she defended you, I finally realized, is because she genuinely believes you are a good person. That you've changed. And I think the only reason she's able to believe it as she does is because she's changed too. It takes one to know one, etcetera, etcetera."

"And what do you think?"

I appreciated the question and answered gladly. "I'm less prone to believe it. Because if it were true, you'd know it was possible she's changed too. You would recognize the signs. You wouldn't be campaigning so hard to keep the upper hand. You wouldn't be so afraid." I chuckled. "Ironic that she's the one you fear. It should be me. I should frighten the hell out of you."

This was the kind of threat I was used to delivering, and a part of me expected the usual fawning and backtracking from Hudson that I had heard from countless other foes.

But Celia had warned me about the man for a reason— he was legitimately formidable, with his own threatening countenance. A man who wouldn't back down.

"Do you want to know why I don't?" he asked, sure of himself as ever.

"Please. Tell me."

"Because you love her."

I did love her. I wouldn't deny it. Yet, it felt almost like he was reading *my* journal the way he announced it, as though this piece of knowledge gave him insight into all of me.

I picked up my cigar to distract from how vulnerable it made me feel.

But he'd spotted my weak spot, and he pressed on it further. "Speaking from one man who is very like another, you'd move heaven and earth for the woman you love. You'd protect and defend her, no doubt in my mind. But you'd also honor her. From what you've just told me, hurting me would mean disregarding her wishes."

He did understand me. Because he was the same kind of man. Younger and more vain, perhaps, but still a king who bowed only to the woman he adored.

"You're smarter than I gave you credit for. Celia said that about you, too." I puffed thoughtfully on my cigar. "You're right. She doesn't want me to go to war with you, and that should be reason enough not to. I'm sad to say that it wasn't enough. She begged and bartered, and..." I shook my head, thinking about how painfully stubborn I'd been. "Didn't matter. I didn't care. I was determined. Because I knew what was best for her. Better than she knew for herself."

He nodded his head, knowingly. Then his brow creased. "Are we at war, then?"

"No. We aren't." I had to take a breath after I said it. It was like laying a heavy weapon down, and the effort of carrying it lingered after it was on the ground. "The thing is, she finally got through to me, and when she did, it wasn't her conviction in your character that made me change my mind. It was just her. It was realizing that she's everything, and anything that isn't her isn't worth my time."

I'd been wrong. My love for Celia wasn't a vulnerability. It was my strength. It was my bastion. It was my greatest weapon.

"I don't care who you are," I said, emboldened by my epiphany, "or what you've done to repay your debts. I only care about her and our child and what she's done for me. She hasn't changed me, but she's accepted me for who I am, and with that acceptance, my focus has shifted. I no longer see you or the battle I meant to wage. All I see is her."

He let a smile slip, but quickly tucked it away. "So you didn't meet with me to discuss the shares?"

I shook my head. "I don't bloody care about the shares. Whoever owns them, I already have what I need. Celia does too."

He pressed me with a quizzical expression.

"Then why are we here, you're wondering." I sighed. "I probably didn't need to meet with you at all since you weren't aware of my vendetta. Honestly, I'm here for selfish reasons. Closure, somewhat. Mostly, I'm here for Celia. She doesn't need me to stick up for her or fight any of her wars, nor would she appreciate it if she knew that's why I was here. If she knew I was here at all, that is. Regardless, I didn't think it was right that you didn't know what she's done for you, and my place or not, I needed to make it known. If she's what one of your enemies looks like, I'd advise you to get more of them."

The man was unreadable, another admirable quality, but I sensed he'd heard me. He gave the impression that he heard everything, including much that wasn't actually said. Rolling his cigar between his fingers, he stared vaguely into the distance. "It's funny, after everything that's occurred between us, I still think of her first as friend rather than foe. And what she did to help find Alayna...I know she was reluctant to help at first, for whatever reason—

"That was my fault," I interjected. "She would have been helpful from the beginning if it weren't for me, guaranteed."

He took a second to digest that. "I wouldn't have found my wife without Celia. I know that. I have nightmares every time I sleep about it, thinking what might have happened. Knowing how close I was to losing...everything." Emotion shuddered through him, but he recovered quickly. "Celia was there when I needed her most, and maybe that doesn't make up for everything in the past, but as you seemed to suggest, there's not much value in holding a grudge."

Reaching into his tuxedo jacket, he pulled out an envelope, bent from being stuffed inside his pocket, and handed it to me. "It's not what you're here for, but it's what I'm here for. Both my lawyer and financial advisor have already approved the language. Take all the time you need looking it over. Whenever, if ever, you're interested, call my office, and we'll schedule a time to make it final

I tucked it in my own pocket without looking at it. I knew what it was, and though it was a nice gesture, it didn't matter. It didn't change anything.

It was, however, a good note to end on.

I set my cigar back in the sand so it would extinguish naturally, then I held my hand out. "I think we're done here."

He accepted my hand and gave it a firm shake. "I'd say we are."

A vivid memory flashed in my mind of that night with Frank, of the way the fire licked against the night sky, the smoke rising above the flames. I'd stood watching as long as I'd dared, hoping for the finality to sink in. It never did.

It was different walking away from Hudson. The world might have been ablaze behind me. I never looked back to see.

EIGHTEEN

CELIA

I walked into the Werner Media lobby and checked the time on my phone. Twelve after nine. I was cutting it close.

I hurried past reception, flashing my ID to the security guard who knew me by sight, and down the hall to the press room located at the heart of the first floor. It took twice as long to get there because of the clothes I was wearing. A tight pencil skirt and sky-high heels were not conducive to speed.

But hey, I looked good.

I always looked good when Edward dressed me, which had become routine again. Usually, though, since my days generally consisted of mothering, the outfits he chose were simple summer dresses or rompers with easy access to my breasts for feedings. When I'd seen today's selection laid out for me when I woke for Cleo's six o'clock feeding,

I'd been surprised he'd chosen something so businesslike. Then I'd seen the note from Edward who'd come in after I was asleep the night before.

Nine-fifteen today. Werner Media press room.

It had struck me as odd right off the bat. I hadn't been to the building at all since my father retired. Even with the three-point alliance, Edward had little interaction with Werner Media.

Strange as the request was, I'd also been immediately excited. Which might have been unjustified considering how many times Edward had led me into uncomfortable situations without any warning. As distressing as those occasions were, though, they always paid off in the end. If that's what I was walking into, so be it.

Too bad I was walking into it late.

With the handicap of the outfit plus another check-in point outside the press room, I didn't walk in until almost nine-twenty. The room was packed, standing room only. Flash bulbs were going off, cameras pointed toward the front of the room. After weaseling my way to a place where I could actually see, I saw it was Nathan Murphy, the Werner Media CEO, behind the podium. And at his side, waiting to be introduced, was my father.

For whatever reason, seeing my father made my stomach knot. I'd heard him speak at hundreds of pressers and events over my lifetime. It was an ordinary part of his job. So mundane, I hadn't tuned in to one in years.

But he was retired now and had less reason to be representing Werner Media in a conference. His presence suggested an important announcement was to be made. And if Edward had wanted me here for it, I could only guess what it would be in reference to, especially considering what else was going on in the Werner world.

Sure enough, after a short speech from Nate that said pretty much nothing, my father approached the podium with a digital reader in his hand.

A *prepared* speech. This was real serious coming from a man who liked to wing it.

He had my full attention, along with forty other people crowded around me. We all watched, a strange silence blanketing the press room while he took his reading glasses out of his jacket pocket and adjusted the microphone.

"I appreciate you all coming out today. So many familiar faces." His eyes roved around the room, greeting old friends with a nod. He paused when he came to me, the jovial expression he'd had a moment before slipping away instantly.

Somberly, he turned his gaze back to his device. "'Recent events have brought focus to my brother, Ronald Werner," he said, and I forced myself to breathe, to not go numb, to stay in the moment. "While he hasn't had a position at Werner Media nor vested interest in the company for years, we feel it is appropriate to make a statement regarding his criminal charges and the sentence of twenty-six years that was announced last week in the Crown Court of London. It is our understanding that he is in the process of appealing these charges.' That's right, right?" He looked to the men gathered behind him. "That's what we hear anyway," he said after the man that I recognized as his lawyer nodded in confirmation. "'Many of his friends and colleagues have already come forward to testify on his behalf and more will likely show up in the coming days. My wife and I as well as representatives for Werner Media have been urged time and again to make our own statement, which we have refused to issue until now.'"

It was hard to not check out. Hard to not pay attention to his words when I was certain I knew where they were going. *These charges are false and egregious. I'll stand behind my brother no matter what.* A whole bunch of horseshit I didn't want to hear. Why did Edward want me here for this? To show that my father was the bastard he'd always purported he was?

Yeah, like I needed proof.

Fuck that. I didn't need to be here for this.

I turned, intending to push my way out of the crowd as he went on. "'Today, I am standing here to formally say that neither I nor my family nor any part of Werner Media Corporation stand behind Ron in any way.'"

I froze, sure I'd heard wrong. But the murmur of reporters across the room suggested they'd been shocked by what they heard too. I wiggled back into my place, attentive now.

"'The acts that Ron has been accused of are abhorrent and inexcusable. He's been found guilty of these terrible acts in a court of law. Anyone wishing to believe him innocent hasn't taken a look at the proof, which is irrefutable. There is no doubt in my mind that he has committed these heinous crimes and that he has been willfully abusing and assaulting children for decades.'"

He took a beat to remove his readers and look at his audience. "I wish I could have understood earlier," he said, with more heartfelt sincerity than I'd ever seen from him. His eyes found mine again. "With all my heart, I wish I could have understood his nature and the danger he posed to those around him so that I might have intervened. So that I might have confronted his predatory behavior and rescued countless little girls from harm. I wish I could have prevented him from ever laying a hand on..." For a moment, I thought he was going to say *you,* but he caught himself. "Laying a hand on a child. It is a regret I will take to my deathbed."

My eyes pricked, and even several blinks weren't enough to stop the tears from falling. How long had I waited for this? Not even for an apology, but just an acknowledgment that it happened. That I hadn't lied.

It was validation that I hadn't believed my father capable of giving.

It repaired something broken between us. Not everything because it was still too little and oh so late, and because I knew this would be all I got from him. There would be no more talk of Ron after this. I knew that as well as I knew anything.

But it was something, and I could appreciate it for what it was. I gave him a tight smile, and his shoulders relaxed as he put his glasses on again and continued reading. "'While I can't undo my brother's actions, and while Werner Media assumes no responsibility for his crimes, we are committed to looking after those he has victimized. I am honored to unveil "For Our Children," a twenty-million-dollar fund dedicated to directly serving boys and girls who have been abused and assaulted by Ron or other predators.'"

I slipped out after that. There would be questions and accusations and details of Ron's crimes would come up, and I didn't want to be there for any of that. I'd gotten what I'd come for.

Everything else I needed was waiting for me back at the hotel with Edward.

I walked into the living room of our suite to find the ottoman upended against the window, the desk moved back against the wall, and the sofa pushed out of the way to make room for all three of the baby gyms we'd had folded up and stored under the crib in Cleo's room to be laid out and fully assembled. Various farm animals and nature figures were strewn across the floor under fabric-covered arches. Cleo lay on her back under the one nearest me, her legs kicking excitedly at the plush stars above her head.

The best part, though, was that Edward was stretched out on the floor with her, dressed only in a pair of pajama bottoms, his back to me, and God what a gorgeous back it was. He hadn't seen me, yet, so I took the opportunity first to ogle, and then to swoon as he played out a nursery rhyme using a stuffed animal and the plush moon hanging from the arch.

"The cow jumped over the mooooooooon," he said, elongating the last vowel as he jumped a stuffed horse through the air, over the crescent shape, and onto Cleo's belly.

She erupted in giggles and Edward did it again. "The cow jumped over the mooooooooon. The little dog laughed to see such fun and the dish ran away with the spooooooooon."

This time she squealed with glee.

My heart. It felt like it was twisting and bursting all at the same time. How did I get so lucky? It was a profound thought after where I'd just been. My father's statement at the press conference had been moving and much appreciated, but it was a reminder of where I'd come from. Of the disjointed family that barely related. Of my shadowed past where a father placed convenience and ease above the word of his daughter.

From that to this.

From the outside, I was sure my life with Edward didn't look so different from the one my mother had with my father. Living in it, though, the difference was night and day, and as much as it had destroyed me to go through what I had growing up, I'd live through that night a thousand times over if just once it brought me to this beautiful day.

Edward and Cleo. Life didn't get any better than this.

The simple moment was much bigger than one that could be captured, still I pulled out my phone from my purse and clicked a photo. The fake shutter sound wasn't loud, but foreign enough to be noticed. Edward looked up quickly, his expression saying he might have been just a tad embarrassed at being caught playing something so silly.

"I'm weak in the knees," I said, determined to not let him get out of being adored.

He gave me a bashful smile. "You probably should have had more than coffee for breakfast."

"From you, you goof. You're making me swoon." I frowned at the horse in his hand. "Though, that is definitely not a cow."

"If there is one in the bunch, I couldn't find the bloody thing."

My cheeks hurt from grinning. "So when her preschool teacher says she doesn't know her animals, we'll know who to blame."

"Elsa, definitel ."

I laughed and sat down on the upholstered bench. "What have you done to this room?"

"The reason we've never had these out is because there

wasn't enough room."

"You mean the reason we've never had all three out at one time was because there wasn't enough room. Which was fine since we don't need all of them at once." The space was tight, though. Not for the first time, I longed for our home in London.

"Pish posh. Everything's better in threes." He gave the horse to Cleo who immediately put it in her mouth, then he scooted closer and sat with his back against the bench, his legs stretched out in front of him. "She thinks the setup is brilliant. You can't tell so much when she's obsessing over the taste of that horse's mane, but trust me, she loves it."

He leaned over to kiss my thigh, his eyes skimming down the bare skin below the hem of my skirt. "And I love how long your legs look in these heels. Remind me to have you wear them later when I have my face between your thighs."

"Behave," I scolded as I nudged him with my knee.

He responded by reaching out to remove the shoe clos-est to him before rubbing the arch of my foot. I sighed into his massage. "The heels are a bitch, but I loved being in my old clothes today. It felt good just being out in the world, interacting with adults."

"Which is why you need to get back to work soon."

"Should I? I keep thinking about it, but does that make me a bad mother?"

"It does not. It makes you a woman who knows that her own mental health and well-being is essential to being a good mother." He looked toward my other foot. "Give me that one."

I slipped my shoe off then stretched my foot toward him. "You make it sound like such a simple decision. I don't want to miss anything important."

"You only work part-time. You'll miss some things, but you won't miss everything, and that's called balance."

Like he knew about balancing home and career.

Except, that was the old Edward. This Edward was trying. Doing better than just trying, so far. Proving it was possible to have it all.

"I'll think about it," I conceded.

Then I gasped as the foot rub was interrupted by a sharp slap across my sole.

"I wasn't giving you an option," he said with a stern look. The kind of stern look that wasn't to be argued with. The kind of stern look that made my lower regions tingle.

I'd forgotten that look. It had been missing for so long, since before Cleo was born. Now he wore it like it had never left his face.

This is my king, I thought. This is the man who cares for me and rules me and knows just what I need. And here he was rubbing my feet when I should have been bowing at his.

I gave him the next best thing. "Okay," I said. "I'll get back to work." That earned me a calf rub as well.

"Where is Elsa, anyway?" I asked when his hands were tired, and it finally occurred to me she wasn t around.

"I sent her home. Daddy's taken the day off to spend with his girls."

"I like the sound of that." The words turned into a surprised "eek" when he tugged me by the leg to the floor with him, my skirt riding up in the process.

I didn't have time to adjust it before he was climbing

over me, his body stretched over mine. He studied my face, looking for what, I didn't know, but I found something in his as I stared back—a serenity I normally only saw on his features when he was sleeping. His jaw was relaxed, his smile loose. Maybe it was me seeing what I wanted to see, or projecting my own feelings, but he looked at peace for the first time since I'd known him

Eventually, he gave me a brief kiss then rolled to his side next to me. "How did it go?" he asked, twirling a loose strand of my hair.

He meant the press conference. I couldn't believe it had taken this long for it to come up, but that was the way with things that weren't that important.

I glanced up at the TV, which was playing a news channel on mute. "You watched it. There's no way you didn't."

"Of course I watched it. I want to know how it went from your perspective."

But that wasn't as interesting as how he'd gotten my father to say it in the first place. "It was your doing, wasn't it? You wrote that statement for him."

"I didn't put a gun to his head to get him to read it out loud. To the entire world, no less." He traced his thumb across my bottom lip.

"You didn't push him to do it at all?"

He shrugged. "Merely suggested that he should."

I let out a sigh, trying to decide how that made me feel. I'd known Edward had been involved with the Werner Media statement. He'd sent me there, after all. To what extent, though? I'd probably never know exactly what he'd said or done to get my father to read it. I supposed it was enough that he'd read it at all.

It was more than enough that Edward had made it happen. "Thank you," I said, sincerely. "It was...as good as I'll get from him, I think. And that's okay. It's more than I expected."

"Much less than you deserve."

I'd spent years playing games where I made people fall in love with me. I was good at it. My uncle had taught me well. I'd never had a shortage of men willing to give anything, give everything, to be with me.

But the earnest way Edward looked at me felt brand new. Maybe because he was the first one who saw who I really was inside, and he still wanted to keep looking.

"You're besotted," I said, rolling to my side to face him.

"You're bewitching."

"You're super hot." I trailed my fingertips across his pecs. But it wasn't just his body that turned me on. I peered over Edward's shoulder at Cleo, who was now mesmerized with a hanging mirror sunflowe , and the expansive baby playground he'd been inspired to set up all on his own. "Especially with this whole dad thing going on. I thought you were attractive before, but this is next level shit. Fatherhood looks so good on you, in fact, we really should consider having more."

I had to bite my cheek not to laugh, even though I was only half teasing.

Teasing or not, Edward did not take kindly to it. "I should punish you for the mere suggestion."

"That's not a no."

"Oh, you asked for it." He swept his hand up the back of my thigh.

I flipped to my back, a desperate attempt to protect my ass. "You cannot spank me in front of Cleo," I warned. "You'll traumatize her."

"Spanking is not what I had in mind."

"Oh?" But then his hand was under my skirt and inside my panties. "Ohhhh." The man could ignite my pussy with just a brush of his thumb. A second brush, and I was molten. By the time he settled into a steady rhythm across my clit, I was halfway to orgasm. "Fuck."

"Shhh. You'll traumatize the baby."

I giggled. "It's your fault for making me..." Whatever I was saying got lost to the intense wave of pleasure. "God, I never realized how hard it was not to scream when you're doing this."

"Terribly hard?"

"Terribly hard." I bit my lip to suppress a gasp as he slid a finger inside me. Holy shit, it felt so naughty. Like we were teenagers fucking around when we were supposed to be babysitting.

Except we weren't babysitters. We were parents. We were supposed to be responsible.

I lifted my head to look behind Edward. "Is she watching us? I swear she's watching us." Really, she was still captivated with her reflection

"Of course she is," he said, not bothering to look. "She adores us. We're the most absolutely fabulous people in her world."

He added two fingers on his next thrust, and I had to grip my nails into Edward's shoulder to keep from crying out. "Is it bad, though? If she sees this?"

"Do you want me to stop?"

"No! No." She couldn't really see anything anyway. His body blocked her view, and she wasn't even looking, and if she did, she wouldn't possibly understand, and with all that self-reassurance, I was able to relax and let the orgasm wind itself up, tighter, tighter. "I'm almost there," I panted, my eyes closed. "Almost—"

With no warning, the pleasure cut off abruptly. Edward pulled his hand from my panties and sat back against the bench, a smirk on his face.

I sat up, propping myself on my elbows. "Why did you stop?"

"Seriously, Celia. The baby is right there." When I glared, he said, "It was supposed to be a punishment." Then he smugly brought a finger to his mouth—a finger that had just been inside me—and sucked it clean.

I was wound up and blue-balled and I'd never been so happy. "I hate you a little bit right now."

"I always love you best when you hate me a little bit." He missed my scowl because he stood then and walked over to the desk. When he returned, he had an unmarked envelope in his hand. "I have something for you."

"What is it?"

"Open it."

I took the envelope from him, and sat up to open it while Edward attended to Cleo, who had started to fuss in-termittently between her coos. It wasn't sealed, so all I had to do was lift up the flap to pull out the folded document. It was several pages of legalese. A contract of sorts. Or an option to buy, I realized as I skimmed through it, my pulse ticking up when I saw Hudson's name and my name and Werner Media mentioned.

"Edward!" I looked up at him, a magnificent god with

the most beautiful baby cuddled against his chest. "He's selling us the shares?"

"He's selling us the shares."

"Oh, my God. He's selling us the shares." I read on, scanning for a catch, and finding none.

Then suspicion kicked in. "What did you do?"

"Nothing. This was all you. Hudson had it prepared before I met with him." He took his place again on the floo, propping Cleo up in his lap.

My ovaries would have burst if I wasn't so distracted by the document in my hand and the man who undoubtedly coerced Hudson in some terrible way to get it.

"You met with him—?"

"Last night," he said, misinterpreting what I was after, though I hadn't known that bit either.

"...and?"

"And he gave me that envelope. Which I have now given to you."

"You didn't...?" I shook my head in frustration, trying to fit the picture together. "I don't understand. Are you saying it's over?"

"We could counter, if you like. Demand the majority instead of just one percent."

I stared at him, then stared at the paper in my hand. Then stared again at him who was too preoccupied with playing peekaboo with Cleo to notice how intensely I was staring.

I just...

I was shocked, to say the least. Edward had put Hudson on his Revenge list at least three years before. That was when he'd mentioned it to me, anyway. He'd likely wanted to go after him the minute he'd first read my journals, which had been at least six months before that. We'd fought over his desire for vengeance. I'd nearly given up a chance at having Cleo because of it. It was so much a part of our marriage, it was almost a foundation stone.

Which was a shitty way to look at it. I wondered what our relationship might be like without this battle between us. We'd still find something to fight about, I wasn't worried about that. But maybe there'd be more of the good. Less of the jealousy. Less of the spite.

I looked again at the document. Hudson had offered to sell us enough shares to make us equal. We could probably announce it publicly, even, without the detail that Hudson had owned the majority before instead of the other way around. We could once again be partners, on equal ground.

Like Edward and I were partners, but also not like that at all.

"I'm happy with this," I said, setting the document down on the bench out of Cleo's reach.

"Then I am too."

"Okay," I said as I scooted up next to him so our shoulders touched. It was time to feed Cleo. She wasn't complaining too much, but she was rooting around on Edward's chest.

Except I was still stuck on my husband's beef with Hudson. I couldn't believe Edward was able to let it go. He never let anything go. Maybe he was still planning to ruin him behind my back. Or maybe he'd already done something he didn't want to tell me, which, in either case, would mean I was the one who should let it go, because I definitely didn't want to keep fighting about Hudson Pierce for the rest of our lives, and whether it was true or not, it was a gift to believe it was done.

But I could never do what I should. "And nothing else?" I asked. "You really aren't going after him?"

"I'm really not. I realized it wouldn't get me what I want."

"What's that?"

"You."

My breath caught in my ribs. "You already have me."

"Exactly." He shifted Cleo to me so I could breastfeed, but he stayed sitting next to us, his brows furrowed.

I let him be alone with his thoughts and focused on the hungry baby in my arms. When she was settled and latched on, I had my own thoughts to parse through. Edward had basically told me he'd felt second place to Hudson. I, too, had felt second place. Edward tunneled in on his schemes, always seeking retribution from this person or that, looking for something to fill some sort of aching need inside him.

So many times I'd wished I could fill that need. Wished that I was enough. Was that what he was telling me? That I was as much to him as he was to me?

"I've been burning for a long time, bird," he said, breaking the silence. The somber tone immediately grabbed my attention, and before he'd said more I already knew it was something he vitally needed me to hear. "I've been completely consumed with rage and spite, these twin fires that ate everything in their pathway. No matter what I fed them, they continued to burn, burn, burn. Everything was fuel, and there I was, throwing flames at whatever I deemed deserving to be burned down.

"Then you came. And while I'd always been facing backward, always looking to the past, you beckoned me toward the future. It took a while to get me to turn all the way around, but now that I am, my back's to the inferno. If it's still burning, I don't see it. All I see in this direction is you. And Cleo. And whomever else you end up forcing me to love. Everything that seemed to matter so much before is just smoke, rising in the distance."

"Edward..." A multitude of emotions pressed inside me—complicated, enormous emotions that were too multi-shaded to be named. There was love, of course. Over-whelming and boisterous, but saying I loved him didn't feel big enough. "I've never felt like this before," I said when I couldn't find the right words

"I know," he said, cupping my cheek in his hand. "I feel it too."

He leaned down to kiss me, more lips than tongue. Ap-propriate with Cleo lodged between us, and also probably it was exactly the kiss he would have given if she hadn't been there. It was a kiss that made me feel cherished and adored and wanted and all those other unnameable emo-tions that I was feeling about him.

"God, I love you," he said when he broke away.

"Me too," I said, determined not to cry. "And I think you just said we get to have another baby."

"I said no such thing."

"Whomever else I end up forcing you to love? That was definitely a reference to another bab ."

"You are definitely getting spanked when she goes down for her nap."

My belly fluttered in anticipation. "Any other surprises I should know about?"

"Just one."

I raised a brow. I didn't think there was anything else he could say to make me feel more content at the moment or more complete.

It turned out I was wrong because his last surprise, announced in his no-nonsense alpha way of his that I'd missed for so long, was maybe the best surprise of all.

"We're going home."

EPILOGUE
Six years later

EDWARD

"It's beautiful, Edward. I don't know what to say."

I look at Camilla's reflection in front of us as I fasten the choker around her neck. It's an odd match with the silk black robe she's wearing, but it looks fantastic on her. The alternating ruby and diamond jewels catch the sunlight streaming through the window and sparkle in the mirror and somehow bring out the specks of green in her eyes. It reminds me of the pendant I bought Celia years ago for Valentine's Day.

This one is even more valuable, though, since it had belonged to our mother.

"She would have wanted you to have it today," I tell her.

Camilla turns to look at me directly. "You can tell me

the truth, Eddy. Did you get this recently?"

I know what she's asking—she wants to know if I've been hunting down family relics again. More specificall , she wants to know if I've been bullying wrongdoers in the process.

"I've had it for a long time, which is embarrassing to admit because I should have given it to you sooner." I'd been saving it for Genevieve, but now I see the selfishness in keeping this piece from my sister. "As for what you really want to know, I am not involved in that sort of business anymore. I'm far too busy with the present to preoccupy myself with the past."

It's not a lie. My life is full on many levels. Celia and my children take up the majority of my energy, but there's also Accelecom and the three-point alliance and while Nathan Murphy is doing a fine job as CEO of Werner, I have a lot of input as a major stockholder, which means Hudson Pierce is more in my life than ever. It's not a complaint. There's much to admire about the man and much from him to learn. I reckon he'd say the same in return.

Then there's the work I do with Leroy. I don't share the details with anyone other than Celia. A good deal of it is illegal, and I prefer not to involve anyone who doesn't need to be involved, but Camilla is aware of my contributions. Turns out there is a lot of good that can be done by a man with deep pockets and a skill at wheedling into the private affairs of other rich men. There are far too many predators amongst my class, and my obsessive behaviors have found a noble repurposing in tracking them down. *Using my powers for good*, as Celia likes to say.

Since she's the purest of the good in my life, and since she's both the one who put me on the path of bringing down bad men and the reason I do it at all, I'd say she's exactly right.

Camilla turns back to the mirror, her hand fondling the jewels at her neck. "I'm glad you saved it. My wedding day is the perfect occasion to bring it out."

She blinks back tears, and I frown. "It's much too early for the waterworks. I'm going to have a hard enough time seeing where I'm going when I walk you down the aisle."

"Good thing it's a short aisle, isn't it?"

Short it is. Only three rows of chairs are set up in the backyard of Bluntisham House. The only guests invited are family and the closest of friends.

"My best wedding was intimate," I say, sensing she needs validation.

"The first one wasn't so bad," she defends. "But you did come out with a more compatible bride the second time, so I'll give you that. Frank insisted on all the bells and whistles and to-do with my first one, you know. Look where that ended up. I would have preferred small."

"And now that's what you've got." I hope that brings her back to the present, though I appreciate that she may be compelled to talk about Frank today. It's human nature to compare and contrast. When I'd married Celia, my thoughts constantly measured the occasion to my wedding with Marion. Which ceremony did which part better. Who'd been in attendance. How I felt.

My situation had been different, of course, considering I hadn't expected to stay married to my current bride, but even as I planned her demise—a plan I'm convinced now that I could never have carried out—I'd given myself permission to live the fantasy that day. I meant the words when I spoke my vows. I sealed myself to her, til death do we part.

But I'd said those words to Marion as well, and I'd thought I'd meant them then. I *had* meant that. If she hadn't had the courage to leave, I'd likely still be married to her, both of us stuck in an unfulfilling marriage. It shows a great deal of progress for me to be able to look back on our divorce now and be grateful. Another lesson where the moral is keep moving forward and believe the best is yet to come.

All that said, I can't imagine what Camilla must be going through today. She wears a lot of scars from her relationship with Frank, some more visible than others. She learns better how to live with them every day. The short-sleeve, low-back wedding dress hanging on the closet door is proof in point.

Still, moving forward isn't always easy.

"Am I doing the right thing?" she asks now. She worries her hands together, her expression anxious. "Maybe I'm not cut out for marriage. Am I rushing into it, do you think?"

"After six years and two children together, yes, rushing it seems to be an accurate description of the situation."

She laughs, which was the point. "You're right. I must seem crazy. Most people are likely criticizing me for dragging my feet."

"Most people's opinions don't matter. Only mine. Since I only want you to be happy, and since I believe you're the happiest I've ever known you to be right now, then I believe your wedding is happening exactly when it was meant to happen." I pull my handkerchief from my suit pocket and dab at her eyes. "Not that you asked, but I also think you were quite efficient in the order of events. This way, you didn't have to rope other people's kids into being your flower girls. You have two beautiful daughters already lined up."

"If they do what they're supposed to. A three-year-old and a four-year-old are hardly reliable."

"Which is why you still had to recruit a child wrangler. I'm sure Cleo will keep them all to task just fine.

"Thank you for that," she says, and I know she's not just talking about Cleo's help with her daughters in today's ceremony, but she clarifies anyway. "Thank you for all of it, Eddie. You've been the best big brother a woman could ask for, and I'm so honored that it's you who will give me away."

I'm not given time to respond, which is likely for the best since my throat feels extraordinarily tight all of a sudden, before the door to the guest suite bursts open and Genevieve comes bounding in with Freddie on her heels, each of them carrying an assortment of cosmetic bags and beauty accessories.

"I'm late!" she says, scurrying to set her items out on the vanity. "I'm sorry. I should have stayed here last night as Dad suggested. I don't know why I thought it would be easier to come in this morning, but lesson's learned. I'm here now. I hope you're not terribly cross with me."

While I recognize there're more important matters at hand, I'm admittedly self-absorbed. "Where's Abigail?"

My daughter gives me a vexed look. "Chandler has her downstairs. Hello to you too."

I shrug. I'm not going to apologize for wanting to see my granddaughter whenever possible. I see her so little since Geneveive's life is across the pond.

Camilla clears her throat, reminding us she's supposed to be the woman in the spotlight.

"You're perfectly on time. It's meant to be a laid-back occasion," she says, the bride ironically soothing her matron of honor. "If I'd wanted something more formal I would have hired someone to do my hair and makeup. I asked you for exactly this reason—I wanted all of today to be real and authentic, and I hope it wasn't too much of a hassle. I'm so thankful to get to spend this time with you."

Genevieve settles, her aunt's words being what she needed to calm her nerves. "I'm honored to be part of this day. Let's get you sparkled up, shall we?"

"That's our cue to leave," I say to my nephew who I assume isn't needed now that he's done being my daughter's bellhop.

"Unless you'd like to stay. I could always use some help testing out blush tones."

Genevieve is teasing, but Freddie's expression says he's not so sure.

I jump in to rescue him. "He'd love to, but I need him downstairs for something. I haven't decided what yet."

Camilla laughs. "Get out of here, boys."

As soon as the door shuts behind us, Freddie sighs in relief.

"It's okay, kid," I say, ruffling his hair. "We men have to stick together."

"We do." He fist bumps me then disappears, likely off to lose himself in one of the books he's always carrying around or to latch onto Chandler. Between Camilla's daughters and Genevieve's and mine, there are a lot of women around. I understand the boy's need for any male companionship he can get.

I, on the other hand, couldn't be more content with

those that surround me on a daily basis. Peering out the hall window to the backyard, I see them now, three of the people I love most in the world. They're gathered round the maple tree near the hedged garden, and a momentary flash of regret cuts through me as I remember all the times I missed with my older children, days spent in the country where I stayed locked inside.

Instead of holding the regret, though, I let it go. I can do nothing for the moments I lost to distraction in the past. But it means everything that I choose to be present in the now.

CELIA

"Higher," Cleo pleads from the tree swing. "Higher."

"Mm hm." But I don't push her any harder. I don't think of myself as overprotective in general, but since Freddie broke his arm last summer from jumping off this exact swing, I'm perhaps more cautious than I need to be.

Besides, I'm a bit distracted. "Stella," I scold. "Leave those alone. I mean it."

"Mummy," the four-year-old protests. "You said the balloons would fly!"

The strings of the helium balloons are gathered and loosely tied around the fence for later. We'll release them as part of the ceremony, which is still an hour away. "Later. I promise."

Stella's expression says there's no way she's dropping her fascination. She's willful and persistent and never takes no for an answer. A lot like her mother, in other words.

Fortunately, my dark knight has come to my rescue.

"Listen to your mother," he says scooping her up in his arms. It may have been irresponsible getting her dressed up so early—there's every chance she'll be stained and wrecked by the time the ceremony starts—but seeing her bundled in tulle and lace in Edward's arms, I regret nothing.

"You look particularly dashing," I say as he comes over. I've completely abandoned pushing Cleo now, so when my husband leans down to kiss me, I'm there for it.

"Mummy!" Cleo complains while Stella giggles.

"You're breathtaking, as always." He picks at a leaf that has found its way into the bun at the back of my nape.

I pose dramatically to show off my floral embroidered strapless fil-coupe dress. "You think so? My husband picked it out."

"Your husband has good taste."

"That he does. It has pockets." I shove my hands inside the hidden pockets to demonstrate.

"Because a woman can't be carrying a handbag all the time, and where is she supposed to put a binkie or her lipstick?"

He's practically quoting me, and I love it. I've obviously been complaining about it for long enough since both our daughters are long past using a binkie, but the sentiment remains, and my husband, as always, listens. Always looks out for me. Always puts my needs first

What more could a woman want?

Stella wriggles in Edward's arms. "Flutterflies! Cleo! Flutterflies!"

I look where she's pointing and see a swarm of butterflies over the bluebells. Edward puts her down so she can chase them, and Cleo, not wanting to miss out on the fun, jumps off the swing to join her.

"Care—" I wince as she lands on the ground, my warning coming too late. "Ful." But she bounces after her sister, obviously unharmed.

Edward puts his arm around my waist. "You can't protect her from everything. Eventually, they're going to be hurt by something. Our job is to be here for them when they do."

"I know." I hug him back. I know it's just as hard for him to accept that as it is for me. Neither of us want our girls to ever feel pain, and if they are ever hurt maliciously, I am certain that Edward wouldn't let their abuser get off without serious maiming.

And I'm okay with that. I know who I married. While I'm grateful that he's set aside revenging for the most part, I also find peace knowing the lengths he'd go to if provoked. He's not an angel, and I'd never pretend otherwise.

What he is, though, is everything I ever needed. A man who challenges me and puts me in my place. A man who sees the real me and lives to make that me well and whole. He's not just that for myself, but for the children we have together. I hadn't wanted children before him; even after I'd lost my first baby, I'd put the notion out of my mind. After what I'd been through, knowing that there were men who preyed on the innocent waiting around every bend, why would I want to bring a child into this world?

Then, with Edward, I'd felt safe. I knew that he'd never let the things that happened to me happen to our girls. I knew that, if somehow something terrible did happen, he wouldn't turn his back on them. I knew he would be the father I'd wished I had, and every day watching him with them, that void inside me fills a little bit more, my heart is a little more healed.

"Want a go?" Edward asks.

I move my focus from our girls to the swing dangling in front of us. I hesitate, but then I'm climbing onto the seat that was purposefully made wide enough for an adult. For me, specificall . A response to a session, years ago now. Therapy I hadn't known I'd needed.

"Not too high, though," I warn, in contrast to my daughter's earlier pleas.

I know I'll be ignored, that Edward will push me exactly as high as he wants me to go, but I don't worry about it. I trust him completely.

As I sail through the air, I close my eyes, relishing the freedom of flying. When I open them, Stella's obviously been back to her agenda because there's a single red balloon rising in front of me.

Beyond that, all I see is miles and miles of sky.

Acknowledgments and Author's Note

When I said I wanted to write a series for Celia, I got more than a few people complaining. Why on earth would I want to take my most hated character from my most popular series (a very popular series, at that) and make her the heroine? It didn't make sense to most readers, and from a business stand point, it was probably even more of a risk. To be honest, I didn't know if I could afford to devote a year to a project that might very well get skipped by most readers.

So why did I choose to pursue this silly, insane idea?

In answer, I'd like to share the bulk of a blog post I wrote earlier this year:

When I first started talking about writing the Slay books, people told me I was crazy.

Not just one or two people, mind you. Dozens and dozens of comments, emails, private messages. My agent questioned whether it was a good idea. One of my closest beta readers said she'd read anything I wrote, but did it have to be her?

I was pretty sure, based on feedback, that if it had been a man I wanted to redeem, I would have had much less backlash. A good deal of romance is based on a not-so-good hero becoming a better man. There are far fewer stories where a not-so-good heroine is redeemed.

I put off the idea for several years because of the blatant display of disinterest, but all the while the story brewed in my head. Partly because I'm that type of person that when you tell me I'm crazy to do something, I just want to do it more. I'm a challenge-authority kind of gal. The writer who likes to flip tropes on their head. The woman who con-sistently responds with, "Let's just see about that."

If it had just been my stubborn streak, though, I would have abandoned the project. I'm the sole provider for my family, and I'm smart enough to realize that writing a story that my readers don't want is not the wisest business deci-sion.

But it was more than being stubborn that brought me back time and time again to Celia Werner's story. She fas-cinated me as a character. She'd done mean things to good people, things that I see play out in less dramatic ways in the real world, and I couldn't stop wondering why she would do that. What compelled her? What drives people—what drives women—to hurt others?

Lots of reasons came up as I continued to mull over it, but one answer spoke loudest from the crowd—she was broken. People hurt others because they are broken. Wom-en hurt others because they've been broken.

So very often, those women have been broken by men.

In today's culture, that felt like a very important topic for me to explore. Especially when I tend to write alpha men with qualities that are often associated with toxic masculinity in the real world. It seemed relevant to dif-ferentiate masculine from machismo. In other words, dif-ferentiate men who are strong, courageous, and assertive from men who use their strength, courage and assertive-ness to hold power over women.

Besides the aptness, Celia's story was completely on brand. Because broken people finding love—specifically dangerously broken people finding love—is exactly what Laurelin Paige books are all about.

And so I got brave.

I focused in on what it would take to tell such a complicated story. I decided to make it possible to read this series and enjoy it without ever reading any of my other books. I freaked out a little when I realized it would need to be four books (oh-my-goodness-four-books-is-a-ton-of-books!), but when I talked myself off that ledge, I carved out time in my schedule, and put book one up for preorder.

Then I took a deep breath and dove in.

It wasn't easy. The writing itself flowed well enough, but facing the terrible and dark places that Celia has been was much harder. I spent significant time researching and talking to a couple of close friends who were sensitive to the subject matter. I put my blinders on to the many readers who said they would never read this book (which is a decision I support completely—not every book is for every reader). I reminded myself this was a story I believed in, a story I needed to tell. I focused. I meditated.

And when I was done with book one, no matter what the critical response was, I decided I'd be proud of it. And I am.

Now, with the series completed, I'm over-the-moon grateful for the support readers have given me. It's beyond what I expected, and I'm very lucky for that. But even if I hadn't received such great reviews and comments, I would still believe in this story. I wouldn't want to write romance books that didn't include some aspect of redemption in them. To me, that's the truest form of love.

The idea that people can recover, that we can heal, that we can atone, that we can change and become someone better than what we once were, that no matter what we've done we are still worthy of being loved—that notion is essential to the progress of humanity. I can't imagine living in a world where we didn't believe growth was possible. I certainly wouldn't want to.

At the end of this journey, I have to take a moment to thank everyone who helped get me down this road. Take a breath, there's quite a few.

First off, my team is fucking awesome. I couldn't wish for a better one. Candi Kane, Melissa Gaston, and Roxie Madar are as much a part of Laurelin Paige as I am. I depend on them more than is probably healthy, and I love them more than I ever let on. Thank you for being my people, ladies.

Then there's Kayti McGee. She's half team member, half co-conspirator, and one hundred percent best friend. I may not be singing you Phantom of the Opera, but I'm definitely singing you A-Ha. (I'll be coming for you anyway.)

Next, my soul sister and agent, Rebecca Friedman. Even when there are long periods where I don't see you (I miss your face right now! Stupid Coronatine.), we always pick up right where we left off. You're a great friend and one of the few people who gets my neuroses (as well as my family's). Love you to the moon and back.

This series definitely couldn't have happened without Liz Berry. Even when she wasn't sure she wanted a Celia story, she spent a weekend with me trying to sort out my vision. I mean, she really went there, into the trenches, helping me discover what the story really was and the dark places it would go. Very few people have that kind of stamina and even less take the task on with such enthusiasm. I'm so lucky to have such a genuine, compassionate, intelligent woman on my side. Thank you for letting me into your family. You've definitely found your way into my heart.

My betas, editors, and proofers - Erica Russikoff, Amy "Vox" Libris, and Michele Ficht. Without these women, my words would be riddled with errors, but they contribute much more than that to my process. Their notes and ideas and, more than anything, their cheerleading are what keeps me going most days. I appreciate you ladies for everything you are. Thank you for letting me invade your lives like I do.

Marni Coleman at Lyric Audio and Elena Wolfe and Shane East—what a fucking audio team! I am so pleased with how you've made my characters come to life. I couldn't have asked for anything more, and, as always, I'm so appreciative of your patience with my sometimes lack of organization. You all are saints.

Tom Barnes and Melissa Gaston for making my stunning paperbacks and Alyssa Garcia at Uplifting Designs for giving me such gorgeous insides.

I couldn't do anything without running it by Lauren Blakely. She's my sounding board and my mentor, and one of my best friends. It's so refreshing to have someone who never tires of talking business. Our chats and marketing sessions are the highlight of my day.

My LARCS and my Instagram team—you ladies are gold. I don't know what I did to deserve such treasure in my life. I hope you know I'm always grateful, even when I'm absent from the interwebz.

The Sky Launchers—I will never not be amazed that there are people who, don't only want to hear the stories I have to tell, but also love them with such devotion and enthusiasm. Thank you for your unfettered joy. I endeavor to be more like you.

And to all my readers all around the world—thank you for giving me this crazy, fantastic life. It's the best job possible.

To the friends who weren't before mentioned —
Mela-nie Harlow, CD Reiss, Jana Aston, ShopTalkers and
all the other authors who share advice and knowledge and
just life on the regular without any expectations in
return. I can't imagine having better peers. You make the
worst parts of the job bearable and you teach me how
to celebrate the best parts in style.

To my mom, husband, and daughters—we bicker and
we fuss but we sure do love each other too. Even
after more than a month of being quarantined with y'all, I
still look forward to popping the popcorn and going to the
the-ater room to watch Magicians with you. What would
my life be without you? Spoiler: not much.

Finally, to Open Cathedral for teaching me a new way
to worship, and to my God. In this crazy, strange, surreal
time, you've been my touchstone. You give my life meaning and direction and help me remember myself when it
would easier to be lost.